The lady an

Leigh swung her flashlight toward the entry gate, and could see the third of the young tigers pacing. Another young male lay in the leaves, his back against the exhibit fence. Leigh exhaled. Four.

She walked quickly past the gate, passing within a few feet of the tiger on her way. As she passed, she swung the beam full into his face. The light caught his round eyes, making them shine like cut topazes on an already striking landscape of orange, black, and white. The tiger's chin sported even more color—it was bright red.

The giant mouth opened in a hissing scowl, baring similarly stained teeth. A carnivore, guarding its kill. Leigh didn't look long at the object the tiger was guarding.

It was a human leg.

ALSO BY EDIE CLAIRE

Never Buried

NEVER SORRY

A Leigh Koslow Mystery

Edie Claire

A SIGNET BOOK

SIGNET
Published by New American Library, a division of
Penguin Putnam Inc., 375 Hudson Street,
New York, New York 10014, U.S.A.
Penguin Books Ltd, 27 Wrights Lane,
London W8 5TZ, England
Penguin Books Australia Ltd, Ringwood,
Victoria, Australia
Penguin Books Canada Ltd, 10 Alcorn Avenue,
Toronto, Ontario, Canada M4V 3B2
Penguin Books (N.Z.) Ltd, 182–190 Wairau Road,
Auckland 10, New Zealand

Penguin Books Ltd, Registered Offices:
Harmondsworth, Middlesex, England

First published by Signet, an imprint of New American Library,
a division of Penguin Putnam Inc.

First Printing, November 1999
10 9 8 7 6 5 4 3 2 1

PUBLISHER'S NOTE
This is a work of fiction. Names, characters, places, and incidents either
are the product of the author's imagination or are used fictitiously,
and any resemblance to actual persons, living or dead, events, or locales
is entirely coincidental.

For Mark, Aster, Klaus, Scotia, Evan, Grace, and the sea monkeys—in order of age.

ACKNOWLEDGMENTS

The police procedure in this book would be based entirely on my knowledge of *Cagney & Lacey* reruns if it weren't for two truly wonderful people, Siri Jeffrey and her detecting husband, Joe, who answered every one of my five billion frantic E-mails with the patience of saints. I would also like to thank Robert Wagner, VMD, Elisa Long, and Lynn Cameron for their equally fabulous attitudes in answering my pesky questions.

Two points of literary license: 1) There is no zoo in Riverview Park—the zoo described exists only in my imagination. The real Pittsburgh Zoo is in Highland Park and bears some resemblance to my fictional one, but astute Tennesseeans may recognize an even stronger resemblance to the Overton Park Zoo in Memphis, where I once served as a volunteer. 2) A word of warning: If you're planning on committing a homicide in Allegheny County, Pennsylvania, don't expect a petite redhead to pop out of nowhere and arrange your bail. The law says you're not going anywhere.

Chapter 1

Leigh cursed herself for becoming such a scatterbrain. She was fool enough to have agreed to work late, but leaving the zoo hospital without a flashlight was sheer idiocy, and being hopelessly infatuated was no excuse. A zoo is a spooky place to be after dark, and the Riverview Park Zoo was no exception. The hair on the back of her neck prickled as she walked down the steep path toward the employee lot, her imagination spawning unwelcome scenarios of ambush—both guerilla and gorilla. The trail lamps were off, as they generally were after the main gates closed, leaving her to navigate with a combination of memory and moonlight. The trail wound mercilessly through the junglelike exhibits of cat country, each artistically tailored with dense vegetation. It was a lovely part of the zoo, but at 2:00 A.M., she would have preferred savanna.

A cool sensation spread suddenly around her toes. "Blast Mike Tanner!" she cursed aloud, stepping out of the unseen puddle. She tapped her toe against the paved walk, but the action was fruitless. The canvas shoes were soaked. "Not a morning person," she mumbled under her breath, mimicking the singsong tenor of her new boss. "I think surgery's more exciting after hours, don't you?"

But her tone belied an animosity she didn't feel. A

smile spread over her face even as she mocked the zoo veterinarian, for recent events had brought some long-awaited satisfaction to the starry eyed sixteen-year-old she had once been.

Mike Tanner had entered her life as the twenty-four-year-old, soon-to-be-graduated precepteer of her father's veterinary practice, the Koslow Animal Clinic. She was a minor, and he was married. But to a teenaged Leigh, such barriers were only a temporary nuisance. The Southern-talking, turquoise-eyed charmer was destined to be hers.

Fourteen years tended to dull the memory, however, and she hadn't thought about him in the last ten. But after her untimely firing from Peres and Lacey Advertising, fate had intervened. The start-up agency she was forming with her fellow sackees was proving long on promise but desperately short on cash, and she was forced to use her homegrown vet tech skills to pull in some extra money. She hadn't been thrilled about working two jobs, but when she heard that the now-divorced Dr. Mike was looking for a part-timer, her attitude had improved.

Her first three days on the job had even been fun, despite her boss's disregard for the hours she had agreed on. But romantic intrigue or no, no sane person started surgery at 11:00 P.M., and that was that. The fall wind was brisk, and she hugged the light jacket tighter around her, hurrying to reach her car and a heating vent at foot level.

She stopped when she saw the light. The tiger shed was illuminated, not with the full set of white spots normally highlighting the path behind the STAFF ONLY gate, but with a dull yellow glow that seemed to come from a single bulb. Carmen wouldn't still be here—would she?

Leigh hesitated. The cat keeper had been acting weird when she left the surgery earlier in the evening. Not that Carmen ever acted completely normal—but this time she had seemed unusually edgy. Why wouldn't she have gone home?

Leigh's fingers fumbled with the latch at the gate. It was unlocked. She swung the door open and stepped behind the tiger run. A rustling noise stopped her, but after a deep breath, she pressed on. It was only one of the tigers, tramping about in the wet leaves. "Is that you, Jenga?" she called quietly as she walked along the fence toward the barn. "Loki?"

She knew it must be one of the females, since the young males had been out all day. The zoo had more tigers than could stand each other's company, so they had to take turns in the exhibit. Carmen should have put the males in their cages for the night. Leigh squinted into the darkness, but could see nothing.

She turned again to the shed, then stopped. The light was out. Her heart skipped a beat. Was she sure there had been a light? Yes, she was sure.

"Is anyone here?" she called weakly. "Carmen? Security?" The only answer was more rustling of leaves, intensified this time.

She felt a prickling up her spine as she considered her options. She could go back along the fence to the gate, keep heading for her car, and convince herself she was seeing things. Or she could take the last few steps to the shed and flip on the lights herself. The promise of quick illumination proved more alluring, especially since there would be a flashlight inside for the borrowing.

Before she could think better of it, Leigh lunged for the shed door, felt around the wall inside, and flipped the switch.

The first thing she noticed was that the back door of the shed was open. The second thing was the blood.

Red, brown, black. Spotted, smeared. On top of the wooden table. Dripped through the slats to the concrete floor beneath. In ragged, but obviously linear, trails through the open back door.

Leigh's breath caught in her throat. Her eyes fixated on the irregular trails, her mind replaying footage of lionesses dragging antelope. Images of Mao Tse, her own cat, howling in triumph as she paraded about with her stuffed mouse. But the tigers were on the other side of the fence. Weren't they? When the roar came from behind, it hit her already taut muscles like a mallet. She slammed the shed door closed behind her, then lunged to close the back. Grabbing a knife from the tool shelf, she held it against her chest, standing awkwardly in the shed's center, turning from door to door. She decided to start breathing again, and once begun, couldn't stop.

When her hands began to tingle, she realized she was hyperventilating. She dropped the knife and rubbed them frantically. When the second roar came, she closed her eyes and exhaled slowly. *The cages are right against the shed, idiot. It's just one of the males . . . in his cage.*

She took another slow breath and tried to get a grip on herself. There were no man-eating tigers on the loose. It was hysteria—brought on by a walk in the dark, too little sleep, and, probably, too much daydreaming. She ran her hands through her hair and straightened her back.

Her bangs stuck to her forehead. She looked up out of the corner of her eye, and stopped breathing again.

It was blood. In her hair, on her hands. On the knife she had grabbed. She rubbed her hands on her pants madly, then grabbed the flashlight she had come for in the first place. This show was over.

She threw open the shed door and darted out, the flashlight sweeping wide arcs over the path to the gate. Nothing. She could hear the siamangs chattering from the ape house, as could anyone within a mile, but the tigers were silent. She whirled around and shone the light back over the covered cages that abutted the shed. The gates into the cage area appeared shut—the two tigers inside were lounging peacefully on their metal perches. She moved the light to the outdoor exhibit, and could see one of the young males pacing near the cliff edge. Three. The fourth tiger announced his presence with a low growl.

She swung the flashlight toward the entry gate. Another young male lay in the leaves, his back against the inside of the exhibit fence.

Leigh exhaled. Four. She walked quickly toward the gate, passing within a few feet of the young tiger on her way. As she passed, she swung the beam full into his face. The light caught his round eyes, making them shine like cut topazes against an already striking landscape of orange, black, and white. The tiger's chin sported even more color—it was bright red.

The giant mouth opened in a hissing scowl, baring similarly stained teeth. A carnivore, guarding its kill. Leigh didn't look long at the object the tiger was guarding. Her imagination might be in overdrive, but this meal wasn't imagination. It was a human leg.

Chapter 2

Reaching the employee lot was no longer Leigh's goal. Her legs propelled her past that exit and toward the main gates with a speed she hadn't known since high school—and would regret in the morning. She reached the wider road of the concession area and looked over both shoulders, anxious to find anyone with a badge. No one was in sight.

She kept running. The security building was a few hundred yards away, to the left of the main gates. She swerved toward it around the front of a pizza shack.

The collision that followed startled both parties, but the guard, having a larger abdomen with which to absorb the impact, recovered first. "Where the hell are you going?!" he snarled.

Leigh's hands flew to her hip, which had collided painfully with the ring of keys on his belt. She tried to stop panting long enough to speak, but her mouth wasn't working right. "I was looking for someone—" she gasped. "I need—"

The guard stepped back, his eyes wide. "Did you cut your head?"

Leigh touched her hands to her forehead. It was sticky. A wave of nausea rolled up in her stomach. "No," she said, frustrated, "someone else—I mean—there's been—"

The guard took a step back and barked an order into his radio. He eyed her up and down. "You work here?"

"Yes," she answered dutifully, glad of a question she could answer. She tried again to explain herself in reasonable-sounding words. "I need you to call the police. Someone's—" she faltered. There seemed to be no reasonable way of saying it. "One of the tigers is chewing on a person's leg."

The guard's expression, which had wavered from sympathy to cool skepticism, slid into open disbelief. He circled her upper arm with his hand and applied a firm grip. "Come on over to the office," he said gruffly.

In the ten minutes between the beginning of her house arrest in the security shack and the confirmation of her story by another guard, Leigh developed considerable empathy for the legitimately insane. Her captor had eyed her with a mixture of caution and amusement, as though at any moment she might note purple monkeys in the sky. Even after she was vindicated, his wary eyes followed her every move.

Excusing herself to go to the rest room, she hastily washed the blood off her face and hands. It was time to get a grip. She never claimed to be brave, but she refused to appear hysterical. She dried her bangs with a cardboardlike paper towel and curled them under with a finger. Her shirt was a lost cause, but as she couldn't see any alternative, she decided to ignore it.

She emerged from the bathroom feeling much calmer. Unfortunately, her new appearance had the opposite effect on the security guard, whose reaction was close to apoplexy. Apparently, she was supposed to have stayed bloody. He was in the middle of a earsplitting lecture, complete with gestures, when word of the police's arrival came through.

Eager to dispose of his charge, the guard hustled her back up the path to the tiger run, where a small army of blue-coated men and women buzzed about with flashlights and yellow tape. A thin, unnaturally pale man came quickly toward them, blocking their path.

"This is the girl I caught running away," the guard announced with a sense of importance. Then, more irritably, "She snuck into the bathroom and washed all the blood off—I couldn't stop her."

Leigh turned on him with a glare. Enough was enough. "I am a woman, not a girl, and I was running to get help," she said indignantly. "And I didn't *sneak* anywhere. You said I could go."

The pale man held up a hand to quell the guard's response. "I'll take over from here," he said in dismissal.

The guard humphed and left them, and Leigh quickly surveyed her new captor. A detective, she assumed. He appeared to be in his late forties, tall, but with a distinctly unhealthy appearance. A crop of prematurely white hair was well on its way to extinction, and his pale skin seemed yellowish in the dim light. His manner of dress, however, was impeccable, particularly given that it was the middle of the night.

He did not smile as he introduced himself. "Gerald Frank, City Detectives." His thin voice was hoarse, and from the redness of his nose and the puffiness of his eyes, Leigh guessed he had a raging cold. His gaze seemed to center on her chest, and for a moment she was offended. Then she remembered the blood.

"Leigh Koslow," she offered.

He withdrew a hankie from his pocket and blew his nose softly, then folded the hankie into a neat square. "Wretched cold. Could we sit?" He waved to the low brick wall that lined the path opposite the tiger exhibit. Leigh nodded, and they sat.

The first few questions, such as her address and phone number, were easy. The interview went downhill from there.

"Start at the beginning, Miss Koslow," Frank urged between sniffles. "What were you doing here at the tiger exhibit in the middle of the night?"

His tone seemed almost accusing, and Leigh had a sudden, intense urge to make her new boss field that question himself. Unfortunately, the good doctor hadn't the decency to be available. She chose the wording of her explanation carefully, painting herself as a naive new employee who did whatever she was told. It wasn't too far from the truth.

She had been hired to work just three hours a day—from 3:00 P.M., when the full-time vet tech left, to 6:00, when everybody else left. What she discovered quickly, however, was that not everyone left. Tanner was both a workaholic and a night owl, a combination that frequently kept him puttering away into the evening. For obvious reasons, she had enjoyed staying late with him, and had cheerfully agreed to assist in a late afternoon procedure on one of the gerenuk. It was a simple pin removal from a healed broken leg, but when late afternoon arrived, Tanner was not inclined to begin. He had forgotten—he claimed—the famous fifth Wednesday barbecue.

How the tradition started, Leigh still wasn't sure. But whenever a fifth Wednesday rolled around, the zoo staff held a barbecue behind the administration building. The meat went on the grills at 6:00, with drinking before, during, and after. For Leigh, who preferred to keep coworkers as coworkers, the event had been a trial. For Tanner, however, it seemed the stuff life was made of. Though he went relatively easy on the Rolling Rock, he seemed particularly delighted to be introducing Leigh around, and reluctant to leave the action. The "action," such as it was, continued well past 10:00 P.M., and Leigh assumed, logically enough, that the surgery would wait until tomorrow.

She was wrong. At quarter to eleven, Tanner draped his arms across her shoulders and asked if she was ready to set up. Like an idiot—an infatuated idiot—she had agreed.

Leigh explained the scenario to the detective as best she could, omitting, for obvious reasons, the infatuation part. The surgery had taken much longer than expected—Tanner had darted the gerenuk in good order, but the radiographs she had taken showed that the leg wasn't healing right. It would have to be restabilized, and as far as Tanner was concerned, there was no time like the present. Between the setup, the surgery, the cleanup, and the intermissions (also skillfully omitted), she considered herself lucky to have packed it in by 2:00 A.M. She concluded the rather complicated story with a play-by-play of her walk down the path and behind the shed that was both accurate and concise. She hoped the detective appreciated it.

Frank scribbled in a notepad as she talked, but appeared to be only half listening. When she stopped he closed the notebook, draped his soggy handkerchief symmetrically over one knee, and gazed off into the distance.

Leigh waited a few seconds, expecting more questions, then gave up and asked one of her own. "Do you know yet who—" she stammered. For a wordsmith, she was particularly inarticulate tonight. "Whose leg it was?"

The detective took his time answering. "The body has not been identified. Hard to say when it will be." He looked at her with a twist to his mouth that could have been a smile or a scowl. "You have a theory?"

She couldn't tell if he was humoring her or baiting her, but either way, she couldn't resist. "After the barbecue, one of the tiger keepers offered to help us out with the gerenuk. But she only hung around the hospital for a few minutes. She left saying that she needed a smoke and was going to the tiger shed to get her cigarettes. She never came back."

The detective's eyebrows rose. "Were you worried about her?"

Leigh wished she could give a more thoughtful answer. "Well, no. She wasn't big on keeping promises."

"I see," he mused. "So you think the tigers attacked her?"

Leigh's eyes narrowed. How could a detective be such a lousy listener? "Of course not!" she blurted out. "She was obviously killed in the shed. The tigers never left their cages."

"But you were afraid of the tigers being loose, weren't you?"

The smile/scowl had widened, and an uncomfortable feeling began brewing in Leigh's stomach. *Get a grip.* "Only at first, before I was really thinking," she said slowly. She couldn't get annoyed. Getting annoyed got her into trouble. "The blood spooked me, that's all. When I saw the knife, I knew it was a human's doing."

"And you picked up the knife for protection."

"Yes."

"Even though it had blood on it already."

The discomfort increased. "I didn't see the blood at first."

"Then why did you think a person had used the knife?"

"I guess I didn't realize that until later. When I picked up the knife, I was still afraid of the tigers."

"I see." The detective reopened his notebook and scribbled further, the lead weight in Leigh's stomach growing heavier with each illegible word.

"Did you drive a car here, Miss Koslow?"

Leigh responded that she had, and described it.

"I'm afraid you won't be able to drive the car home tonight," he said evenly. "We're examining evidence in the employee parking lot, and your car will be needed for a while longer."

She opened her mouth to protest—and to ask more questions—but Frank cut her off with a pale, raised palm. "Don't worry. One of the officers will give you a ride to the bureau. You can call someone to pick you up from there."

The bureau?

Leigh sat, speechless, while the detective tucked his notebook neatly into its designated pocket. "We'll need fingerprints from you, and everyone else who was in the zoo after hours," he said matter-of-factly, rising. "And of course, your clothes will be taken as evidence."

Leigh looked at the dried streaks on her khaki uniform. Fashionwise, the ensemble was no loss, but taking the clothes off one's back seemed a little third world, and a trip to a police station in the middle of the night was out of the question. Besides, she needed her car. She had important things to do—like be at her other job by 8:00 A.M.

She stood up to protest, but Frank's attention had already been diverted to a younger officer who approached with heavy footsteps. "We can't do any more until we get the vet," the man announced somewhat breathlessly. "The zoo hospital's locked up, but he's not answering at home."

"He's probably en route," Frank answered, turning to walk toward the tiger run. "Ever heard of night court? Well, now we've got night surgery."

The younger man chuckled insincerely at his superior's attempt at humor, and the two moved off.

Leigh fumed silently. She wasn't sure how he did it, but Frank had managed to make her feel like a prime suspect and an unimportant bystander at the same time. *An officer would give her a ride to the bureau.*

When? And what was she supposed to do in the meantime?

She had almost decided to follow Frank and tell him she was calling a cab when she realized why the police were looking for Tanner. For the crime scene to be fully investigated, the tigers would have to be sedated. Yet she knew the police would never find the zoo vet by calling his house all night. If they had asked her, she could have told them that Tanner was probably sacked out in the hospital lounge, by now sound asleep.

She started after the officers, but stopped. She would get the vet herself. Detective Frank could fall all over himself thanking her later.

Though all the walking paths in the zoo were now fully illuminated, every light in the dreary-looking concrete block hospital was off, and the doors were locked. No wonder the police had assumed it was empty.

Leigh lifted the tail on the plastic squirrel affixed to the downspout by the back door. A key hung from a peg underneath. She opened the door, replaced the key, and stepped inside.

"Mike? Are you awake?"

The name sounded strange to her ears. She had certainly always thought of him as Mike, but as a respectful teenager, she'd opted for "Dr. Tanner." Especially with that persnickety wife of his always hanging about watching for indiscretions. What a shrew, Leigh remembered. She had never understood what a man like Tanner had seen in Stacey the Wonder Witch, but at least he had finally got enough gumption to divorce her.

She flipped on every light switch she could find as she made her way to the staff lounge. She was an adult now—she could call him Mike if she wanted to. And if she wanted more, well, that was her business too.

The makeshift staff lounge consisted of one green vinyl couch, a drink machine, and a corroded metal wastebasket. The ambience evidently wasn't a problem for Tanner, who was sprawled out on the couch, dead to the world.

Leigh flipped on the fluorescent lights overhead, but received no reaction. "Mike!" she said louder. "Wake up!"

The form shifted position only slightly. Leigh sighed, but didn't begrudge the opportunity to admire his sleeping form. Mike Tanner was one of the Southern variety of cowboys. He was good with pickup trucks, guitars, and any hoofed mammal— but worthless with a lasso. His long, lean form was crumpled onto the narrow couch, his feet hanging off the near edge and hovering possessively over his disengaged boots. Had she ever seen him with his boots off? She didn't think so.

She plopped down on the narrow ledge of couch that wasn't already occupied, and bounced.

Tanner sat up quickly, looking at Leigh with cloudy eyes. He rubbed his face with his hands, then focused on her and smiled. "Well, this is a nice surprise. I thought you left. Where've you been?"

Leigh smiled back. Actually, she *had* walked out on him, which was why she had left the hospital in such a rush to begin with. The evening had been quite memorable. The camaraderie of a complicated surgery, then—well, the other. But she had her principles, principles that happened not to be in agreement with the clamoring of her hormones. After Tanner had taken the gerenuk back to its stall for recovery, she stayed only long enough to clean up, then vamoosed. She knew he often spent the night at the zoo, and she could take only so much temptation.

"I did start to leave," she answered. "But something happened."

Behind eyelashes any woman would kill for, Tanner's eyes widened with concern. "Are you OK?"

She nodded her head, a wave of sadness suddenly creeping over her. How well had he known the tiger keeper? Had they been good friends? She was certain, despite the detective's vague dismissal, that it was Carmen whose body she had seen. It wasn't just logical—she *knew.* Her sixth sense was finely attuned, and Carmen was, after all, more to her than just a new coworker.

How should she tell him?

"There's been a tragedy. Someone was killed behind the tiger exhibit."

Tanner sat up, fully alert. "An accident?"

Leigh shook her head. "I don't think so."

Tanner blinked twice, then pulled on his boots and started for the door, motioning for Leigh to follow.

"You'll need to load the dart gun," she called, jumping up after him. "All four tigers have to be knocked out."

He wheeled around, incredulous. "Why? You said somebody was killed *behind* the exhibit."

"The body was thrown in," she said simply.

Tanner swore colorfully and strode hastily to the pharmacy cabinet. He collected some supplies in a tackle box, closed it with a bang, and headed for the exit, sweeping Leigh's waist in one arm on the way.

He opened the clinic door and stepped back to let her through. Leigh's heart melted. *Chivalrous—even in disaster.*

She walked outside, then turned. "There's one more thing you need to know," she said to his back as he closed the door. "I think it was Carmen."

Though his face was hidden, the tremor that passed through his body couldn't be missed. He grabbed her arm and took off at a jog.

* * *

Detective Frank stopped Tanner a few paces from the tiger's gate. He did not seem unduly pleased when Leigh arrived with him. "Why didn't you tell me the vet was still here?" His words were calm, but behind his puffy lids, dark eyes flashed.

"You didn't ask," Leigh said defensively, the bad feeling creeping back into her stomach. "I figured I'd just get him myself."

Frank pulled his gaze away from her, somewhat reluctantly she thought, and turned to Tanner. "I'll need to ask you several questions," he said in a more respectful tone, "but right now, we need those tigers out of the way. For at least a half hour, if possible."

Tanner nodded, then drew a breath. "Who was killed?"

"We don't know, and we won't find out until we can get to the body," Frank replied irritably. "Now, how long will this take?"

It took hours, or so it seemed to Leigh. She sat miserably on the brick wall outside the tiger run, feeling slighted that Tanner didn't need her help, but also relieved. Relieved that her eyes wouldn't be given any further fodder for nightmares.

Yet patience had never been one of her virtues, and after ten minutes of torturous inactivity, she decided to see what fate had befallen her car. The employee lot ran along the far side of the tiger run, the entrance being farther down the hill and around a bend. Leigh walked down the path and over to the gate, which was standing open, evidently to admit the police. Normally, the gate stayed locked, except at shift changes when it was monitored by a guard. Employees could leave through the one-way turnstile, but after-hours arrivals had to be more covert. Leigh had been taught on her first day how to sneak under the fence where it crossed a chasm—and she had found the path well worn.

She walked through the open gate and out into the brightly lit parking lot, but didn't get far. Yellow tape outlined a large area abutting the tiger run—and the "secret" entrance. Leigh swallowed. Being basically lazy, she had parked her car as close to the hole as she could get. A cluster of people buzzed about the Cavalier, one pointing at the driver's door, another photographing it. Two other people in uniform walked away from the car and toward the hole, gesturing at the ground.

"You shouldn't be out here, miss," a stern voice called.

Leigh turned around to see a portly, redheaded policeman standing by the employee gate. He hadn't been there before. Had he followed her?

"Come on back and have a seat," he urged, more politely. "We'll be leaving shortly."

She saw no point in arguing, as her car was clearly going nowhere soon. It was only as she turned back toward the gate that she saw the lot's only other occupant, a red Grand Am, parked on the far side of the entrance. Leigh's eyes were drawn instantly to the vanity plate adorning its rear. CAKY-10. She sucked in a breath, then let it out slowly. There could be no more question about it. Caky was Carmen's nickname, and she had always thought of herself as a ten.

C.A.K. *Carmen Andrea Koslow.*

Chapter 3

Leigh sat miserably on the stone wall for another fifteen minutes before Detective Frank reappeared, a defeated-looking Tanner in tow. Tanner put a sympathetic hand briefly on her shoulder, then sat down beside her. Frank, Leigh noticed, did not miss the gesture.

"Miss Koslow," the detective began, his voice assuming an edge that made her nervous. "We have reason to believe the deceased may indeed be a keeper here, Miss Carmen Koslow. Is she any relation to you?"

Leigh took in a deep breath. It was a question she had been asked countless times before. Once, on an occasion she preferred not to remember, by another policeman. She gave the same answer she always gave, and was glad it was the truth. "Not that I know of. But there are several Koslows in the area—we might be related way back." *And if we are, I'd rather not know about it.*

The detective didn't scribble this time, but stared at her with penetrating dark eyes—a stark contrast to his pale face. "Did you know Carmen Koslow before you came to work here?"

Leigh swallowed and nodded. "We went to middle school and high school together. At North Hills. We were thrown together because of our names, but we weren't close. Until I came to work here, I had no idea where she was or what she was doing."

Frank had decided to scribble after all. He pulled out his notebook, propped his leg up on the wall, and started to write on his knee. The action brought on a coughing spasm so severe it made Leigh's own lungs hurt. When he had recovered, he spoke. "Before you started working here, how long had it been since you last saw her?"

Leigh paused. She had grudgingly attended her ten-year reunion a few years ago, but Carmen hadn't been there. "Not since high school graduation," she answered.

Tanner, who had sat through the interrogation with his head in his hands, turned to look at her. "You weren't friends?" he asked quietly, a puzzled expression on his face.

Leigh couldn't help casting a glance at Frank, who of course had heard the question and was now watching her like a hawk. "Not particularly," she answered vaguely, wishing Tanner would keep his mouth shut. What had Carmen told him, anyway?

Frank looked at her for a long moment. She was normally good at staring games, but the detective was better. She looked away, her anxiety growing. "Are we going to the bureau now?"

The detective stopped staring at her and began nibbling on the end of his pen. "In a few minutes," he mumbled. "You two stay here until we call you."

Frank returned to the tiger run, and when he was out of earshot, Leigh turned to Tanner. "Can't you just drive us in your truck?"

Tanner shook his head sadly. "They're doing something with it, I don't know what. It's parked way over in the main lot, so I'm not sure why it's important." He stretched out his long legs in front of him and sighed.

"I can't believe this. I never thought anyone would do this to her."

Leigh watched him closely. His voice was filled with sorrow, his deep-blue eyes moist. He must have known Carmen fairly well. Furthermore, he must have known a side of her that Leigh didn't.

"She told me you were one of her favorite people in high school," he continued morosely. Then he gave a small smile. "I wasn't surprised. You seemed like a fun girl to be around."

Leigh forced herself to smile back. So Carmen had spoken well of her. That wasn't too surprising. One learned not to be surprised by anything Carmen did.

A sudden roar from one of the tigers sent prickles up her spine. The big cats were awake already. And the body?

She turned to Tanner. "You are sure it was Carmen?"

He winced suddenly and turned away from her. After another moment with his head in his hands, he answered, "They haven't recovered the whole body. At least not yet. There were—" He broke off, then cleared his throat into a fist. "They found legs and one arm. That's all."

Leigh's stomach made a move for her throat, but she willed it down. Two legs and an arm? Where was the rest? She asked the obvious question. "Could the tigers—"

Tanner shook his head violently. "No way. They were well fed. They weren't eating what they had, just—"

He stopped, but Leigh knew enough about cats to guess the statement's unpleasant ending. *Just playing with it.*

"The police think the rest of the body was dragged out under the fence," he stated flatly.

Leigh thought of the rustling leaves she had heard when she first approached the shed, and her heart rate increased. "Did Detective Frank tell you this?"

Tanner shook his head. "Frank didn't tell me anything. I overheard the cops talking while I was monitoring the tigers."

"Then they can't really know for sure that it's Carmen," Leigh offered, though personally she had no doubts.

He shook his head again. "There's more. Her purse and keys were still in the shed, along with her torn clothes—and there was a clump of hair on the floor, stuck in the doorjamb."

Leigh didn't have to ask what type of hair it was. Carmen's waist-length jet black mane had been her pride and joy.

"And there was another thing," he said miserably. "The tigers left—" He stopped, swallowed, and continued, "There were rings still on her hand. I recognized one."

Leigh's stomach performed another odd maneuver, and she wondered if it would ever feel normal again. She was not, and had never been, a bosom buddy of Carmen Koslow's, but she *was* sorry the woman was dead. Coming upon the gruesome scene had unsettled her thoroughly, and as if that wasn't disturbing enough, she had Detective Frank's odd demeanor to worry about too. Now, adding insult to injury, there was a look of pain in Tanner's eyes that no self-respecting woman could misinterpret, and she didn't care for it one bit.

"You recognized one of Carmen's rings?" she blurted out.

Tanner nodded, and sighed again. "Yep," he said softly, falling back into an even thicker Southern accent. "I gave it to her."

The Central Detectives Bureau would not have been Leigh's first choice of a location to spend her predawn hours, but her preferences seemed not to matter. She was whisked away in a patrol car before she had a chance to pry further into Tanner's relationship with Carmen, and was fingerprinted before she had a chance to sit down. To add further insult, Frank had insisted that a female officer accompany her into the rest room while she traded her bloody uniform for jail apparel. The bright orange jumpsuit put her at a distinct psychological disadvantage as she faced Frank across the table in the interrogation room. To make matters worse, she couldn't get the ink off her fingers, and she was pretty sure there was still blood in her hair.

"Now," Frank began offhandedly, "I know you've already answered questions at the scene, but we're going to need an official statement on audiotape as well. You have the right to remain silent. If you give up the right to remain silent, anything you say can and will be used against you in a court of law. You have the right to speak with an attorney and to have an attorney present during questioning. If you so desire and cannot afford one, an attorney will be appointed for you without charge before the questioning begins. Do you understand these rights as I have read them?"

Leigh's mouth had dropped open on the second sentence. "Excuse me," she said when her senses were partially recovered, "did I miss something? Am I being arrested?"

The detective closed his red-rimmed eyes and sighed heavily. "You people watch too much TV. The Miranda warning isn't only for individuals under arrest. Before we take a statement from anyone who's a potential suspect, we read them their rights."

Leigh's eyes narrowed thoughtfully. She didn't entirely trust Frank, but she had no reason to assume he didn't go by the book. The words "potential suspect" were not reassuring, but she had done nothing wrong, so what did it matter?

"Do you waive and give up those rights?" Frank pressed impatiently.

Leigh ground her teeth. Even if she didn't do anything, she *should* probably still get a lawyer. But who? Criminal defense lawyers cost money she didn't have. A public defender? She looked at her watch. 4:00 A.M. Did PDs work night shifts? Fat chance.

She sighed and shifted in her seat. Surely there would be no harm in just telling her story straight and getting it over with. Any funny stuff and she'd clam up.

Frank drummed his fingers on the table and stared at her.

"Fine," she said, a little more obstinately than she intended. "Tape away."

At the detective's prompting, she repeated her story, careful not to say anything more than was absolutely necessary. When she had finished, he began with a new line of questions.

"How would you describe the relationship you had with Carmen Koslow when you were both still in high school?"

She blinked. Why would he care? "Casual."

"You never spent a great deal of time together?"

An image flashed in Leigh's mind of another police station, another day. Of the attorney's bill her father had dutifully paid.

"No," she answered firmly.

Frank followed up with a few questions about her relationships with other zoo employees. When he moved to her relationship with Tanner, she'd had enough.

"I'd like to go home now," she said politely, not wanting to look guilty of anything. "I'm too tired to think. Can we continue this some time when I've been up less than twenty-four hours straight?"

Frank looked at her thoughtfully, but nodded.

"That'll be enough for now. In the meantime, don't leave town. We may be speaking with you again."

Leigh wanted to say she was looking forward to it, but that would be a bald-faced lie.

"Do you need a ride home," he asked with uncharacteristic chivalry as he showed her back to the waiting area, "or is there someone you can call to pick you up?"

Without thinking, Leigh glanced around the room. The detective was quick. "Dr. Tanner is still being questioned. If you want to wait for him, fine. But it may be a while."

She cursed herself for being so transparent. The last thing she needed was to encourage Frank's sniffing around her interest in Tanner. Particularly if Tanner and Carmen—

"I'm going home now," she said quickly, interrupting her own thoughts. "I can call someone to pick me up."

"Suit yourself," Frank replied, and left her alone in the waiting area.

Someone to pick me up. And who might that be? There was a difference in the kind of friend you'd go to a movie with and the kind of friend you'd drag out of bed at a quarter to five in the morning to pick you up at a police station. In the latter category, Leigh's options were limited. Her cousin was out of the question—Cara had a new baby to take care of. There was her old college pal-cum-politician Warren—she could always count on him. But for this particular dilemma, special expertise was needed.

She took a deep breath and picked up the phone. Her experiences in waking up her ex-college roommate, Officer Maura Polanski, were never pleasant. But desperate situations called for desperate measures.

The phone rang only once.

"Yeah?" an alert voice demanded.

"Hi. It's me," Leigh began sheepishly. "Sorry to wake you, but I kind of need your help." She paused. "Don't worry—I mean, I'm fine and everything, but I'm stuck at the Central Detectives Bureau in East Liberty, and they're holding my car—"

"I'll be there in about twenty-five minutes."

Leigh's brow furrowed as she removed the phone from her ear and stared at it for a moment. "Maura, are you awake? Did you hear what I said?"

"Yes."

"I'm at a police station in the middle of the night. Doesn't that surprise you? Shock you? Just a little bit?"

"No."

Leigh sighed. She was in no position to quibble about the slight to her character. "You're coming then? Thanks. And if it isn't too much trouble—could you bring me a change of clothes?"

"No problem."

Leigh began to explain, but didn't get a chance. Maura had already hung up.

Twenty-three minutes later, Maura Polanski's six-feet-two, 210-pound frame filled the doorway of the waiting area. "Here," she said gruffly, holding out a pair of sweats. "Are they done with you?"

Maura had on her best countenance of disapproval, which could scare the pants off anyone under six feet tall and unarmed. Leigh knew better, however. When the policewoman wasn't trying to intimidate, she had a baby face that was absolutely cherubic—and the heart to go with it.

Leigh ducked into the rest room and quickly traded her prison togs for the sweat suit. Reemerging, she wondered if she should have bothered. Maura's pants were so baggy she had had to tie the waistband in a knot just to keep them up, and constant vigilance was needed to keep the gaping collar from exposing her bra straps. Leigh couldn't help but wonder if Maura had picked out this outfit on purpose, given how easily she could have borrowed clothes from one of her more normal-sized aunts. But protesting now seemed unwise.

Maura didn't speak until they were in the car headed home. "All right, Koslow," she began, sounding resigned. "Start talking. You've got half an hour. I go on duty at six."

Leigh's eyes narrowed. Maura clearly assumed that she was somehow responsible for her own predicament, which was terribly insulting. On the other hand, given Leigh's record as a magnet for calamity, Maura could hardly be blamed. Leigh tried not to bite the hand that was feeding her. She swallowed, then told her story once again. A specialized version—conveniently vague on matters relating to Mike Tanner, yet heavy on the disconcerting actions of Detective Frank. Maura listened without any visible reaction.

"Well?" Leigh asked when her story was finished. "Don't you think I've been treated rather shabbily in all this?"

Maura cleared her throat, then twisted her mouth into a grim line. "What I think," she said firmly, "is that you need a lawyer."

Chapter 4

As Leigh trudged up the four floors to her Ross Township apartment, her mind spun with worrying thoughts of circumstantial evidence, bloody legs, and something disturbing that Tanner had said that she couldn't quite remember. Maura had insisted on asking around about a good lawyer, which wouldn't have been so alarming if the policewoman was the fretting type. But Leigh knew her friend too well to delude herself. Overreacting was Leigh's forte—Maura was into stoicism.

She fumbled with her key in the lock, stumbled into the bedroom, and collapsed on the madeup bed. She couldn't think—or worry, anymore. Her brain cooperated by slipping into self-preservation mode, convincing her as she drifted off that the last few hours had been just a bad dream.

Her slumber was deep, but not long. The phone at her bedside rang at the tender hour of 6:30 A.M.— and rang, and rang. Leigh had trained herself to ignore phone calls, letting the answering machine pick up on the second ring whether she was home or not. Unfortunately, her cat, Mao Tse, had a nasty habit of walking on the OFF button. After the eighth ring, she gave up.

"Hello?" Her head was still fuzzy, but for having

less than an hour's sleep, she felt surprisingly rejuvenated.

"Leigh, it's me. Sorry to wake you, but I need a favor. A big one."

The pleasant tone of her old friend's voice was soothing, despite the hour. It seemed a nice distraction from whatever bad thing it was that her brain didn't want to remember, but that was making a pit in her stomach anyway. "What is it, Warren?" she yawned. "Nothing that can't wait a few hours, I hope."

"Sorry—I need you now. *Right now.* Can you come down? I'll explain later."

She sighed. She would have had to get up in another half hour anyway. She tromped down the two flights of stairs that separated her apartment from Warren's and knocked on the door.

It flew open almost instantly, and a long arm pulled her inside. "Did you see anyone in the hall?"

Warren Harmon III had made Leigh's acquaintance when they were freshmen at the University of Pittsburgh, vying for the least valuable player award in Volleyball 101. Warren had been an unattractive teenager—tall, scrawny, a poster child for Clearasil. But in the decade since, the nonthreatening geek that Leigh had so enjoyed debating with had metamorphosed into a successful local politician. And, as she had recently forced herself to admit, not a bad looking one. Particularly in the blue silk robe he was wearing now.

"Of course there was no one in the hall," she answered sleepily. "What sane person would be at this hour?"

The arm continued to drag her back toward the bedroom. If it had been anyone but Warren, she might have been worried. He stopped in front of a closet, took out a man's fuzzy velour bathrobe, and held it out for her.

"Put this on, OK?"

Leigh smirked. "I don't know. Maroon isn't really my color. I like the one you're wearing better."

Sighing with exasperation, Warren turned her around and slipped the robe over her arms. He stepped back and studied her. "There. You look stunning, as usual."

She rolled her eyes. "Enough butter. I'm here already. Now how about you tell me why?"

Warren started to answer, but was interrupted by the doorbell. He snatched Leigh's arm again hastily. "Sit down at the table," he ordered. "Hide those god-awful sweatpants. And here," he said quickly, pulling an empty mug from the cabinet, "pretend you're drinking coffee."

Leigh sat down and took the cup. "But who—"

"Just play along!" Warren whispered, advancing on the door.

He opened it to reveal a stout, sixtyish woman wearing the sort of stiff-looking outfit Queen Elizabeth II might appreciate. Warren greeted her with a full dose of the Harmon charm—which could be considerable.

"I'm so sorry to disturb you at this hour," the woman pleaded apologetically. "Myran just can't function without his reading glasses, and he's such an early bird. I've told him he needs to take better care where he leaves them—but he doesn't always listen to me, you know."

Warren responded with both insistence that she was not imposing and chastisement of Myran for not taking heed of her wisdom—all the while moving gracefully backward toward Leigh.

Eventually, the woman looked into the kitchen. She had been in the middle of an indulgent giggle (having taken Warren's blatant flattery at face value) when her hand flew to her mouth, her face suffused with red. Leigh took a sip of imaginary coffee and waved.

"Oh, I'm so sorry, Mr. Harmon!" the woman bubbled. "I had no idea—"

"Of course not, Mrs. Wiggin!" Warren soothed. "It's no problem at all. This is Leigh Koslow. Leigh— Mrs. Barbara Wiggin."

"Nice to meet you." Leigh grinned broadly.

Mrs. Wiggin smiled back hesitantly. Warren picked up a black eyeglass case from the table and pressed it into her hand, then whispered something in her ear. She seemed to relax. "Oh," she said solemnly, "I see."

"Would you like a cup of coffee?" Leigh offered. "It's vanilla almond."

Warren's eyes widened.

"Oh, no, dear!" Mrs. Wiggin said quickly. "I really must be going. Myran will have my head. It was nice meeting you." She threw a conspiratorial glance at Warren, then looked back at Leigh. "I'm sure I'll be seeing you again soon."

As soon as he had gallantly ushered his guest out the door, Warren turned on Leigh with an accusing glare. "*Vanilla almond?* Please! What if she had said yes?"

"She wouldn't. Not in a million years." Leigh laughed, pulling off the heavy robe. "This thing is hot. The least you can do after compromising a woman is give her your best robe."

Warren took the robe defensively. "There's nothing wrong with this. And you're one to talk about taste in night wear, anyway."

Leigh looked down at the elephantine sweats bagged up from her ankles to her knees. She realized one shoulder was completely uncovered. "These aren't mine," she said hotly, jerking up the neckline.

"That's what concerns me," he said, sounding serious. "Did *I* interrupt something?"

Leigh scoffed. *Not likely.* "These are Maura's," she answered. "Enough about me. I want real coffee. And a nice long explanation for this little performance."

"Fine," Warren agreed, "but I'm fresh out of vanilla almond."

Ten minutes and a change of clothes later, Leigh was again sitting at Warren's kitchen table, this time drinking a full-strength brew.

"Myran Wiggin is the chair of the Allegheny County Democratic Party, as every good Pittsburgher should know," Warren explained. "He's extremely influential. To make a long story short, he can make or break my chances for the new county council."

Leigh tried not to let her gaze wander. She loathed politics, as Warren well knew. But changing the world through channels was his life goal. That—and being president, of course. She used to laugh at his aspirations, but now she wasn't so sure. He had won his first election—to become the county's Register of Wills—by a landslide, then gone on to collect considerable accolades for his cost-cutting innovations. Now, with the revamping of the county government under way and the extinction of his current post looming, he was vying for a charter membership on the new Allegheny County Council. Warren was brilliant at all matters financial, but she could never quite figure out how he succeeded in politics, given the fact that he was basically honest.

"It appeared that I was standing in pretty good favor with Myran," Warren continued, "until last weekend."

Despite her efforts, Leigh's gaze wandered to a water spot on Warren's ceiling.

He waved a hand in front of her face. "Yoo hoo, Leigh? Stay with me—the good stuff's coming."

She redoubled her efforts.

"We were having drinks at a hotel bar after a committee meeting—standard stuff, and Myran was feeling unusually festive. So festive, in fact, that he offered to serve up a couple of female companions for the evening—his treat."

Leigh was back with the program. "And you said—?"

"I declined, of course. Gracefully—or so I thought. He sulked through a few more drinks, then I put him in a cab and sent him home to Barbara."

"Where he belonged."

"Granted."

"So what was the problem?"

"The problem was that when he came over last night to talk shop again, he seemed uneasy. He kept looking around my apartment like he was trying to find something."

"Thought you'd squeal on him, eh?"

"Hardly. I don't think he loses much sleep over his reputation. Barbara is well aware of his weaknesses."

"Oh," Leigh said, disappointed in the little woman. Any man who tried that on her would regret her knowledge of the neutering procedure.

"I got the distinct impression," Warren continued, "that he thought I didn't share his taste for women. *Any* woman."

"Aha . . ." Leigh cooed, catching the drift. "The single, slender, and neat thing, eh?" She smiled. "You are awfully neat for a man, you know."

Warren glared. "Don't start with me. The point is, he had his suspicions. And as conservative a Democrat as Myran is, those suspicions could be the death knell of my campaign."

Leigh laughed as she poured herself a second cup of coffee. "Hence the sleepover facade."

"Right, although that was sheer luck. He called before dawn this morning to tell me he'd left his glasses, and that he was sending Barb to pick them up."

"The little woman again." Leigh scowled, sitting

back down. "Fetch, dear! What a jerk." She took a long drag of coffee.

"Myran is no saint, but he has political talent," Warren defended. "Besides, you'll be happy to know that he doesn't know as much about his wife's whereabouts as he thinks he does."

Her eyes widened. "Really? Mrs. Prim and Servile herself? Do tell!"

But Leigh's prurient interests were not to be satisfied. Warren's telephone rang, and he was quick to take advantage of the distraction.

"Hello? Mo-Mo! How're you doing? Bust any politicians lately?" he began happily.

The sick feeling that Leigh had so successfully been ignoring came back in full force. Warren was the only person who had ever called Maura "Mo-Mo" and lived to tell about it. Like Leigh, the policewoman seemed to have a giant soft spot for the future president. They had made an odd trio in their college days, but they'd shared a lot of laughs.

"Criminal defense attorneys? Sure, I know a few. Why?"

Leigh sank down in her chair, the pit in her stomach growing. It hadn't been a dream. *Damn.*

There was silence on Warren's end of the line as he turned and fixed her with a hard glare. "She's right here," he said heavily. "She didn't say a word."

Leigh sank low enough to see the underside of the table, then decided that her back hurt. She slithered back up into the chair and polished off cup number two.

When Warren had finished his conversation, he hung up the phone, poured decaf grounds into a fresh filter, and restarted the coffeepot. "OK, Leigh," he said solemnly, sitting down. "Let's talk."

The Hook agency was headquartered on Pittsburgh's North Side, close to downtown, but with more affordable rents. Both were necessary for the fledgling advertising agency that Leigh was starting up with three other ex-employees of Peres and Lacey Advertising, Inc. They had all been unceremoniously sacked after two major clients withdrew their accounts—rather capriciously, in Leigh's opinion. None of the four took the matter lightly, least of all Leigh, who had already lost two copywriting jobs to Pittsburgh's dog-eat-dog advertising climate.

The venture was a gamble, and Leigh had already had cause to regret it. Though she hadn't been required to invest any of her own money, her savings were needed just to cover her expenses until the agency could pay her. So far they had done well, swiping a third of their previous accounts from Peres and Lacey and picking up several others from past contacts. The sad fact, however, was that without nepotism, they'd still be nowhere. They were afloat purely because Carl Ooms, their production manager, happened to have a Fortune 500 uncle who was willing to steer a sizable contract their way—payable up front.

She thanked Warren for the ride and skidded through the lobby of the remodeled warehouse and into the suite marked HOOK, INC., a loose acronym for the principals. She passed through the reception area, which was empty of both people and chairs, and on into one of the three back offices, which she shared with designer Alice Humboldt. Alice was out, but Jeff Hulsey—account representative, financial planner, and two-bit motivational speaker—swept in immediately after her.

"Leigh—good news. I think we've got a chance with Major's Pizza. They're thinking print ads with radio spots—I told them you were their woman."

"Do they know I don't do jingles?"

"They don't have to," Jeff said, waving a hand dismissively. "We can contract it. I know a guy."

Leigh smiled. Jeff Hulsey knew everybody. He was a one-man white pages. He was also the driving force behind the new agency, and without him they'd be sunk. "Cool. Let's go for it."

Jeff beamed his approval and disappeared.

Leigh threw the thick wallet she used as a purse into an empty drawer of the painted metal desk she had bought at a flea market. Her computer, at least, was new—even if it was an off brand. Jeff understood the necessities of life.

She adjusted the small stack of papers on her desk, booted up the PC, and commenced staring at the monitor. She was good at staring at monitors. Unfortunately, she was no longer doing it on salary.

The headline of the Geisler Chemicals press release blurred in front of her. Warren had made her repeat every detail of her harrowing night, and had promised to find her an attorney by the end of the day. The problem was, she didn't want one. She'd only met a few trial-type lawyers, and she hadn't liked any of them. Plus, it was very unlikely they'd be willing to take her on as a charity case, which she was. Even if Warren could convince them to agree to a benevolent payment schedule, it would be money she badly needed otherwise.

A loud sigh escaped her lips. She didn't *really* have anything to worry about. Did she? She hadn't done anything except find the body. So what were the police doing with her car? Tanner had said the rest of Carmen's body was dragged under the fence, and the Cavalier had been parked within ten feet of that spot. Could the killer have left some evidence on it? And how long were they going to keep her car, anyway? She was tempted to call Frank and ask, but she doubted she could get off the phone without having to answer more questions. And there were at least two lines of questions she didn't want to answer.

She had spent several unproductive hours at her

desk when the phone rang in the reception area. It didn't ring often; since their newly hired business manager hadn't started work yet, important callers were given Jeff's direct line. Leigh poked her head outside her door. Carl wasn't in today either, and Jeff was busy on his extension. It appeared the copy-writing department would field the call.

"Hook, Inc. Innovative Advertising and PR. How may I direct your call?" *As in, six feet in which direction?*

"Hey there," answered a smooth, Southern male voice. "Sorry I got hung up last night. Are you OK?"

Leigh smiled and sat down on the floor next to the phone. "I'm fine. Seemed like Frank grilled you for a while, though."

"It was nothing. The man's just doing his job," Tanner said charitably. "He's been nosing around here again this morning; the staff's pretty shell-shocked. Listen, I need to tell you that Leo's laid down the law on after-hours procedures."

As well he should, Leigh thought. Leo Martin was the zoo's largely incompetent director, and he was undoubtedly in severe gastric distress over what Carmen's murder would mean for the park's image.

"No one's allowed to be here after closing, period, unless there's an emergency, and then you have to have a security escort. So we may have to adjust your schedule a little."

Leigh sighed. If she was never in a dark zoo again, it would be too soon, but she needed the money. If the zoo wanted her earlier in the day, she'd have to go back to Hook at night or on the weekends to make up the time. It was not a pleasant prospect. "When do you want me there?" she asked, trying not to sound as unenthusiastic as she felt.

"Actually," Tanner said softly, "I was hoping you might come in right after lunch today. I'm still planning on shaving Ollie, and I know you wanted to help."

Leigh smiled. She had been looking forward to seeing the orangutan get his new doo. It was sweet of Tanner to think of her.

"I'll be there," she said decisively. Hook, Inc., could live without her for a few hours. Besides, she had to talk to Tanner. There were things she had to know.

She headed out the door at noon, and was all the way out into the parking lot before realizing she had no car. As if on cue, a neon-blue VW beetle pulled up alongside her.

Warren stretched out a long arm and pushed open the passenger door. "Going somewhere?"

"To the zoo," she replied, getting in. "The vet needs my help. Could you give me a lift?"

"I'll give you a lift all right," Warren quipped, speeding off. "But it won't be to the zoo. You have an appointment with an attorney in twenty minutes. And you're going to keep it."

Chapter 5

"I'm really not comfortable with this," Leigh repeated for the third time as they stepped off the elevator onto the fourteenth floor of Grant Street's Oxford Centre. "I can't afford an attorney and I shouldn't have to pay one. I didn't do anything wrong."

Warren had already stopped trying to reason with her. He merely pulled her along with a gentle grip on the arm. "This is it," he said, reading the brass doorplate. He checked his watch and smiled. "Perfect timing."

He opened the door and ushered her inside, where an efficient secretary sent them straight into the office of Katharine Bower, Attorney-at-Law. A petite, fortyish woman in a sharply cut business suit stood up and flashed a broad smile at Leigh's escort. "Warren!" she said warmly, "I'm so glad you came in. We really need to do lunch sometime." She looked at her watch. "Are you free at two P.M.?"

Leigh surveyed the lawyer skeptically. So, this was Warren's "shark among women"—the attorney who'd saved one of his previous employers from a trumped-up fraud charge? Judging from the sparkle in the counselor's eyes, she had matters other than criminal defense on her mind at the moment. *Lunch at 2:00 P.M.? Please.* By that hour, Leigh was long past lunch and into the Snickers zone.

Warren graciously requested a rain check, explaining that the clock was already ticking on his lunch hour. Unlike most elected officials, the Allegheny County Register of Wills seemed to feel he owed the taxpayers a full day's work. He introduced the two women, then headed for the door. "I'm off to lunch," he said, looking at Leigh, "Can I bring you back something?"

The timing was appropriate, but Leigh shook her head. When it came to unappetizing adventures, a lawyer appointment was right up there with the gynecologist.

Katharine Bower said good-bye to Warren with a calculated toss of her extremely short, extremely red hair, then turned to her client. "Now, Ms. Koslow, let's get down to business, shall we?"

Leigh sat up in her overstuffed leather chair and studied the lawyer from across the shiny black desktop. A pair of wire-framed glasses had materialized on Katharine's nose, and her voice had lost its warm edge. Evidently, business meant business. The shark had merely been on a flirt break.

"Call me Leigh, please."

Katharine nodded briefly in assent. "I understand you've been questioned by the city detectives in regard to a homicide, and that they first advised you of your rights?"

Leigh nodded glumly.

"That means they're considering you a potential suspect. It's important that you don't offer any more information unless I'm present. Understand?"

"Fine," Leigh agreed charitably. "Detective Frank can stew."

Katharine's potent green eyes looked up. "You've got Gerry Frank on this one?"

"Yes," Leigh answered, a little worried. "Is that good or bad?"

The lawyer's facial expression gave away nothing, but there was an intensity in her eyes Leigh couldn't miss. "Frank does his job," Katharine answered impassively. "You could do worse."

She pulled a laptop computer in front of her and began quizzing Leigh on possible reasons the police might have for suspecting her. Unfortunately, Leigh was able to list several. The blood was a big one. Her "running away." And whatever the heck had happened with her car.

Katharine typed rapidly, occasionally tilting her nose down and peering at Leigh over the wire-rims. Her face became increasingly grim. "Anything else?"

"I can't imagine what else they'd have," Leigh said uncertainly. "I've only been working at the zoo a few days."

"So you and the victim had never met?"

Leigh squirmed. She was going to get this one wrong too. "Well, actually, we went to high school together. But after that I didn't see her for thirteen years." *Why couldn't it have been fourteen?*

"You were friends in high school?"

Another strike. "Acquaintances," Leigh answered carefully. "Have you read the statement I gave the police?"

Katharine shook her head without looking up. "The police won't give me jack unless you've been charged with something. Then we get the works. Statements, forensics reports. We'll hope it doesn't come to that."

Leigh agreed wholeheartedly.

"Now," Katharine continued, "I want you to start from your first day at the zoo, the first time you saw the victim as an adult, and tell me every significant thing that happened between then and when you walked into my office just now."

Leigh sighed. It was a story she was tired of telling. It was also a story she was tired of editing. She began doggedly, got derailed several times by specific questions, and finished with a faintly nauseous feeling.

Katharine took off her glasses and leaned back in her rather impressive-looking office recliner. "We need to talk motive, Leigh. It will make or break any case against you."

The nausea increased. "I have no motive."

Katharine smiled suddenly. "Tell me something. You said that during the day you work at an advertising agency?"

Leigh nodded.

"Have you ever pulled an all-nighter over a tough deadline?"

"Sure—usually when somebody else drops the ball and screws up the schedule. But I'm working for myself now, and I intend to make all-nighters a thing of the past." The words sounded naive, she knew, but one could always dream.

"But what about when you were an employee? If your boss wanted you to put in some extra evening hours for his convenience, even though it wouldn't strictly be necessary to get the project in on time? Would you agree?"

"Of course not." Before the words were completely out of Leigh's mouth, she saw through the attorney's questions. *Damn.*

"Do you have a romantic interest in Dr. Tanner?"

The question hit Leigh like a load of bricks. She was tired of being self-conscious about her emotions. The fact was, she still wasn't sure how she felt about Tanner, and it certainly wasn't anybody else's business—homicide investigation or no. She had nothing to do with Carmen's death—why should it give perfect strangers the right to know what she was thinking?

"No!" she said forcefully.

Katharine blinked. "Fine. And was Tanner involved with Carmen Koslow?"

"I don't know!" Leigh answered honestly, if a little too vehemently.

The lawyer studied her closely. Leigh made an effort to relax. She knew such people were trained to read body language, and it annoyed the heck out of her. Why couldn't she do all this on-line?

Katharine typed a few more lines, then closed the lid on her laptop. "Look, Leigh. I'm not accusing you of anything. I'm just trying to figure out where Frank's head is at. He's out there even as we speak searching for a motive. And I can tell you right now what he's thinking. He's thinking love triangle."

Love triangle? Leigh's face grew hot, but she kept her mouth shut. A few innocent kisses, and she was on trial for bumping off the other woman. And who said Carmen was the other woman, anyway? Who said there even *was* another woman?

"That's all I need from you for now, Leigh," Katharine announced. "Lab results may come in as early as this afternoon. Blood matches, hair, fibers. Fingerprints."

"I'm not worried about that," Leigh said honestly. "I didn't touch anything in that shed except the doorknobs, the light switch, the knife, and the flashlight. And I don't know why they were all over my car— I parked it yesterday afternoon and haven't touched it since."

"Good." Katharine looked at Leigh pointedly. "Frank may find you today, or he may call and ask you to go back down to the bureau. When he does, you call me immediately." She handed Leigh a business card. "And don't say a word until I get there. Understand?"

Leigh nodded. Frank was definitely *not* getting any more out of her.

*   *   *

When Warren's VW delivered Leigh into the main zoo parking lot, it was after 1:30 P.M., and Leigh was worried that Tanner had been waiting for her.

"Are you going to take her advice?" Warren repeated, since Leigh wasn't listening to him.

"Yes, yes!" she answered. "But I'm not going to use her any more than necessary. I can't afford it."

"I already told you, it's a no-interest loan."

Leigh squirmed uncomfortably. "I appreciate that, Warren. But at the rate my finances are going, it will take me years to pay you back, and I don't like owing you. I don't like owing anybody. Can you understand?"

He smiled. "Of course I can. But you can't get cheap on something this important. You're in trouble, and Katharine's the best. You deserve the best."

The events of the last twenty-four hours were beginning to wear on Leigh's emotions, and her eyes watered. Warren could be so damn nice sometimes.

He stopped the car and she jumped out quickly. "Will you need a ride home?" he asked.

She shook her head. "You've done enough for me already."

"If you change your mind, just call me at the City-County Building."

Leigh nodded and turned her misty eyes away.

The zoo seemed more crowded than usual for a Thursday, and as Leigh began walking up the long hill to the hospital, she noticed that many of the visitors were heading toward the Asia section—and the tiger run.

Fabulous. The word is out.

She veered off in the opposite direction, taking the long way around goat mountain and the round barn. As she passed the administration building, her stomach gave a faint, healthier rumble. Evidently it remembered that she'd had no lunch. It also remembered that the vending machines in the employee lounge stocked Whatchamacallits.

She opened the door to a smoky, medium-sized room buzzing with conversation. By the time the door closed behind her, there was silence. She looked out nervously at the half-dozen pairs of eyes that were staring at her. It took a second, but she regained her composure.

"Well, I didn't have lunch," she announced to the crowd. "So I know there's no giant piece of broccoli in my teeth. What gives?"

A round of nervous laughter broke the tension. "Hi, Leigh," came a voice from the corner table. "Sorry. It's just—we didn't think you'd be in today."

The voice was that of Lisa Moran, the floater who had helped out at the hospital two days ago. Lisa was a tiny, perky natural blond, the kind of woman other women loved to hate. Leigh was not above such primal feelings, but right now, Lisa was her best candidate for an ally.

Leigh got her candy bar and walked over. "Gotta work," she replied. "You know how it is."

The other three keepers seated at the table nodded. Leigh knew two of them: Tish Holly, the rather frightening six-foot, 135-pound elephant keeper, and Tonya Rawlings, a thrice-divorced twenty-something who worked in the bird house. The third keeper was a young man with fuzzy red hair who Leigh thought worked with the reptiles.

"So you found her, huh?" the redheaded youth asked. His nametag said ART FAIGEN.

Leigh swallowed a large bite of candy bar and nodded. She should have expected an interrogation. The other keepers were bound to be dying of curiosity. If the deceased had been anyone other than Carmen, they might have been grieving too.

"We've all been watching the news reports at lunch," Lisa chattered. "None of them mentioned your name, just that a zoo employee found her, and that parts of her body were in the tiger run."

"You gotta wonder where the rest of her is," Tonya chimed in. "Whoever did it was pretty stupid if they thought the tigers would eat everything."

Lisa nodded solemnly. "No way. Now the polar bears—maybe. But nobody who worked around here would throw her to the tigers. Not unless they were starved first."

"Hell, it still could have been anybody!" Tish broke in loudly. Her tone might have sent the uninitiated ducking for cover, but nobody at the table flinched. Tish always sounded angry. "They won't never figure out who did it. Too many people got screwed over by that bitch!"

The other keepers nodded in agreement, and Leigh noted that none of them seemed worried that Carmen's murder had been a random act of violence. They just assumed it was personal.

"She was, like, *with everybody*, wasn't she?" Art asked with a rakish grin.

Lisa and Tonya looked at each other and smirked. "Well, we don't know, Art," Tonya gibed. "*Was* she with *everybody*?"

All three women looked at the redheaded youth, who couldn't be more than twenty, and burst out laughing. He blushed crimson. "Hey, man, I'm not saying nothing."

The candy bar Leigh had wanted so badly lay in her stomach like lead. She hadn't expected Carmen to have been well liked. But the indifference of her coworkers was disconcerting. That, and the other thing they were implying.

She crumpled up her candy wrapper and threw it in the trash. "I've got to get to the hospital," she said casually, "I'm running late."

"Tell Dr. Mike we all said 'hi!' " Lisa called out in a singsong. Leigh walked out and closed the door behind her, not quick enough, unfortunately, to shut out the ensuing laughter.

Leigh wondered if a person could get used to this sour stomach, fleeting nausea thing. Didn't pregnant women do it? She trudged the rest of the way up the hill and walked in the door to the hospital. Doris, the full-time vet tech, looked at her disapprovingly. "She's here, Doc!" she called over her shoulder, then turned back to Leigh. "He's been waiting on you to do Ollie. I told him we could get it in this morning, but he said no. I'm off—got a doctor's appointment. Told him that two weeks ago."

Doris, a heavyset woman in her early fifties, was highly competent and knew it. Unfortunately, she didn't seem to hold Tanner in the same high regard she had held his now-retired predecessor. She banged out the door without another word.

Tanner appeared in the doorway. He looked at Leigh and smiled. "She loves me, you know." He grinned, nodding toward the exit. "She just doesn't know it."

Leigh took one look at the welcome in his sparkling blue eyes and wanted to launch herself into his arms. But she didn't.

Tanner clapped his hands together with energy. "Well, shall we get going? Ollie's so nasty they can smell him in Cleveland."

Leigh picked up her share of the supplies, and they headed toward the ape house. When it was built in the early sixties, the ape house was state of the art; but now that outdoor gorilla runs and rain forest motifs were commonplace, the rather plain concrete-and-glass exhibit had become passé. A new exhibit was already in the works, but would take several years to complete.

Tanner led Leigh to a locked back door, and knocked. In a few seconds, a greasy-haired, heavyset man in his thirties swung open the heavy metal door. He motioned for them to come in, then retreated. They filed through the door and into a dark, foul-smelling room with two chairs, a desk, and a small black-and-white TV set. Charlie Maxwell, the keeper who had let them in, settled back into one of the chairs. In the other sat Detective Frank.

Leigh's heart stopped for a second, but she willed it to start back up again. She had to quit acting nervous around this man. *She hadn't done anything wrong.*

"Detective Frank," she said nobly, extending her hand, "so nice to see you again."

"Likewise, Miss Koslow." He smiled broadly. He seemed more chipper than he had last night, but still looked as though he needed a blood transfusion. He nodded to the vet. "Dr. Tanner."

Tanner returned the nod. Frank stood up. "Mr. Maxwell and I were just finishing. I'll be speaking with you two again later, I'm sure." He popped the foreboding notebook back into a pocket, smiled again, and exited through the door they had just come in.

Leigh felt her blood pressure drop with the swoosh of the closed door. She wasn't the only one relieved. Charlie Maxwell pulled a handkerchief from his pocket and wiped beads of sweat from his brow. "I ain't never been questioned by police before," he said nervously. "This whole thing gives me the heebee jeebees. Cutting her up like that—damn. Some psycho, gotta be. Don't you think?"

Leigh made a mental note that at least one zookeeper *did* think Carmen's murder was the act of a nondiscriminating lunatic. She also realized that she didn't agree. It wasn't hard to imagine Carmen making a mortal enemy, even one with cannibalistic tendencies. The idea of a serial killer being in their midst, however, was too disturbing to contemplate.

Tanner looked distinctly uncomfortable. "We'd better get started, Charlie," he said evasively.

The keeper nodded and led them down the narrow corridor that ran behind the exhibits. "I got him by himself in the back. He ain't too happy about it."

Leigh leaned in close to Tanner as they walked. "Why would Frank be questioning *him*?" she whispered.

Tanner looked back at her, and his eyes seemed sad. "He's questioning everybody Carmen worked with. He's been here all morning."

Leigh found that revelation comforting. Carmen had to have enemies—plenty of them. Frank was merely ferreting them out. That was, after all, the logical way to find the real killer. And she hoped he succeeded—soon.

The corridor widened out into a small U-shaped room that surrounded a cage made of steel bars. A door with a sliding gate connected the cage with the public part of the exhibit, a ten-by-twelve-foot concrete run with a front wall of glass. Ollie, the two-hundred-pound patriarch of the zoo's orangutan collection, took one look at Tanner and began to snarl and grunt frantically. He retreated to the far corner of the cage, his eyes shooting daggers at the hated vet.

"That's the trouble with intelligent animals," Tanner said sadly. "They remember you." He loaded the anesthetic into the blow dart and aimed. The orangutan's cries escalated in pitch, and he covered his head with his long arms. "Watch out," Tanner warned Leigh behind him.

"Why?" she asked playfully. "I thought you had good aim."

"I have great aim," he answered proudly. "But Ollie's not half bad either."

Leigh put herself on alert. Tanner shot the dart with a puff of air, and it landed in the muscle over Ollie's left shoulder. With an ear-piercing screech, the orang pulled out the dart and flung it straight back toward the vet.

Luckily, Tanner and Leigh had both ducked, and the missile collided harmlessly against the wall behind them, its needle bent from the force of the impact. "Get that, would you?" he asked.

Within a few minutes, the indignant orangutan lay sleeping peacefully, and Charlie opened the cage door to let them inside. "I got the extension cords ready, Doc," he offered.

Leigh plugged in two pairs of electric clippers, and she and Tanner went to work. It was a messy business. In the absence of normal wear and tear, Ollie's coat grew unusually long, and personal hygiene was not high on the old ape's priority list. Leigh shaved off huge mats of stiff, fecal-coated orange hair, happy she had remembered her gloves. Tanner watched the ape closely to make sure he was deep enough under, and Leigh worked fast—having no desire to be nearby when a perturbed Ollie started coming out of it.

Fifteen minutes later, they were almost finished. Charlie swept away the vile piles of hair while Tanner got on ground level to attack a stubborn mat under Ollie's chin. Leigh watched him. Tanner was the kind of guy she'd always wanted—intelligent, sweet, fun-loving, handsome. And for whatever reason, he seemed fond of her. Few men did, and they were always the ones she wasn't interested in. But with Tanner, everything seemed to be going right. It was scary.

With an evil gleam budding in her eyes, she put her arms under Ollie's armpit and levered the huge, limp arm above Tanner's toiling form. She then lowered it just enough that the orangutan's long, dangling fingers brushed the vet's cheek. Tanner sat up like a shot, eyes wide, and Leigh burst out laughing.

"You're a sadist, you know that?" he chided good-naturedly. He picked up a shock of filthy hair and threw it at her. "Get to work, you!"

When the job was done and a trimmer, cleaner Ollie was starting to stumble around, Tanner and Leigh headed back toward the hospital. On the way, the vet pulled her off the trail into the wooded area beside the aquarium and led her to a bench. "You're doing a great job, Leigh," he said softly. "Plus, I've really enjoyed your company this week. I'm sorry you had to get mixed up in—" he faltered, evidently not sure what to call the previous night's events.

"It's not your fault," Leigh interrupted. "I have a way of walking into things. Call it a gift."

He smiled and draped an arm around her shoulders. "I still feel bad about getting you into all this. Your dad will have my head."

The warmth of his arm radiated straight into Leigh's heart, and she wanted to move closer. She wanted to sink into his arms and forget that fourteen years had passed since she had first fallen under his spell. She also wanted to forget that he had ever been married. But reality reared its ugly head, and she held back. Too many things were still bothering her. She didn't want to talk about Carmen, not at this particular moment, when they were finally alone again. But she couldn't stand not knowing.

She shifted in the seat to face him, dislodging his arm. "You said you had given Carmen a ring. Why?"

He answered without hesitation, his voice somber. "It was a friendship ring. Carmen was always a friend to me, from the first day I started working here. I know she was—how shall I put it—'morally challenged,' but she had a way about her, you know? She did have a lot of problems, and I tried to help her. She helped me with some of the baggage I was carrying around from the divorce too."

He sighed. "A lot of people around here really

hated Carmen, but she didn't hate them. She just lived her life. She was—well—different, you know?"

Leigh studied him, hard. The pain in his voice was sincere, and she believed the words were too. He was going to miss Carmen, whatever it was she meant to him. But it didn't sound like a romantic entanglement. She leaned back against the bench, and the arm slipped around her shoulders again. It felt nice.

He leaned over and kissed her gently on the forehead. "We need to spend some time together away from all this, don't you think?"

Leigh nodded and laid her head on his shoulder. Far away sounded good.

"How about coming up to my cabin this weekend? It's quiet, and the trees are beautiful this time of year. What do you say?"

Leigh raised her head and started to answer, but never got the chance. A figure on the trail had spotted them, and was advancing rapidly.

It was Detective Frank.

Chapter 6

Leigh briefly considered jumping up out of Tanner's arms, but what would be the point? Besides, as she reminded herself hourly, she hadn't done anything wrong.

Frank covered the distance to the bench in a few long strides. His complexion had turned from yellow-white to yellow-pink, and he had a ghost of a smile on his face. Nevertheless, the exertion brought on a lengthy coughing fit, and it was a while before he could talk. Leigh and Tanner disentangled themselves and stood.

"There's a drinking fountain right over there," Tanner said helpfully, pointing.

Frank waved away the suggestion. "I'm fine," he croaked. "You know these first colds of the season—they're always the worst."

The detective's overly courteous manner set off Leigh's suspicion-o-meter. Frank was hard to read, but she was getting better at it. There was bad news. At least, it was bad news for them.

"I'm sorry to inconvenience you again," he began, confirming her fears, "but I'm afraid I'll have to ask both of you to come back down to the bureau for questioning. Forensics has some new information we'd like to clarify with you."

Leigh looked instinctively at Tanner. Since the po-

lice couldn't possibly have any forensic evidence that
didn't fit her statement, she wondered what they
might have that would be a problem for him. Surely
they knew his job took him all over the zoo? His hair
or fingerprints could be anywhere.

Tanner didn't seem concerned. "Sure, no problem," he said agreeably. "I don't have anything else
pressing this afternoon." He looked at Frank pointedly. "I want this person caught, you know."

The detective looked squarely back at him and
nodded. "So do I."

Since Tanner's pickup truck had somehow escaped
the impound-lot purgatory in which Leigh's Cavalier
was still lingering, he drove them both to the station.
Leigh was not surprised to find the maximally efficient Attorney Bower waiting for her, patent-leather
laptop case in hand.

"I'm glad you called," Katharine said shortly. "I
was expecting this." The lawyer surveyed the booted
vet with a fleeting look of disdain. She sniffed the
air, then quickly averted her eyes.

Leigh hid a grin behind her hand. Evidently eau
d'orangutan was not to Ms. Bower's tastes. Neither,
apparently, were cowboys.

Within a few minutes, Leigh and her attorney were
seated in the interrogation room. Frank's manner was
still disturbingly courteous, though when he greeted
Katharine, a flash of venom traveled through his
dark eyes. "The lab has matched the blood on Miss
Koslow's clothing with that of the victim," he began.

Katharine Bower wasted no time breaking in.
"That merely confirms my client's statement," she
said tersely. "Is there anything else?"

"As a matter of fact, there is," Frank said slowly,
leaning back in his chair. The gleam in his eyes as
he glared at the lawyer made Leigh's stomach flip-
flop. She looked back and forth between the two of

them, neither of which seemed to care that she was in the room. Clearly there was no love lost between Frank and her lawyer. *Fabulous.* And how did Ms. Bower get along with the D.A.?

"Yes?" the lawyer demanded.

Frank spoke evenly, but Leigh swore he was enjoying himself. "A bone saw was left at the crime scene, and forensics has concluded that it was the same bone saw that was used to dismember the body."

"And?" Katharine demanded.

"And—" Frank continued, dragging out each word, "your client's prints are on it."

Leigh sat and stared. "Your client"—that would be her. But her prints couldn't possibly be on any bone saw. What bone saw?

"Was this bone saw part of the zoo hospital's inventory?" Katharine asked without missing a beat.

Frank held up his hands and shrugged. "Perhaps your client can tell me."

"We'd like a moment alone," Katharine asked, without even looking at Leigh. Frank nodded in agreement and left, a distinct jaunt to his step.

Katharine turned to Leigh. "You are employed as a vet tech?"

Leigh nodded.

"Is it your responsibility to clean, put away, inventory, or otherwise handle the surgical instruments?"

Leigh nodded again. "Although I don't remember—"

"You don't have to remember anything," Katharine broke in. She got up and opened the door, waving Frank back in. "Handling the zoo's surgical instruments is one of my client's job responsibilities, Detective. I'm sure her prints may be found on any number of items in that inventory. If that's all you have, we'd like to go now. Unless, of course, you want to charge my client with something?"

Leigh watched Frank's face closely. Although Ms. Bower appeared to have won this round, his countenance was disturbingly smug. "You're free to go," he said charitably.

With a few admonitions to Leigh about keeping her mouth shut when—not if—the police next made contact, Katharine picked up her briefcase and left. Leigh watched as Tanner headed in for his own turn into the interrogation room, unfettered by any lawyer. "Waste of money," he had told her on the way over. "I just tell the truth."

She sat miserably in the waiting area, bored and puzzled. When had she handled a bone saw? If the zoo hospital had a large one, which she was certain it must, it would probably be in one of the drawers in the necropsy room. It would probably be kept with the— She smiled and snapped her fingers. That was it! The bone saw must have been in the same packed drawer as the rongeurs she had been searching for on Tuesday. She had picked up and moved aside virtually everything else in the drawer before finding them. If Frank checked some of the other instruments for prints too . . .

She started to get up, but stopped herself. Her lawyer would have a fit. Plus, it really wasn't incumbent on her to do Frank's job for him. Even if he was wasting a lot of time on her and Tanner when he should be looking for the real killer.

And who might that be? Leigh had no idea who Carmen's current enemies were, but surely Frank did, if he had spent all morning questioning the zoo staff. And what about Tanner? He obviously knew a lot about Carmen.

Maybe too much.

She shook her head to rid it of the unproductive thought. Carmen was dead; it wasn't as though they were in competition for Tanner's affections. Yet even as she reasoned with herself she realized that it was principles, rather than jealousy, that was the issue. She didn't think she could respect, much less fall for, any man who would get involved with Carmen Koslow.

And she was definitely falling, despite the horrors of the last twenty-four hours. It seemed like months ago that she had first walked into the zoo hospital for an interview, but it had really only been two weeks. She hadn't seen Tanner in fourteen years—he could have put on weight and gone bald for all she knew. Yet there he was, handsome as ever, and he appeared just as pleased with time's effect on her.

She remembered the sparkle in his eyes as he'd looked her up and down. "Leigh! You look great!" he'd said. Most flattery made her suspicious, but from him, it made her feel wonderful. No more of the "nice little boss's daughter" routine—he had treated her like a woman from day one. And on day three of her zoo employment, he'd made his intentions clear.

Had it only been last night? She hadn't even had a chance yet to enjoy the memory. They had been talking and laughing as they prepared for what should have been a simple procedure—and as she brushed past him to load the X-ray machine, he swung out an arm, pulled her to him, and kissed her. Not an urgent, lust-filled kiss—it was one of the warm, soft, feathery kisses that merely hinted at more to come. There was more to come. And then, as she recalled ruefully, they were interrupted.

Leigh sat up in her chair in the waiting area, suddenly jerked out of her reverie. She had pulled herself out of Tanner's arms that night because she thought she had heard a noise. He had laughed at her and told her it was just one of the cockatoos, clanging about with its water dish. She hadn't thought so, but she wasn't inclined to argue with him. She had thought it was a door shutting.

She breathed in deep. If her prints were on the bone saw, the killer must have taken it from the hospital between Tuesday and last night. And they wouldn't need it until after they'd killed Carmen.

The air in the stuffy waiting area seemed to have developed a chill, and Leigh put her legs up on the chair and hugged her knees. *Could the killer have been in the hospital with them last night?*

"Are you OK?" a voice asked tenderly. Leigh looked up to find a concerned Tanner staring down at her. "You look upset."

She forced a smile. "I'm fine," she said quickly, bouncing up from the seat. "Let's get back to work."

The tape in the zoo hospital's answering machine was completely full, and the light blinked frantically. Half a dozen messages were from reporters; three were for Leigh.

The first one was good news—her car was ready to be picked up at the tow pound. The second—an invitation from her cousin Cara to visit the farm and see the baby—didn't seem urgent, but Leigh knew better. What her mystery-obsessed cousin really wanted was to pump her for information about the murder. The third message made her muscles tense and her head start to ache.

"Hello, this is Frances Koslow, calling to leave a message for my daughter, Leigh Eleanor Koslow. Please inform Leigh that she is to call home *immediately*. Thank you very much."

She sighed. It was inevitable, of course, that her mother would get wind of the tragedy. By now, almost everyone in Pittsburgh must know. Dismemberment in a zoo was, after all, not your typical noon news. The trick would be finding out how much Frances knew without inadvertently adding to the arsenal. Lisa had said that the television reports had not given Leigh's name, and the murder had happened too late to make the morning papers. Perhaps there was hope. If Leigh could get to her mother before she found out who actually found the body, perhaps—

She shook her head and smiled sadly. It was pointless. Her mother would find out everything regardless. She always did. The questioning, the lawyer. A bad memory swept across Leigh's brain. The last time she'd needed a lawyer, her mother hadn't handled it well. Dr. Koslow didn't illegally script valium to relatives for nothing.

The last message on the machine was for Tanner, from Leo Martin, the zoo director. It cut off at an inopportune point, namely, "I want to see you immediately because—"

Tanner left in a huff, and Leigh picked up the phone and dialed. The receptionist at the Koslow Animal Clinic answered promptly, but as usual, her father took his time getting to the phone. "Leigh?" he said finally, over a background of barking dogs.

"Hi, Dad. Could you tell Mom I'm OK?"

"Be happy to. That the truth?" Randall Koslow, DVM, was not one to get excited unnecessarily. Leigh was sure he knew everything her mother did about the murder, but wasn't too worried about it.

"Yes," Leigh said weakly, unsure if she was lying. "I found Carmen's body. It wasn't fun, but I'll survive. Just tell Mom I'm really busy running back and forth between the two jobs. And tell her that the zoo has quadrupled security—or some such thing."

Dr. Koslow gave a muffled order to an employee, then returned to the conversation. "OK, honey. Anything else?"

"Yes," Leigh thought quickly. "The business in high school . . . didn't the lawyer say my record would be wiped clean?"

"I believe so." Dr. Koslow paused. "Should I ask why you want to know?"

"Probably not. I'll talk to you later, Dad."

Leigh finished the afternoon hospital chores, and when Tanner had not returned by five, she decided to take off. She'd given the zoo overtime already, and the lack of sleep and food was beginning to wear on her. Warren picked her up at the main gate, having graciously agreed to drive her to the strip district to reclaim her car. They arrived back at their apartment building in tandem.

"Did you ever get any lunch?" Warren asked, concerned.

Leigh shook her head. "I've got bologna in the fridge, and maybe I could make some macaroni and cheese. I'm out of milk, but if you double the butter—"

Warren raised a hand. "Enough with the violins already. You're invited. But since we're in a hurry, I'll just order pizza."

Leigh smiled. She could have really gone for some of Warren's homemade quesadillas, but she wouldn't push it. She owed him too many meals already. She hiked upstairs to her apartment, shucked the odiferous zoo uniform, and took a quick shower. Clean and ravenous, she ignored the blinking of her own answering machine and headed back down to Warren's place. Pizza—followed by a prolonged state of unconsciousness—sounded great.

But Warren was not alone. And given the two large pizzas laid out on his kitchen table, he hadn't expected to be. Maura Polanski shoveled in a mushroom-laden piece of pie, offering Leigh a wave in lieu of a greeting.

"I asked WonderCop to join us," Warren explained, using Maura's college tag line. "I thought you could use some more good advice. And moral support."

Leigh didn't want to think about anything but food and sleep, but she smiled weakly. "The more the merrier. Provided I get enough pepperoni." She dug into the second box, elated to see that Warren had ordered thin crust—her favorite. She ate two pieces almost without chewing, then felt more sociable. Looking at Maura, she suddenly realized that despite the policewoman's healthy appetite, she looked awful, with blue-red bags under both eyes.

"Are you OK?" Leigh asked, concerned. "You're not working double shifts again, are you?"

Maura shook her head and finished swallowing a hefty mouthful. "No, we're staffed now." She paused uncomfortably. "It's Mom."

Leigh's heart felt heavy. Maura had lost her father, a police chief and community idol, just last year. Now her mother was battling Alzheimer's, and deteriorating quickly.

"Her sense of day and night is off," Maura explained. "She keeps waking up and trying to leave the house. My aunts used to stop her when I wasn't home, but Charlotte's hearing is going, and they're exhausted besides. Mom's been out twice in the last week."

Warren and Leigh both listened with sympathy. Maura had left the city force, and her plans for making detective, for a position on the suburban force of her home borough of Avalon. Twenty-four hour close proximity was the only way she could adequately care for her mother. Though the two aunts who lived in the other half of the Polanski duplex tried to help, they were elderly themselves.

"Maura," Leigh said seriously, "don't you think it's time?"

The policewoman's eyes moistened. "Maybe." Her tone indicated that the discussion was over for the time being.

Leigh knew better than to push, so she returned to her pizza and polished off half of it with ease. She put her dirty dishes in Warren's dishwasher and slipped a five surreptitiously into his cookie jar. For a financial genius, Warren was exceptionally generous, but she had always insisted on paying her share, which is why the thought of a hefty legal tab galled her. She had nothing to pay it with, and she had no choice but to accept a loan. It was a rotten feeling.

"Katharine Bower's the best," Warren was telling Maura, "so unless our Leigh actually is a homicidal maniac, I'm sure everything will be fine."

"That's a big 'if,'" Maura joked. "You know these creative types and their violent outbursts."

Leigh glared at them both. "Thanks for the moral support. By the way, Warren, do you have any idea why Detective Frank hates my lawyer?"

Warren gave her a puzzled expression. "Who says he does?"

"Nobody. But I could tell. There's history there, trust me."

They both looked at Maura. "Do you know Frank?" Leigh asked.

Maura cleared her throat. "Not personally. I've heard good things about his work. He's thorough." She stopped talking, but it was clear there was more.

"Spill it!" Leigh insisted impatiently. "Does he hate all women lawyers or what?"

Maura's eyebrows rose as Leigh's words hit near the truth. "All right," she sighed. "I'll level with you. Frank's got a rep as a misogynist. He went through a nasty divorce a few years ago—nearly bankrupted him. I think he's fair enough, but in your situation, I wouldn't push his buttons."

Leigh sat and stared. So it wasn't her imagination. Frank hadn't liked her from the get-go. This was all she needed.

Warren attempted to lighten the mood. "Leigh will be an angel in khaki, won't you, dear? Anyway, I'm sure Frank will fixate on a more likely suspect soon. One with a motive, for instance."

Leigh's stomach had begun to complain after the misogynist comment, and was now back to peak acid production. She hadn't told Frank—or her lawyer either, for that matter—*everything* about her past with Carmen. It had seemed wise at the time, but now she wasn't so sure.

"Maura," she asked nervously, "do you think Frank would care, I mean, would the trouble I had in high school be relevant?"

The policewoman looked at her, puzzled. Then she smiled. "Oh, you mean the possession thing?"

Leigh nodded.

Maura chuckled under her breath. "Come on, Koslow. You were seventeen and you were acquitted. Get over it already. Nobody cares."

"Frank will."

"Why should he?"

"Because the whole thing was Carmen Koslow's fault."

Chapter 7

Maura was silent for a moment. "Maybe you'd better tell me the story again," she said finally.

"What story?" Warren demanded. "Why haven't I heard about this before?"

Leigh looked at him and sighed. "I didn't think the future president of the United States would look too kindly on a teenage drug trafficker."

"Don't be ridiculous," Warren said irritably. "What really happened?"

Leigh had no desire to relive the experience that had ruined her senior year of high school, but in comparison to what she'd been through the last twenty-four hours, it seemed trivial.

"It was just a few months before graduation," she began. "My dad was at a veterinary conference out of state, so my mom let Cara and me drive to school in his car—a major coup at that age, as you can imagine. I had just let Cara out at the front door when Carmen came running up."

Leigh could picture the seventeen-year-old Carmen quite clearly. Medium height, thin as a rail, with Cher-like black hair cascading over her shoulders. Her cheeks had been flushed with excitement—rosy circles on her smooth olive skin. "Leigh!" she had said, flustered, "scoot over!"

Carmen had opened the driver door and started to

slide in behind the wheel. Leigh had the choice of either moving over or having Carmen in her lap. She had moved.

"I left my history paper at home!" Carmen had bleated. "I've got to get it fast!" She had pushed the accelerator, and they were off.

"Didn't you protest?" Warren interrupted, surprised. "If somebody tried that now, you'd poke their eyes out with the car keys."

"Maturity helps," Leigh said with regret. "I didn't have the guts back then. Carmen was like an alien being to me. She was so unlike anyone else I knew—she was fascinating."

The years rolled back in Leigh's mind. She herself had been a plain, book-smart, and sheltered youth. Carmen, who thanks to alphabetical seating had been assigned to the next desk every morning during homeroom, was a wild woman. From the seventh grade on, Carmen had regaled Leigh with tales of older boyfriends, petty theft, promiscuity, and generally raucous independent living. Leigh knew better than to believe it all—but the entertainment value was high, regardless. Over time, Leigh became a regular confidante for Carmen's escapades, living them vicariously from the safety of her orange plastic chair.

So when, that fated morning, Carmen had wanted a favor, Leigh felt compelled to help. She didn't trust Carmen, and she doubted that the teenaged Morticia look-alike had ever completed a history paper, much less worried about turning one in late. But she couldn't say no. Carmen wouldn't understand why—and that could be a problem, since they had no choice but to sit next to each other every morning till graduation.

Leigh sighed again at the memory, and at her own idiocy, then returned to the story.

"Carmen drove in the opposite direction from her

house almost immediately, but since she didn't really care if I believed her story, she didn't bother to explain the inconsistency. She drove to the parking lot of an apartment complex about three miles from the school, then took the keys and jumped out. A scummy-looking guy in his mid-twenties was sitting in the front seat of some rusted old gas guzzler, and she hopped in the passenger door. She sat there about a minute and a half, then popped back out with a collection of plastic bags."

"Did you know what she was up to?" Warren asked.

"I wasn't *that* sheltered," Leigh answered. "I was furious. We were going to be late to school, and I was going to get detention. I'd never had detention, and I certainly didn't want to get one just so Carmen Koslow could get high. When she got back to the car, I ripped the keys out of her hands and took over the wheel."

"Much better." Warren grinned. "That's the Leigh we know and love."

"Carmen just shrugged and smiled," Leigh went on. "She had what she wanted, and my outrage only amused her. I drove back to school like a bat out of hell—I was mad, and I was *not* going to rot in detention with a bunch of delinquents like Carmen."

"I take it you didn't make it?" Warren asked.

Leigh shook her head. "I was pulled over two blocks from the high school for doing forty-five in a twenty-five zone. Here I was, my first chance to drive my dad's good car, and I was getting a speeding ticket. At that moment I didn't think things could get any worse. I was naive. When the officer asked for my car registration, I reached over and opened the glove compartment."

There was silence for a moment.

"She didn't," Warren said incredulously.

"She did!" Leigh fumed, getting mad just thinking

about it. "It all toppled right out onto her lap—in nice, perfectly *clear* plastic bags, in full view of the officer."

Maura chimed in. "That was a bad break, you know. The officer would have had no right to search. But when you wave it right under his nose . . ."

"I know, I know," Leigh said irritably, thirteen years evaporating in her mind. "The lawyer did a great job of explaining to my parents exactly what fantastic odds I overcame in order to get myself arrested."

"You were actually arrested?" Warren asked.

Leigh nodded glumly. "The works. I'd never been so humiliated. We were charged with possession of marijuana. I called my dad; he called a lawyer. Some old guy with a beard who smelled like cigars. I was mortified. But the lawyer had no trouble getting me off—he convinced the judge I had nothing to do with the drugs, since I was a stellar student and my prints weren't on the bags. So, I was off the hook and my record was wiped clean." Nevertheless, she thought to herself ruefully, her dad had gotten a hefty legal bill to remember the incident by.

"And Carmen?" Warren prompted.

"It was her first real offense, so she got community service. Weeding, mowing, washing police cars. She got a kick out of the last part. 'Fraternizing with the fuzz,' she called it. Bragged that she was dating a parole officer."

"You were still on speaking terms?" Warren asked with surprise. "Was she sorry she got you into trouble?"

Leigh laughed. "That's just it. Carmen was never sorry about anything."

She turned to Maura. "You remember that Abnormal Psych class we took together junior year?"

"How could I forget?" The policewoman grinned. "You diagnosed everyone you'd ever known."

"I did not," Leigh said defensively. "Just a few—and only one I was really sure about. We were studying personality disorders, and I told you that I knew a girl in high school who was a sociopath."

Maura thought for a moment. "The girl who would steal clothes from gym lockers, then wear them around school?"

"That's her. People would recognize their stolen clothes, but Carmen would act like nothing was wrong. All the time, she'd be perfectly nice to you. Once she volunteered to be treasurer of some club—future homewreckers of America or something—and a few days after dues were collected the money 'disappeared' from her locker. She had the nerve to report the theft to the police, even as she was wearing a whole new outfit she couldn't possibly afford. It was like she had no conscience at all. She assumed everyone liked her—she saw no reason why they shouldn't. She was charming and friendly, but the moment your back was turned, she'd do just about anything."

"Sounds like a couple of women I've dated," Warren mused.

Leigh glared. Warren hadn't been much of a ladies' man in his college days, but in the last few years he had dated no small number of politically eligible women. He never got serious about any of them, however, a fact that evidently had not escaped the notice of Myran Wiggin.

"Were you ever openly hostile to Carmen?" Maura asked seriously, trying to keep Leigh's thoughts on the subject.

"Of course not," Leigh said defensively. "I wanted to wring her stringy little neck, but I was a wuss. She acted like nothing had happened, so I played along. It was easier that way."

"And there were no real lasting consequences for you?" Maura probed.

"Besides my dignity? The horror of being arrested when you're such a straight arrow you're voted 'Most Likely to Lead a Boring Life'?" Leigh smirked, wondering if her old high school yearbook staff had been watching the news lately. Her life wasn't so boring now, was it?

"Koslow," Maura said heavily. "Pay attention. This is your butt in the sling, remember? I asked if there were any real, lasting negative consequences from that arrest."

Leigh sighed. "I suppose not. Although I did miss a calculus quiz that morning—which cost me a letter grade." She ground her teeth at the memory, then remembered the purpose of Maura's questions. "It was nothing worth killing anyone over, of course. That would be ridiculous."

Maura considered a moment, then agreed. "High school trauma is pretty lame, for a motive. But it would have been better if you'd told the police about it yourself."

"But they won't find out," Leigh countered hopefully. "The lawyer said my record would be wiped clean, remember?"

Maura shook her head. "Yours might have been, but Carmen's wouldn't."

Crap. Leigh bit her lower lip. "So Frank will find out?"

Maura sighed. "He probably already knows, Koslow. Did he ask you any leading questions? Give you the opportunity to mention it?"

As a matter of fact, yes. Leigh's stomach was back to its old tricks. She needed to pop some antacid—quick. "I suppose he might have," she mumbled.

"Ask your lawyer if you should get it out in the open," Maura suggested. "They'll have trouble getting a warrant if all the motive they have is a petty thirteen-year-old grudge. They'd need something else. Like blackmail. Or a love triangle."

A love triangle. There it was—again. Leigh tried hard not to look at Maura. The policewoman was trained to read people, and knew guilt when she saw it. Leigh asked Warren where he kept the Mylanta and made a hasty exit to the bathroom.

The buzzing of Leigh's alarm clock the next morning announced the end of eleven hours of sleep that seemed more like twenty minutes. She stumbled through the morning routine on autopilot, scalding her wrist with coffee and stubbing her toe on a basket of dirty clothes. To top it off, Mao Tse was having serious attitude problems—undoubtedly miffed at the irregular hours Leigh had been keeping and the fact that there had been no canned food since Tuesday.

"Herring in prawn jelly this weekend," Leigh said with a yawn as she left. "Promise." Unlike the day before, Hook, Inc., was buzzing with activity. The new business manager had somehow wrangled a desk and chair, and was setting about the professional task of lifting the phone off the floor. Jeff Hulsey was once again schmoozing potential clients over the phone, and Carl and Alice were arguing over whether her flashy layout would make the Techmar Industrial brochure go over budget. Leigh gave each of her coworkers a wave, and as Alice and Carl had the decency to be arguing in the other office, she shut her own door and sat down to work.

The print ads for X-M Mold Remover should have been a snap job. On a better day she could have rolled out a half-dozen great slogans—with copy— by noon. Not this morning. Her mind was enveloped in a haze that three cups of coffee had yet to touch, and the pressure in her sinuses was building up like a powder keg. She was staring at the blank document on her monitor, debating whether Frank had given her a cold in addition to an ulcer, when the door to her office opened slowly. Two women of equal height and build shuffled quietly inside and stood looking at her.

The one wearing two strands of pearls and carrying an embroidered handbag cleared her throat. Leigh looked up at the women and smiled weakly. Like many identical twins, the two were a study in contrast. One in full Barbara Bush regalia, the other in shiny pink sweats. "Leigh, dear," said the proper one, "we're sorry to interrupt, but you never answer your phone anymore, and we're worried about you."

"I'm fine, Mom." Leigh answered with as much cheer as she could muster. She offered the women seats, then realized there weren't any. She pulled out her chair, dragged over Alice's, and settled herself on the desktop. "How do you like the place?" she asked, waving an arm to show off the red-painted concrete-block walls and exposed pipes.

Frances Koslow pursed her lips and looked at the floor.

"I think it's got character," Leigh's Aunt Lydie said approvingly. "Definite potential."

Leigh smiled.

"Let's not pussyfoot," Frances said heavily. "We're here because we know that you were the one who found that Koslow girl's body, and it's all over the morning papers that the police have several suspects. You're one, of course. Your father and I agree that you need your lawyer again. He's retired, which is unfortunate, since he knows your history. But his firm is still operating. I called them this morning—"

Leigh quietly clenched her heels together—a tried and true alternative to screaming her guts out. "I already have a lawyer, Mom. Warren found one for me yesterday."

"Did he?" Frances's face lit up. She had always thought Warren Harmon made prime son-in-law material, and made no secret of it. "What a nice thing to do. You should write him a thank-you card."

The muscles in Leigh's calves were starting to fatigue when Lydie jumped in. "Have you met with the lawyer yet? Did he reassure you?"

"The meeting went fine, thanks. And it's a 'she.'"

Frances gasped. "A woman lawyer? Do you think that's wise?"

Leigh leaped off the desk and shook out her arms. It was the next stage of self-control therapy. She hoped she wouldn't need the third, which required an exercise mat, or at least plush carpeting.

"For heaven's sake, Frannie!" Lydie said indignantly. "Why on earth shouldn't a woman make as good a lawyer as a man?"

Frances clutched her handbag defensively. "I'm not saying one couldn't, in some fields, but criminal defense is a male-dominated area. Men deal better with other men—" She stopped. "Leigh, will you please quit that ridiculous exercising? Can't you do your sit-ups at home? This tile will ruin your back."

"I think I hear my phone," Leigh said hastily, springing up. "Back in a jif!"

Ten carefully counted seconds later, she returned. "Isn't this your phone?" Frances asked accusingly, pointing to the mute instrument on Leigh's desk.

"That's Alice's," Leigh answered truthfully. It was Alice's. Alice's and hers. "Listen, Mom, Lydie, I really appreciate your coming down, but everything is under control. Warren says my lawyer is the best. But I have a headache coming on and a ton of work to do, so . . ."

"I'm sure you have a lot more time now that you're not running back and forth to the zoo every day," Frances quipped. "Although you do need the money. I'd be happy to talk to my friend Doreen down at Mellon Bank. They're always hiring for something . . ."

Leigh sighed. She knew that Frances Koslow wouldn't rest until her only daughter had a boring, stable desk job that came with a 401K and a dental plan. The threat of a call to Doreen had hung over her head ever since college graduation, and her uncertain employment of the last decade had done nothing to lessen it.

"I'm fine, Mom. Please don't stress poor Doreen. I already have another source of income." *The same one I've had.*

Frances eyed her daughter skeptically. She knew her well enough to know that although she generally didn't lie, her verbal acrobatics were well seasoned. "Really. And what might that—"

"Leigh!" shouted Carl from the abruptly opened doorway. "Sorry to interrupt, but we really do need you in here."

"Sorry, Mom, Lydie." Leigh apologized happily, pushing the women toward the front door with the subtleness of a backhoe. "Sounds important." With mutterings of discontent and commands for Leigh to keep in touch, the visitors departed.

Leigh leaned heavily against the back of the door. Carl and Alice watched her and smiled.

"It was my turn, wasn't it?" Carl probed. "Sorry if I lost track of time. But I think I was still within the requested five-minute range."

"You did good, Carl," Leigh praised. "Next cappuccino's on me."

Deep in the Avalon Borough Police Headquarters, Maura Polanski tapped a pen against the stack of papers littering her narrow desk. She stared, as she had off and on all morning, at the black telephone balanced precariously over the desk's right edge. Should she, or shouldn't she?

She was used to bailing Leigh Koslow out of trouble— she'd been saving her friend from herself on a regular basis ever since college. But this time, things were especially complicated. Maura sighed heavily, picked up the phone, and dialed the city detective's desk.

"Vincent Fanelli, please."

The deep booming voice on the other end of the line seemed pleased at the interruption. "Polanski! How the hell you been and why the hell haven't you made detective yet? We were supposed to do this together, remember?"

"I'm with the Avalon force now," Maura answered cheerfully, trying to keep the regret out of her voice. "Things move slower here. But someday I'll come show you guys how it's done."

Vince Fanelli gave a deep chuckle. "So what's up?"

Maura took a breath. "Bad news, Vince. A friend's in trouble."

"What kind of trouble?"

"Your kind."

Vince gave a low whistle. "Homicide?"

"Yeah. Name's Leigh Koslow."

There was a short pause. "As in the zoo murder?"

"Right." Maura paused a moment. "Leigh can irritate the fire out of you, but she's no killer. You got my word on that. She just has a knack for being in the wrong place at the wrong time."

Vince said nothing.

"I'm not asking you to leak anything," Maura said firmly. "But I thought maybe you could tell me how worried I should be."

There was a rapping sound as the detective tapped his own pen on his desk. Then he sighed. "It's like this, Polanski. Circumstantials add up. Publicized case means pressure for an arrest. To sum up—your friend better have a damn good lawyer. *Today.*"

Maura's spirits sank. It was worse than she thought. "Thanks, Vince. Appreciate it. Keep a seat warm for me over there, will you?"

"Will do."

Maura hung up the phone with a new weight on her shoulders. This was going to get worse before it got better.

She had to do something.

*　　*　　*

If the worst thing about having your own business was lack of a paycheck, the best thing was setting your own schedule. After giving the X-M Mold Remover account one more miserable shot, Leigh gave up and decided to take a couple hours off to clear her aching head. She took a brisk walk to her favorite coffee shop and invested in a cup of espresso and the morning paper.

Surprisingly, Pittsburgh's intrepid reporters seemed to know even less about Carmen's murder than she did. As a potential suspect, she had gotten off relatively easy—the media seemed to have missed the "running away from the crime scene" tidbit, and mentioned her merely as the employee who found the body. Her name still hadn't surfaced, thank goodness.

Leo Martin had managed to contribute his typical inept plug—noting merely that the murder had occurred after regular zoo hours. Lisa Moran, who was probably the nearest thing to another tiger keeper that the reporter could find, was more forthcoming. When asked if she was concerned for her own safety in the zoo, Lisa was quoted as saying: "No, not at all. I think it was just a personal thing . . . if I thought there was some psycho on the loose, I wouldn't be here."

Leigh's eyebrows rose. Lisa seemed awfully sure of herself. She almost made it seem as though the murder was justified. What exactly did she know about Carmen's sins?

When the last drop of her espresso had been drained, Leigh downed a handful of mints from the counter and set off again. It was time to cock an ear to the zoo grapevine and find out what had been going on with Carmen. Maybe it mattered to the murder investigation. Maybe it just mattered to how she felt about Tanner. Either way, she had to know.

Chapter 8

After changing hastily into her uniform, Leigh drove to Riverview Park and entered the zoo through the main gates. She didn't know if the employee gate would still be manned, given that the morning staff should have already arrived, and the "secret" entrance was no longer an option. She couldn't help but imagine what was left of Carmen's body being dragged under the fence, and it was an image her peace of mind could do without.

Fighting an urge to head straight for the hospital, she instead went looking for Lisa Moran. It wasn't easy to get her feet walking in the direction where Lisa was most likely to be. The tiger exhibit had been temporarily closed to the public, but the tigers and Carmen's other big cats still had to eat. Mercifully, Leigh found Lisa taking a smoke break on a tree stump just outside the leopard enclosure. Breathing a sigh of relief, she approached.

Lisa acknowledged her visitor with a smile and a nod, then began examining her fingernails with fervor. "Chipped again," she moaned. "I really should wear work gloves."

Leigh's mind drifted back to a long forgotten ritual—the state-of-Carmen's-nails address. "See, Leigh," the teenaged Carmen would begin as soon as she had taken her seat in homeroom. "This one's tearing now, and I had got it all the way out to here." She would demonstrate the loss, giving the history of each nail in stunning detail. She wasn't asking Leigh's advice, just keeping her informed. As a courtesy.

"Did Carmen wear work gloves?" Leigh asked suddenly.

Lisa looked up from her own hands, assuming a puzzled expression. "I don't know. A lot of women here do. Why?"

"No reason," Leigh muttered, embarrassed.

Lisa studied her. "You're worried, aren't you?" she asked sympathetically. "I heard that you have some kind of history with her. But don't flatter yourself. You're only one in a long line of suspects, as far as I can tell. Carmen had plenty of enemies."

"She did?" Leigh asked innocently.

Lisa wasn't buying. "Yeah, right. Did you know her or not?" She leaned toward Leigh conspiratorily. "I gave that detective a notebook full when he talked to me. I hear everything around here, you know, as a floater."

Leigh could imagine.

"Carmen had only one real friend here—and that was Kristin. And I happen to know that even they didn't part on the best of terms."

Leigh searched her memory bank for mention of a keeper named Kristin. None came to mind. "Kristin who?"

"Kristin Yates," Lisa answered. "They used to work the big cats together before Kristin took over the bears. She and Carmen went way back."

A sinister image suddenly bored its way into Leigh's mind, giving her a slight chill. *Kristin Yates.* The frightening, horse-faced delinquent whose reign of intimidation had oppressed North Hills girls throughout the early eighties. Kristin had the kind of cold gray eyes and haughty air that made for good adolescent horror fiction. She could play the evil ringleader who would slip the good girl Ex-lax, lock her in the bathroom, and steal her clothes. Preferably on prom night.

"Kristin Yates worked here?" Leigh said stupidly.

"Yeah, like forever," Lisa answered, watching her. Then Lisa's face lit up. "They went to high school together, didn't they? So you must have known them both."

Leigh nodded. "Vaguely."

"Kristin was all right," Lisa said charitably. "She was easy to work with. At least she stayed out of everybody's business."

Leigh's eyebrows rose. The Kristin Lisa was describing was a far cry from the one she remembered. But then, people change. Most people, anyway. "Where is Kristin now?"

"She left a couple weeks ago," Lisa chatted merrily, looking at her nails again. "She got a job offer at the zoo in D.C. She's been wanting to move there for a long time, because she's really into pandas. She's starting off with hoof stock, but she figures at least she's got her foot in the door."

Leigh couldn't imagine the Kristin she knew caring about much besides where her next Marlboro was coming from. In any event, she was glad Kristin was out of the picture. "I wonder if she knows about Carmen yet."

Lisa shrugged. "I guess she'll find out the next time she calls anyone back here. I'd call her in D.C. if I knew her number. But like I said, she and Carmen didn't part happy."

"What happened?"

A cloud passed over Lisa's face, and she took a long drag on her cigarette. "Let's just say it was man trouble," she said flippantly, watching Leigh's eyes. She stood up. "Gotta get back to work. See you around."

"Wait!" Leigh called after her. "Are you saying

Carmen was serious about somebody?" A ray of hope had emerged. She had assumed Carmen was a love-'em-and-leave-'em kind of girl, but if she had a significant other, the accursed "love triangle" theory wouldn't hold water, no matter how Leigh felt about Tanner.

Lisa's eyes looked at her with something between pity and disgust. "That depends," she answered cryptically, "on who you ask."

Leigh trudged up the hill to the hospital more frustrated than ever. Why did Lisa always have to clam up just when she was getting interesting? She had done it before, on Tuesday. Lisa had been chattering on about staff romances, and she had started to say something about Carmen, but Tanner had walked in and interrupted, and Leigh had forgotten the whole thing.

She opened the hospital door aggressively enough to bang it against the wall, startling a tall, stooped man standing just inside the doorway.

"I'm sorry," Leigh apologized quickly, recognizing Leo Martin, her boss's boss. "I'm not sure how it got away from me."

Leo scowled at her without any pretense of politeness. His appearance was forbidding enough even when he was in a good mood—thanks to his Ichabod Crane stature and cigar-stained teeth. How this man could be expected to put on a good PR face for the zoo was beyond Leigh, but since the zoo was her employer and not her client, she didn't waste time worrying about it.

"There'll be no more of this after-hours nonsense," he said to her sternly, poking a finger in her face. "And I don't want you or anyone else talking to reporters. Got that?"

Leigh bristled. Boss's boss or no, she didn't appreciate being talked to like a petulant child. Especially when this wasn't even her real job.

"Excuse me," she said, as sweetly as she could manage, "have we met? I'm Leigh Koslow, an advertising copywriter. I'm here helping out Mike in my spare time."

Some of the creases in Leo Martin's scowl flattened. He looked at her as if studying a stinging insect—patronizing, but cautious. "Leo Martin," he said gruffly, "director."

He cast a scathing glance at Tanner. "Fill her in," he barked. Then he was gone.

After the door banged closed, Tanner burst out laughing. "What are you doing here so early?" he asked, gathering Leigh up in his arms. "You're a hoot, you know that?"

Leigh wasn't sure if being a "hoot" was desirable, but all indications were positive. Tanner kissed her soundly. "Leo needs somebody to shake him up once in a while. I remember once, Carmen—"

He broke off the sentence abruptly, the merriment draining quickly from his eyes. He let Leigh go and stepped back.

"It's OK," Leigh said softly, "you can talk about her. In fact, that's why I'm here." She didn't want him to talk about Carmen at all, certainly not fondly. But there were secrets lurking in that gorgeous head of his that she had to know. She dragged him to the couch in the lounge and sat him down.

"Look, Mike," she began. "I know nobody wants to speak ill of the dead, and I know you considered Carmen a friend, but let's get real here. I knew Carmen too. She was a sociopath. Or a psychopath, or an antisocial personality—whatever the jargon is nowadays. The point is, she had no conscience, and she used people. Most everybody in the zoo hated her for some reason. You know all about that. And if you have any theories on who killed her, I'd really like to know about them."

"Carmen wasn't a psychopath," Tanner defended uncertainly. "She was just . . ." He broke off and sighed miserably. "I don't like talking about it. It's the police's job to find killers, not ours." He stood up suddenly, then added, "I still can't believe somebody would do this to her."

The words struck a chord in Leigh's brain. He had used them before—the night it happened, and they had struck her then too, but now she knew why. "I can't believe *somebody* would do *this* to her." Not "I can't believe this happened," or "I can't believe she's dead." It was as if he wasn't surprised she was dead, wasn't surprised somebody wanted her dead, but the way it happened—that he couldn't grasp.

Leigh stood up beside him and tried again, the words running out of her mouth before she could censor them. "What is it you know? Are you trying to protect someone in the zoo?"

Tanner looked at her incredulously. "Of course not! How could you think I would do that? This person's sick, for God's sake!"

"I'm sorry," Leigh apologized quickly, cursing her impetuousness. "I didn't mean that you'd condone anyone hurting Carmen, I just thought that maybe you had some suspicions about somebody, maybe even an accident—"

"Look, Leigh," Tanner broke in tiredly. "You're starting to sound like Frank. If it'll make you feel better, I'll tell you what I told him. I don't think anyone at the zoo could actually kill Carmen like that, no matter how much they hated her. There's a much more likely explanation."

Leigh waited. He sighed and began. "Carmen had money problems. Serious money problems. She was into illegal gambling. Dogs, horses, daily number, football, you name it. When she won, she spent it all within twenty-four hours. When she lost, she borrowed. I think she finally borrowed a little too much."

"You mean loan sharks?"

"Probably something like that," Tanner said with a nod. "Maybe a little more personal. Carmen ran with a rough crowd when she wasn't here. She was so fascinating, so alluring. She could attract any man she wanted—well, you know."

Leigh nodded. She knew what Carmen was capable of at age thirteen; she shuddered to think what maturity might have added to her repertoire. She also shuddered to think *who* she might have added to her repertoire.

"Her death was so violent, so out of the blue," Tanner continued, "I'm certain it was a professional job. What bugs me is that Frank doesn't seem to be buying that. And he's got to know I'm telling the truth about the gambling. There'd be evidence of that."

Leigh considered. A professional job certainly sounded plausible to her. And from a purely selfish standpoint, it was a convenient solution: neat, faceless, no risk of further harm to anyone else. She could buy it. Couldn't she?

The memory of the shutting door that had interrupted her first tryst with Tanner shoved its way back into her mind. Had someone come to get a bone saw? Surely no professional hit man would do that. How would they know where to look? Why would they risk getting caught? And if the whole thing was premeditated, wouldn't they have come prepared?

She shook the thoughts out of her head. No door had slammed—the noise had been one of the cockatoos. Maybe Carmen herself had taken the bone saw to the tiger shed, to saw—well, to saw something— and it just happened to be there when it was needed.

She looked into Tanner's liquid, Robert Redford

eyes. Why couldn't romance work out right for her? Just once?

She took his hand in hers and pulled him back down to sit on the couch again. "I think you're right," she said firmly. "I think it was a professional job."

Tanner smiled at her warmly and leaned toward her, but the sound of the front door opening intervened.

Damn.

Light footsteps trekked down the short hall. "*Mike!* Where are you?"

An old memory snapped into sharp focus. Leigh would know that nasally, high-pitched whine of a voice anywhere. Her first reaction was to hide under something, but she bravely suppressed it. This beast would have to be faced.

The footsteps stopped at the lounge doorway, and Leigh looked up boldly at the woman who stood there. She was five feet two, counting her retro wedge heels, and barely one-hundred pounds, but psychologically, she packed a wallop. She stared at them—but mainly Leigh—with a trademark sneer/ smile. The look in her eyes was hard to determine, given that her oversized plastic glasses were tinted a bizarre pinkish-red color. Her short, bleached-blond hair was swept up with a yellow gauze bandana, clashing in acceptable retro style with her tight-fitting striped shirt.

"*Well, well,*" she whined, "what have we here? Miss Koslow, how you've grown! Physically, at least. But I see you still want the same thing you always did, eh?"

Leigh forced herself to look squarely at Tanner's ex-wife. Part of her wanted to run, another part wanted to grab a wedge heel and start bludgeoning. Luckily, neither of those ideas won out. Her rational mind took charge, reminding her that she was now a thirty-year-old woman, not a sixteen-year-old girl, and that the woman in front of her was now firmly on the wrong side of thirty-five.

"Stacey," Leigh cooed sweetly. "So nice to see you again. It has been a long time, hasn't it? And you're right, time certainly does age people!"

The sneer/smile dissolved into a clenched jaw, and the pinkish-red lenses turned slowly toward Tanner. "Hello, dear."

"What the hell do *you* want?" Tanner said rudely, standing. "If you're after the clothes on my back, forget it. They're zoo issue."

Stacey Tanner stood unfazed. "Actually, you can keep those. I'm here for the cash."

"What cash?" Tanner bellowed.

Stacey didn't answer immediately, but wedged her petite derriere onto the couch next to Leigh. "The insurance money. I know you don't have it yet, but you will. There's no doubt it was a homicide. Why Little Miss Mafia should make you her beneficiary is beyond me, but I'm no longer interested in the sordid details of your sex life."

"Shut up!" Tanner snapped.

Leigh rose. The atmosphere in the tiny lounge had deteriorated to trailer-park level—she didn't want to be there when it sank down to talk show. "I'll just be outside," she announced. She shut the door behind her and went into the treatment room next door. It hardly mattered—she could still hear every word.

"How the hell do you know about Carmen's life insurance policy?" Tanner fumed.

"I work at Eastern Central Trust now, remember? Records Administration is a grind, but in this case it was terribly convenient. Considering that you would never in a million years admit you were coming into money—even though you know perfectly well that fifty percent of it is mine."

There was silence for a moment, and Leigh could

picture Tanner struggling for control. "I've paid what I owe," he growled. "And as for Carmen's money, I'm not getting a dime of it. Nor, I'm so sorry to say, are you."

"And why not?" Stacey screeched.

"Because first crack goes to Carmen's creditors—and there's a long, hungry line of them."

Another moment of silence. "Surely there'll be some—"

"Nada."

"There has to be something!" Stacey screeched again. "I *need* that money!"

"Oh?" Tanner said derisively. "What for? Your own creditors getting testy?"

Leigh heard a scuffling noise, then the rattle of metal hitting metal. *Trash can on vending machine?*

"Calm down, Stacey," Tanner said gravely.

"I am calm!" she barked. "How about the cabin? Have you sold it yet? I'm still waiting."

"I told you it's going slow."

"And no wonder! One lousy FOR SALE BY OWNER sign tacked up in the middle of the winter! You promised to get a realtor working on it. Do I have to call my lawyer again?"

"Forget the damn lawyer, OK? I'll sell it next spring. That's when the market's best anyway."

"I want my share *now*," Stacey threatened. "You have a month. If it's not on the market, my lawyer will be calling. And I suppose that antique rifle is still sitting in the cabin?"

"And what if it is?" Tanner snarled.

"SELL IT. I want that money, I need that money, and I deserve that money. NOW."

"Get out." From the tone of Tanner's voice, it wasn't a suggestion.

"With pleasure!" Stacey said haughtily, opening the door. She slammed it behind her and left.

A dull thump issued from behind the closed lounge door. *Fist on couch?*

Leigh waited for Tanner to come out. She had no intention of going in. After a few long minutes, he opened the door and looked for her.

"Still here, eh? I'm sorry you had to hear that."

Leigh shrugged. "No big deal." She knew this was the part where she was supposed to be noble and insist that the argument was none of her business. But then, she'd never been good at that sort of thing.

"So, you're Carmen's beneficiary. Does Frank know that?"

Tanner nodded, his face grim. "Oh, yeah. He was all over me about that. But it doesn't matter. He knows that I know Carmen was in debt—it's not like I could have been expecting anything. Even if I was—all she had was the standard city-issue employee life. It's not like she was leaving a fortune."

"But why—" Leigh faltered. Did she really want to know? She watched him as he absently ran a tanned hand through his tousled, sandy-blond bangs. Oh, yes. She wanted to know.

"Why did Carmen choose you?" she asked flatly.

As usual, Tanner didn't miss a beat. "I have no idea. I didn't know anything about it until Frank threw it in my face yesterday. I suppose because she didn't have any family, and she knew I was having my own money problems."

Leigh considered. In high school, Carmen's only family had been an alcoholic mother with a bad liver, so her being alone now was no surprise. Nor were Tanner's monetary problems. Zoo vets, especially those employed by smaller, low-budget parks, did not make nearly as much as the average practice owner. It was true that Stacey had supported Tanner all through college and vet school, and if she had made a claim to half of his future earnings . . .

Don't need lawyers, he had said. *All I do is tell the truth.*

It was easy to see how he'd gotten fleeced.

"I'm sorry," Leigh said, suddenly remorseful. "This has been harder on you than it has on me, and here I am bugging you with questions."

He smiled at her warmly, then took her hand and led her back to the couch. "You've got nothing to be sorry for. It's not your fault I married the first girl I ever dated. Now, I know better." He spoke in a whisper, tracing her cheek with his finger. "Where exactly were we?"

She had just started to demonstrate when a rapping at the hospital door intervened. "Come on in," Tanner yelled testily. "Door's open."

They waited in frustration as two pairs of footsteps squeaked toward them on the ancient linoleum floor. When the visitors arrived at the lounge doorway, Leigh wasn't surprised. Some people had a flare for dramatic entrances. And bad timing.

"Afternoon," Detective Frank began amicably. "Leigh Koslow, you are under arrest."

Chapter 9

The hours that followed marked a new low in Leigh's life. Being arrested as a teenager was far from fun, but being arrested as a responsible adult was worse. First off, and of little consequence in the grand scheme of things, was that Frank had caught her and Tanner alone. Again. He had also interrupted them. Again. That Frank should arrest her in front of Tanner, then proceed to parade her out of the zoo in handcuffs, was supremely humiliating. The detective didn't even have the decency to exit with her through the nearer employee lot—nothing but the main entrance would do. The only positive notes were that most of the keepers were busy behind the scenes and that no representatives of the press were visible. Even then, she did manage to get her picture taken by one photographer—a prepubescent boy who seemed to prefer women in chains to giraffes and elephants.

Leigh said nothing as Frank chatted idly, letting his uniformed assistant drive the patrol car. She went through procedure at the Central Detectives Bureau in a semiconscious haze of mortification and annoyance. The routine was grimly familiar—and interminable. She had left an emergency message with Katharine Bower's assistant; now there was nothing else to do but sit on the hard metal chair in which her current escort had placed her, and wait for something else to happen.

The whole thing seemed so surreal, she was almost able to pretend it was a charade. By rights, she should have been petrified. This wasn't possession of marijuana—it was murder. But in those moments when she did allow herself to think, she was certain her arrest was just a terrible mistake. They did have some circumstantial evidence against her. But they couldn't possibly have enough, because *she hadn't done anything wrong.* She refused to think in any terms other than that this was a misunderstanding—one that would be cleared up shortly. Very shortly.

"You'll be arraigned at the coroner's office," Frank said casually, appearing out of thin air beside her. "From there, it's the county jail." Leigh tilted her head up at him, trying hard to look bored. She should be charitable, she knew—the evidence did make her look bad, and Frank didn't know her well enough to know what a colossal mistake he was making. But she wasn't feeling charitable. In fact, she was beginning to think she really was capable of murder.

"We'd like to ask you a few more questions before you go. Do you mind?"

Leigh lowered her head and considered. She hadn't said a word to him so far, and she had no intention of doing so without her lawyer. But neither the coroner's office nor the county jail was an enticing prospect, whereas jerking Frank's chain was. She nodded in consent and rose.

Frank led her back to the interrogation table, where she sat in stony silence. Determined to meet his gaze—even as she completely ignored his first three questions—she pondered how to improve his appearance. A nose ring, perhaps? Purple sideburns? She decided on a metal stud in one eyebrow, with a matching one on the lower lip.

"Ms. Koslow," the detective said with growing exasperation, "would you care to explain what you're smiling about?" His complexion was slightly more pink today, and he hadn't coughed all afternoon. Leigh wondered if the euphoria of a false arrest was good for his immune system. It certainly wasn't helping hers. "I'm beginning to think you don't want to cooperate after all," he said tightly, the anger in his voice now unmistakable.

Leigh shrugged.

Frank rose, his face reddening. He slammed out the glass door, gesticulated with another plainclothesman in the hall, and walked away. The second man opened the door quietly and sat down across from Leigh.

"Hi. I'm Detective Stefanou. Would you like a drink of water or something?"

She shook her head and surveyed the newcomer. He was short, solid, and dark, possibly of Greek extraction. His words were kind, but his eyes gave no clue to his thoughts.

"You'll have to excuse Frank. He's had a rotten week, you know?" The detective leaned back casually in his chair. "I guess he hasn't been listening to you too well."

Leigh smiled. It was straight out of a TV cop show—in her case, *Cagney & Lacey*. "I don't mean to be rude," she said sincerely, having nothing against this particular man, "but you're wasting your time if you think I'm going to fall for the good cop/bad cop thing. I'm not talking about the case because my lawyer isn't here, and as you know, that's the smart thing for me to do. But you're a good actor. Did you ever do community theater?"

Stephanou's eyes widened for a second, then he laughed heartily. "High school—Albert Peterson, *Bye Bye Birdie*. Want to hear 'Put on a Happy Face'?"

Leigh laughed with him. "I'll pass. Perhaps under more pleasant circumstances." She caught Frank's pale visage peeking around the corner of the hall, and she smiled wider. "So it's Frank's time of the month, eh? Is he ever in a good mood?"

Stephanou studied her thoughtfully. "He's happy when he gets his man."

Leigh smirked. "Well, no wonder he's down."

The detective spoke softly. "You saying you're innocent?"

Leigh smiled sadly and shook her head. "You're good, Detective, but as I told you, I'm no idiot. If you want to talk about the weather, fine. But until my lawyer—" she stopped, smiling happily out the interrogation-room window. Warren's "shark among women" had arrived.

Attorney Katharine Bower blew into the room like a small hurricane, angry and building up steam. "My client will not answer any questions until we've had a chance to review the evidence," she said authoritatively, glaring openly at Frank as he followed her through the door.

Frank's dark eyes shot daggers back at her. "Your client hasn't said beans," he said with a pained smile. "If I didn't know better, I'd say she was stalling to avoid transport."

"Then she's damn smart," Katharine snapped, still looking only at Frank. "But in this case, we'll have to hurry up the process. She's got a bail hearing in"—she glanced at her watch—"exactly three hours. So juice up the paddy wagon."

Leigh's heart jumped, warmth quickly radiating through her chest. She was going to get out on bail. Today! She beamed at her attorney with the kind of visual worship she usually reserved for confectioneries.

"How the hell'd you do that?" Frank exploded.

Katharine shrugged. The lawyer and detective continued to spar with frightening glances and frosty words, but Leigh paid little attention. What mattered was when she got out, not how.

She endured her tour of Pittsburgh's criminal accommodations with a mixture of hope and creativity: the hope that she would never be back, and the creativity of pretending she was never really there. Imagining she was an undercover reporter proved helpful—by the time she was piled into a van for final transport to the courthouse, her piece on the treatment of local prisoners was already half written in her head. She even had a marketing strategy for selling it to the *Post*.

But her optimism couldn't last forever. It was not until after the hearing had begun that she realized bail might require money. She considered the sum total of her assets, and hoped that the judge was having an extraordinarily good day. She was already indebted to Warren for Katharine's bill, which could be enormous if this nonsense carried on. Her parents would do what they could—but they certainly weren't wealthy. How bad would it be?

Leigh waited anxiously as the prosecutor impressed on the judge the heinousness of the crime, requesting that bail be denied. She was certain for several horrifying minutes that this logic would prevail, but she had underestimated Katharine Bower. The attorney quickly took charge of the proceedings, convincing the judge that choir-girl Leigh, active member of the Greenstone United Methodist Church, was not going anywhere. Katharine was so persuasive that Leigh found herself hoping for a bail with four digits. She was to be disappointed.

When the judge announced the final figure, Leigh's heart fell into her shoes. She didn't know exactly how bail bonding worked, but even ten percent of that awful number was more than she could make in a year. Her parents couldn't quickly pull together that kind of money either.

She was going back to jail.

Katharine noticed the horror in her client's eyes, but instead of sympathy, she offered reproach. "You should be smiling," she chastised. "Do you have any idea what kind of odds we just beat?"

Leigh laughed sadly. "Half a million dollars? What good does that do me?"

Katharine softened. "Relax, will you? The money's being taken care of. I assumed you knew."

The blank look on Leigh's face urged Katharine to continue.

"Your policewoman friend Maura Polanski called me early this morning and tipped me off that your arrest was imminent. I made a quick call to the docket clerk—who owes me a few. Not just everyone gets a same-day hearing, you know, so keep that under your hat. Your cop friend also said that she was making bail arrangements, and that price would be no object. So cheer up."

Leigh continued to stare blankly. How did Maura know she was being arrested? And what was this nonsense about price being no object? Had she lost her mind? With her mother facing assisted living, Maura had worse money problems than Leigh did.

"I'll meet you back at the jail," Katharine continued. "You have to be processed out before you can go home." She looked at her watch. "Warren should already be there waiting for you."

The faint tinge of jealousy overriding Katharine's last comment was not lost on Leigh, but she had other things on her mind. The handcuffs, the escorts, arrangements mysteriously made—the day's events were making her feel very much like a marionette.

Her escort (a stocky young man with a trace of BO) reapplied her handcuffs and led her out of the courtroom. She stopped cold in the hallway as a familiar figure started toward her.

"Leigh! Are you all right?"

She looked up into the genuinely concerned, ridiculously handsome face of her cousin-in-law. "I'm OK, Gil," she answered, marshaling all the dignity she could for someone whose hands were cuffed behind her back.

"The bail's taken care of," he said quickly. "You don't need to worry. You're getting out, and you're not going back in. This whole arrest is ludicrous!"

So that was it. Maura had gone straight to Cara, knowing that Cara would offer the money in a minute. Leigh looked at her cousin's husband with a mixture of gratitude, embarrassment, annoyance, and some other feeling she refused to acknowledge. He was even more gorgeous when he was angry, and this anger was righteous indignation toward the police, a sentiment she wholeheartedly approved of.

"I'm sorry you guys got dragged into this. Cara's OK, isn't she?" she asked.

"She's worried sick about you, of course," Gil answered honestly. "We're both anxious to help. Just let us know what you need, all right?"

"How about a one-way ticket to Rio?"

He looked at her sternly, and Leigh laughed out loud. Some people had no sense of humor. "I'm just kidding, Gil. Make sure you tell Cara I was cutting up in my hour of darkness, OK?"

He smiled slightly.

"And—" Leigh's voice broke. This was the hard part. She hated taking charity from her cousin, much less her cousin's husband. No one should have to bankroll an in-law. But no way was she rotting in the county jail out of stubborn pride. She wasn't that noble—or that stupid. She cleared her throat. "Thank you."

He started to answer, but Leigh's escort gave her arm a visible tug. "We'll see you later," Gil said instead, turning to leave. "Take care of yourself."

Leigh watched his perfect, photo-ready form stride away before the guard moved her along. He and Cara made such a perfect couple. She was glad she had set them up. Really, she was.

*   *   *

With her clothes returned and her orange jumpsuit abandoned, a released and unshackled Leigh was able to meet Warren with some trace of dignity. Neither Maura nor Warren had chosen to show up at the hearing, and she was grateful. There was a fine line between providing moral support and adding to one's humiliation. Warren rose to greet her without a trace of worry in his face, and Leigh suspected he'd worked hard to look that way. She would soon get all the worry she needed from her mother—Frances Koslow's worry capacity being equal to that of ten regular mothers.

Warren smiled warmly and stretched out his arms, and she fell into them gladly. They had always been affectionate pals, and he knew when she needed a lift. An awkward moment of silence followed, heightened by Katharine Bower's distinct look of disapproval, which Warren seemed to find extremely amusing.

"It's about dinnertime, by my watch," he said cheerfully. "And I'm starving, as usual. Can I take you ladies out?"

Katharine's eyes danced a little at the invitation, but she declined, saying something about billable hours. Leigh knew that she was a third wheel as far as Katharine was concerned, but she didn't particularly care. Warren was her friend first, after all, and she had had a rather despicable day. Leigh thanked Katharine profusely for her stellar work, promised to meet with her first thing in the morning, and headed toward the door with Warren.

Ignoring the small throng of reporters awaiting them outside the jail, they took off in the VW and drove back to the North Hills, where Leigh assuaged a small portion of her guilt by covering the bill for takeout heaped off a Chinese buffet. Ordinarily, she would have taken a seat and stuffed herself silly on General Tso's, but she was weary of crowds, and Warren didn't seem to mind.

As they carried their paper-sack booty across the parking lot and up to the main entrance of their apartment building, they nearly collided with a startled Tanner, who was just turning to leave.

"Leigh! Thank God!" He hugged her close, squishing some duck sauce out of the bag and onto her shirt. She reddened at the greeting and held the food out to the side.

"Mike! What are you doing here?"

He smiled and shook his head. "What do you think? You were whisked away in handcuffs, was I supposed to just go on about my business? I called around and found out you'd been released—I was hoping you'd be home. Are you OK?"

Leigh's heart warmed. "I'll be fine. Thanks for coming by."

"Warren Harmon," said the forgotten man at Leigh's other side, who knew his friend too well to wait for an introduction. "I presume you're Mike Tanner?"

Tanner nodded, and the men shook hands. Leigh noticed absently that Warren was taller—she would have guessed the other way around.

"Would you like to come up to my place for some Chinese?" she asked Tanner, smiling. "I think we loaded up enough for three."

Within a few minutes, she was playing hostess to two attractive, single men in her own humble kitchen—a rare event indeed. Warren didn't officially count, but the illusion was nice.

"So who paid your bail?" Tanner said curiously, digging into some twice-fried pork. "And what about that fancy lawyer? I thought you were having money problems."

Leigh wished he hadn't asked, since it really wasn't any of his business, but she couldn't very well dodge the issue under the circumstances. She opened her mouth to answer, but Warren cut her off.

"Leigh has some rather wealthy family connections," he said smoothly, "but she doesn't like to advertise it."

Tanner's eyebrows rose, but he said nothing. Having worked with Leigh's father, he no doubt knew she couldn't expect any windfalls from that quarter. Randall Koslow was an excellent veterinarian, but no one would ever accuse him of being a shrewd businessman.

Tanner surveyed Warren with a suspicious look, though his tone remained casual. "Are you a relative?"

Warren smiled. It was a smile Leigh knew well—the one that said he was secretly amused by something. "Just an old friend," he answered.

"Do we need more rice?" Leigh asked nervously. There was something about Tanner meeting Warren that she didn't care for. Warren was one part of her life, Tanner was another. They should have stayed that way.

"You make rice?" Warren teased.

Leigh whacked him with an empty carton and got up. "I am capable of boiling instant rice, yes. But only when absolutely necessary. More Coke?"

She went to the refrigerator and pulled out two more cans, the last cold ones. She'd have to make do with a lukewarm one herself, since the ice cube trays had been empty for weeks. No matter. It was a bonus there were cans at all—she'd have never found three matching tumblers.

She returned to her plate of the General, and joined Warren in steering the conversation away from the obvious. They talked first about the weather, then national politics, which led quickly to Pittsburgh politics and a heated debate over the necessity of new sports stadiums. Given that Warren was a professional debater and well versed on the facts to boot, Tanner wasn't coming off too well. Leigh grew annoyed, making an ill-fated attempt to change the subject to methods of rodent anesthesia. When dinner was finished, Tanner threw an easily interpretable look at Leigh. *Are we going to be alone soon?*

Leigh tried to send Warren a visual invitation to leave, but not only did he avoid her eyes, he started clearing the table. A noble gesture that Leigh ordinarily approved of, but in this case, blasted awkward. He drifted comfortably around the kitchen, giving every indication he knew it intimately. In reality, he almost never went near the place, declaring it woefully inequipped.

It soon became apparent that Warren had no intention of leaving first, and though Leigh would ordinarily feel no compunction about booting him out, something about his footing her legal bills made that seem crass. Tanner eventually gave up, made an excuse to leave, and asked Leigh to walk him out.

"I can't tell you how terrible I feel about all this," he said for the umpteenth time as they walked down the hall and boarded the elevator.

"You have," she answered, "repeatedly. And as I keep telling you—it's not your fault. It's not anybody's fault." *With the possible exception of one Detective Gerald Frank.* "It's just my dumb luck. But I'll be OK. The worst is over, you know. I'm not going to jail. No way."

Tanner smiled. "You've got guts, you know that?"

"Not guts," Leigh answered honestly. "Just a good self-defense mechanism for blocking out reality."

He laughed, then looked at her with his deep blue eyes in a way that made her spine melt. "I'm going up to the cabin tonight. Why don't you come with me? We can forget about all this—at least for a little while."

The offer that had been so tempting the day before only saddened her now. She could block out only so much reality. Tanner was wrapped up in all this mess somehow, and there were things he was hiding

from her—she was sure of it. She was tired of not
knowing what to believe, and nothing was going any
further until she had all the facts. But she had to talk
to him alone, without interruption. She had to get
him to trust her. And vice versa.

"I can't go tonight," she answered as they stepped
out of the elevator into the lobby. "I'm meeting with
my lawyer tomorrow morning. But if you're going
anyway, I could drive up afterward and meet you."

She had expected disappointment, seeing how an
invitation for the weekend generally implied something more than fishing and canoeing. But Tanner
smiled happily. "Sure, if you'd rather. I'll head up
early tomorrow then. Do you know where Eau
Claire is?"

She looked at him blankly.

"I'll write down some directions. It's not hard to
find . . ."

They walked outside to Tanner's pickup, where he
rummaged about until he'd found a pen and an old
copy of the *Journal of Zoo and Wildlife Medicine*. Finding an ad for stainless-steel live traps that had a fair
amount of white space, he began to scribble. Leigh
tried to listen to the directions, but such things bored
her to excess. She took the map and rolled it up
carefully. She would figure it out tomorrow.

"Are you sure you can leave the county?" Tanner
asked practically.

Leigh had no idea, but knew she would go anyway. "Sure. I'll send Frank a belly-gram with my
exact location. He won't mind."

Tanner laughed again, and pulled her into his
arms. "You know why I like you? You crack me up."

Given the demonstration that followed, Leigh
wasn't inclined to be insulted that he didn't like her
for her looks. But just as she was really beginning to
enjoy herself, and just when she was seriously wondering how bad an idea it would be to stand up her

lawyer tomorrow—she saw something disturbing out of the corner of her eye. She had seen a lot of it lately. It was that unmistakable shade of navy reserved for police uniforms.

She jumped, pulled out of Tanner's arms, and swung around. But it was only Maura Polanksi, leaning casually against a Ford Escort ten cars down. Maura had been watching the scene shamelessly, munching on an apple in the process.

"Who's that?" Tanner asked.

"Don't worry," Leigh answered, though she was a little worried herself. "That's my friend Maura, checking up on me."

"That's great," he said, smiling, "just don't bring her along tomorrow." Heedless of Officer Polanski, Tanner opted for a warm good-bye kiss, then drove away. Leigh was sad as she watched him leave. It would be nice to get away from everything tomorrow. No police. No orange jumpsuits. No interruptions. And hopefully, no more doubts.

"I guess you're doing all right after all," Maura said flatly, approaching. "And to think I was worried about you all day."

Leigh smiled. She had no idea how Maura had found out about her forthcoming arrest, but she hoped that the method was ethical. Maura Polanski was the most honest person she'd ever known, and she certainly didn't want their friendship to be Maura's downfall.

"Thanks," Leigh said simply. "You helped me out a lot today. I would have hated asking Cara for money myself, you know."

"I know."

Leigh knew not to be any more effusive. If Maura was forced to hear a big sloppy speech, she'd never help Leigh again.

"So what do you think?" Leigh said cheerfully,

tilting her head in the direction of Tanner's exit. "My new boss. Not bad, eh?"

Maura didn't smile. She wasn't frowning either, but her disapproval was clear. "He's a witness, Koslow. This is a parking lot. You should see a problem with that."

"He's not a witness," Leigh said defensively. "He's a veterinarian. And our relationship has nothing to do with Carmen's murder. Absolutely nothing!"

Maura's face assumed the distant look it always got when she was trying to read Leigh's mind. Leigh averted her gaze quickly. Maura wasn't flawless at the task, like Warren was, but she was darn good. Leigh cursed her own transparency. It was incredibly annoying not to be able to lie to your own friends.

They walked the rest of the way to Leigh's apartment in silence, where Warren, forgotten and unfazed, had settled himself in front of the television with a carton of lemon blend. Mao Tse, who had retreated to the bedroom when the first visitors arrived, had ventured out as far as the recliner to glower at Warren more noticeably. One look at Maura and she was off again, hissing in protest.

"Unsociable beast," Warren said dryly.

"Doesn't like you either, eh?" Maura chuckled.

Warren rose and turned off the television. "I'm afraid your arrest made the evening news . . . and it will be all over the papers tomorrow."

The chagrin in his voice was deep, though Leigh wasn't sure why bad publicity for her would upset him so much. Having her name broadcast all over Southwest Pennsylvania as a murderess wasn't pleasant, but it wasn't like she had an adoring public to disillusion. On the other hand, it did mean her mother would find out.

"My mom's going to freak," she said dully, dropping onto the couch.

"She did OK, actually," Maura answered.

Leigh sat up straight. "She what? She knows?"

Maura motioned for Leigh to relax. "I talked to your folks myself this afternoon. I didn't want them to hear it from the media. Or from some buttinsky who happened to catch the first newscast."

Leigh pictured her mother picking up the phone. *Hello, Frances? It's Viv. I just heard about your daughter being arrested for that awful dismemberment thing. And she was such a sweet little girl! Hello, Frances? Frances?* Leigh shuddered.

"Thanks, Maura," she said sincerely. "That was good thinking."

The policewoman shrugged. "I tried to reach you this morning, but I couldn't track you down. It was just as well—I wouldn't want Frank to know you were expecting him."

Leigh considered herself a good actress, but calmly sitting around waiting to be arrested and then acting surprised was a bit beyond her. She nodded dumbly.

Warren threw a brotherly arm around Leigh's shoulders. "Are you going to be OK tonight? Should we hang around a while longer, or just let you sleep?"

Leigh considered. Company was a nice distraction, but unconsciousness was better. A few Sominex and some warm milk, and she'd be angst-free till morning. "I think I'll hit the hay," she answered.

Maura tossed her head in the direction of Leigh's phone. "I told your folks you'd probably be pretty strung out tonight. Your dad promised they wouldn't call until tomorrow, but I'm not sure your mom was sold. If you really want an undisturbed night, you'd better turn the answering machine on and the ringer off."

"Already done," Warren answered.

Leigh smiled warmly at her defense team. She was going to need them.

Chapter 10

Despite the horrors of the day, Leigh would have had no trouble sleeping even without the Sominex. She was exhausted. A few dreams came and went, some involving knocks on the door that may have been real, but for the most part, she was out. When her alarm clock rang at 6:30 A.M., she looked at it through heavy lids. Her brain was still foggy, but she knew enough to know that it was Saturday, and any alarm clock of hers that valued its gears knew better than to go off on a weekend.

She reached out to hit the snooze button and found it obstructed by a yellow sticky note. She pulled it off and held it close to her face in the dim light. "Katharine. Seven A.M. SHARP." The bold letters, print rather than cursive, were unmistakably Warren's. Mr. Punctuality himself. Grumbling, Leigh rolled out of bed. Would a 10:30 A.M. appointment have been a crime?

She barely had time to dress and stuff down a breakfast bar before Katharine Bower rang her buzzer—at precisely 7:00 A.M. A woman after Warren's own heart, Leigh thought cynically. *In more ways than one.* As soon as Katharine came in she unloaded her laptop and a thick sheaf of papers on Leigh's kitchen table and began.

"We have a lot to get through this morning," Katharine announced, more with relish than regret. "We'll begin with the evidence—specifically, data from the crime scene." Her voice was mechanical, her whole manner eminently professional. Leigh wanted to go back to bed.

"It's extensive, but I'll summarize the relevant points for you. Two human legs and one arm were found within the tiger enclosure. The limbs were in poor condition—for obvious reasons. The left hand had been extensively gnawed but still bore two rings. The rings were identified by Mike Tanner as belonging to Carmen Koslow. Other personal items found at the scene included torn clothing, a purse, keys, and a jacket, all eventually confirmed to be those of Carmen Koslow. A car registered to Carmen Koslow was found in the employee parking lot. The victim had type O+ blood, matching Carmen Koslow's medical insurance records. Hair, consistent with that obtained from a hairbrush in Carmen Koslow's apartment, was found both on the floor of the shed and on the ground under the fence where police believe the body was dragged. Type O+ blood was also present in the shed, on the ground in a trail leading under the fence, and—here's the interesting part—on the driver-side door and on top of the trunk of a vehicle registered to Leigh Koslow."

Leigh swallowed. "There was blood on the car?"

"Evidently," Katharine answered. "Any ideas?"

Leigh shook her head.

Katharine shuffled through a few more papers. "A zoo security guard claims he found you running away from the scene of the crime, and that you were covered in blood. That blood, incidentally, also matched the victim's. He also claims that you attempted to wash the blood off before police arrived."

Leigh scowled. "I explained that a hundred times."

Katharine raised a hand. "We'll go through your explanation again in a few minutes. Your prints were found on the bone saw, as you know, but they were not recovered from the knife or the flashlight. Undoubtedly because both were smeared with blood. That's it for the physical evidence."

Thank goodness. Leigh rose. She couldn't possibly deal with this on less than three cups of coffee. She stumbled over to the pot and poured in enough water for five cups, graciously offering Katharine one.

The lawyer shook her head and continued. "Now here's the rest. Another security guard claims to have seen two women in zoo uniforms standing outside the tiger shed about 11:15 P.M. One fit Carmen Koslow's description. He described the other woman, whom he saw only from the back, as being medium height, medium build, with shoulder-length hair, probably brown."

"That could fit several people besides me," Leigh answered, dumping extra grounds into the filter. "Anyway, I was at the hospital then, setting up while Mike darted the gerenuk."

"There's more. A zoo employee named Dena Johnson claims she saw you walking through the staff gate into the tiger run sometime soon after 11:00."

Leigh wheeled around. "Who the hell is Dena Johnson?"

Katharine raised an eyebrow. "I was hoping you would know. She identified you quite specifically."

"She's lying through her teeth, whoever she is!" Leigh raged. "I was never there. I wasn't behind the tiger run that night at all—well, not before the murder anyway—and certainly not at eleven. Mike can testify to that!"

Katharine sighed slightly and took off her wire-rimmed glasses to look at her client. "That's another thing. Tanner. He's not your alibi, Leigh. He's your motive."

Leigh felt her legs begin to quiver, and she sat back down at the table. "What do you mean?"

"I warned you about the love triangle angle," Katharine said evenly. "Several zoo employees, not to mention Detective Frank himself—nice touch there—witnessed some type of romantic overture occur between you and Tanner."

Leigh's face was so hot it burned. She felt embarrassed and guilty, and she had no reason to feel either, which made her mad. "How I feel about Tanner is my own business!" she quipped.

Katharine didn't reply, but sat quietly and waited for Leigh to calm down. It was a practiced technique, and it worked.

"Why does it have to matter?" Leigh asked more sedately.

"Because according to every zoo employee Frank asked, Carmen Koslow and Tanner had been involved for years."

Leigh's heart sank down into her shoes. The arrest was bad enough—now her most private hopes were to be dragged out and bludgeoned. "Define 'involved,'" she asked quietly.

Katharine looked at her with uncharacteristic sympathy. "The exact nature of their relationship can't be determined from what I have here—the witnesses can only provide their impressions. There is Tanner's statement."

She had to ask. "And what did he say?"

Katharine replaced her glasses and looked down at one of her many documents. "'I knew her before, during, and after my divorce,'" she quoted. "'It was a platonic relationship, although Carmen wasn't happy with that. I told her I didn't want to make any commitment to anybody else for a long time. She seemed to understand, but she was still very possessive. She got incredibly jealous whenever I so much as looked at another woman.'"

Leigh's brow wrinkled. "That doesn't make any sense," she thought out loud. "Why would Carmen be possessive if their relationship was platonic?"

Katharine looked at Leigh as if she ought to know the answer to that question. "Tanner's statements about the relationship aren't completely consistent," she said heavily. "And they disagree with the impressions of the witnesses. To say the least."

Leigh stood up again. She'd had enough. "If Frank thinks a mild-mannered model citizen like me would chop up another woman over a man—any man—he's crazy."

"'Crazy' is strong," Katharine responded quickly, "though that scenario is not very plausible, I agree. Unfortunately, I believe Frank has another scenario which was easier for the D.A. to swallow."

Leigh looked at the lawyer expectantly.

"Carmen Koslow has quite a colorful past. If you were the dead one, she'd have been jailed before dawn. She has a history, according to witnesses, of jealousy over Dr. Tanner, and on a few instances she has reacted aggressively toward other women he's been involved with."

Leigh didn't want to think about the implications of the last statement, so she ignored it.

Katharine continued. "I suspect Frank is basing his theory on Carmen's having attacked, or planned to attack, *you*. Somehow or other, she was the one who wound up dead. The dismemberment could have been a frantic attempt to cover up whatever 'accident' killed her. You and Tanner could have disposed of the rest of the body together."

Leigh sank back down into her chair, speechless. The scenario made a sick kind of sense. The only problem was, it was completely untrue.

"If that didn't happen, the scenario won't hold up," Katharine said firmly. "Our job is to go through every minuscule detail of your story looking for supportable contradictions with that scenario. I can think of several offhand. There were no indications of your being involved in a struggle. Neither your car nor Tanner's bore any evidence of having the rest of the body *inside*, and both engines were cold when the police arrived. No blood was found on Tanner's clothing—no other bloody clothing was found at the zoo. And as for your running from the scene, the report overlooks the fact that although you were running toward the main gates, you were running *away* from the employee lot where your car was parked."

Katharine paused. "But punching holes in the state's theory is only half our job. We not only need to show that you didn't and couldn't have done it— we need a defense theory. We need to figure out how it actually went down."

Leigh rose and headed instinctively for the coffee-pot. She pulled down a double-sized thermal travel mug, filled it to the brim, and gulped two uncomfortably hot swallows. The sad truth was, she hadn't given all that much thought to what had really happened to Carmen. The killer could, after all, have been just about anybody. She liked Tanner's theory of a professional hit because it was more comforting than imagining a murderer on the zoo payroll, but otherwise the details didn't concern her. Carmen was dead and Leigh was sorry about that—really, she was—but finding the killer wasn't her problem.

Until now.

A pot and a half of coffee later, Katharine Bower closed her laptop and straightened her papers. "We'll need to interview everyone involved—I'm sure all the zookeepers have theories, even if some were reluctant to share them with police. And if you insist on talking to Tanner before I get a chance, don't go soft—make it clear that his failure to be truthful with us could seriously jeopardize your case."

A thought that should have struck Leigh earlier

finally surfaced. "Am I allowed to leave the county? I was planning to meet him at his cabin this afternoon—up past Butler."

Katharine's mouth hardened into a grim line. "I wish you weren't involved with him at all—but there's no point continuing some lame cover-up." Leigh bristled a little at the implied criticism, but let it go. One had to pick one's battles—and one's opponents.

Katharine didn't think a day trip across the county line would be a problem, but wasn't happy that Leigh could provide only vague directions and no phone number. "Don't stay long," she warned. "We'll need to keep in touch." She headed for the door, then turned. "Warren lives in this building too, doesn't he? Could you give me the number? I need to speak with him about something."

The lawyer's voice was practiced in neutrality, but Leigh wasn't fooled. She gave the number with somewhat of a smirk, which Katharine ignored.

"One more thing," Katharine yelled back as she started down the hall. "The reporters will keep on you for a while. Whatever you do—don't say *anything*!"

Leigh nodded and smiled slyly. No, she wouldn't be talking to any reporters. Not until the charges were dropped, anyway. Then they'd get an earful. She crossed to the front window to survey the reporter situation, and was happy to see only one holdout of the few that had been waiting for Katharine outside the apartment building this morning. But so far none had gotten close enough to harass Leigh in person. Buzzer systems were a definite advantage of apartment life. Especially ones with volume controls.

She glanced at her answering machine and sighed. It hadn't worked for ages, now it was blinking its little heart out—the tape was probably full. She sat down beside it, turned up the volume, and hit PLAY, taking a deep breath to fortify herself. The messages started from the night before—reporters chiefly, a few concerned friends and coworkers. Then the one she'd been dreading.

"Leigh, it's your dad. Maura just left, and she did a very good job of explaining everything. Your mother's doing all right, but it would help if you could speak with her yourself. Give us a call tomorrow morning."

Leigh smiled sadly. Her dad was a rock in a crisis, but he was known to underplay everything by a factor of at least five. If he said her mother was OK, he meant that she didn't require hospitalization. He also never said things he didn't mean. The call home was not an option.

She downed another breakfast bar before picking up the phone. It was almost noon, and she was starving. Hypoglycemia and a call to her mother did not mix well.

A thin voice answered on the first ring. "Yes?"

"It's me, Mom. I'm absolutely fine. The arrest was no big deal, everybody treated me just fine, I was out before I knew it, and my lawyer is confident that the case won't go much further. The charges are probably going to be dropped and everything is absolutely A-OK hunky dorry. All right?"

There was no answer for a moment, and Leigh awaited the sound of a clunk on the floor, but none came. The thin voice came back on, strained but steady.

"I'm glad you're taking it well. Maura assured me that you have a fine lawyer. But you need your family now. I'm already organizing a family conference."

Leigh's blood froze. The fact that her mother wasn't babbling hysterically was frightening enough, but the dreaded family conference was a fate too horrific to contemplate. "Um, Mom," she said weakly, "can I talk to Dad, please?"

"In a minute," Frances said firmly. "First, you're going to agree to a family conference. At two o'clock."

With every cell in Leigh's body shrieking "Avoid! Avoid!" the wheels in her brain began to churn. "I really can't today, Mom," she insisted, "I have an important meeting this afternoon with a witness. The lawyer gave me instructions and everything."

Frances paused only briefly. "Tonight, then."

"I don't know when I'll get back. It's a pretty good drive from here. And I've been going to bed early lately—"

"Sunday morning, right after church. We'll have lunch. Lydie can make lasagna and Cara and Gil can bring the baby over."

Leigh's body slumped in defeat. She couldn't avoid it forever. They all meant well. "OK, Mom. I'll be there."

"We'll see you at church beforehand. Shall I have Reverend Albers bring you up as a—"

"No!" Leigh uttered the exclamation automatically, then reconsidered. After another day every man, woman, and dog in Pittsburgh would know she'd been arrested for murder. What did it matter? A little prayer couldn't hurt.

"Um, sure, Mom. That'd be great. Thanks." She bit her lip. Her mother's behavior in all this was disturbingly rational. Not half as bad as the time Leigh had attended the church picnic in a midriff shirt with a snake tattoo.

"Take it easy, Mom. OK?"

"You can talk to your father now."

What, no parting advice? Leigh began to panic. There were muffled noises, then a voice came back on the phone. It was Frances again.

"Oh, and dear—be careful what you wear. The television reporters may be watching for you, and you don't need to be seen running around in those awful blue jeans or you'll look guilty for sure. I've read that the camera puts ten pounds on, you know—"

Leigh smiled. Frances might make it after all.

Leigh held the scribbled map to the right of the steering wheel, trying to read it as the Cavalier bounced helplessly on the pitted gravel road. Tanner was better at surgery. The map began all right, but by the time he drew the last road he had cornered himself in so tiny a space that the cabin location was indecipherable. She tossed the journal on the seat and decided to use her instincts.

Her stomach growled. The two tacos she'd picked up on the way were good, but insubstantial, and her next meal in civilization could be a ways off. She sighed and thought again of her conversation with Katharine.

It was a platonic relationship, Tanner had said in his sworn statement. Why would he lie? He couldn't have known that Leigh would read the report. Maybe he was the only man who ever told Carmen no and that's why she was so attracted to him . . .

I knew her before, during, and after my divorce, he had said. *Before?* When had Tanner started working at the zoo, and when had he and Stacey broken up? She envisioned the jealous and overzealous Stacey going bonkers after one look at Carmen's zoo uniform, which on every occasion Leigh had seen it was unbuttoned conspicuously low. Had Carmen caused the divorce?

Leigh sucked up the last of her Diet Coke, now diluted to pale brown swirls in melted ice. If Carmen had been the catalyst, it could help explain Stacey's generous divorce settlement. What was it she had said in the hospital lounge? *I'm no longer interested in the sordid details of your sex life.* Stacey was talking about Carmen.

Leigh tipped up the cup to finish off the ice, and was suddenly hit with cold in more places than one. *The divorce settlement.* What if his defense in the divorce was to claim that he hadn't cheated? If Stacey's case had included proof of infidelity, Tanner would be foolish to lie about that to police—they could find out about the divorce settlement. But if she hadn't been able to prove it, which seemed more likely, he couldn't very well admit it later—knowing Stacey, she'd haul him right back to court and have him brought up on perjury charges. So if he ever claimed there was nothing going on with Carmen during his marriage, he'd have to keep claiming that.

The possibilities swam circles in Leigh's brain. Did he lie both times, or was he telling the truth? Even if he covered up an involvement before the divorce, why cover up an involvement after? He was a free man now. He said that the relationship was platonic, period. It might very well be. Mightn't it?

She slammed on the brakes as an energetic young rottweiler suddenly darted out into the road in front of her, followed closely by a grubby little boy of three or four. She hadn't been going fast, but stopped only a few feet short of the dog and uncomfortably close to the child as well. The boy looked at the Cavalier only briefly before running back into his own yard, followed happily by the dog. Leigh looked for a supervising adult, and saw an older woman, probably the boy's grandmother, hanging out laundry beside a double-wide trailer. The woman looked at Leigh as if to say "watch out where you're going, will you?" and continued with her work.

Leigh shook her head and kept driving, this time at a snail's pace. But the few small houses and trailers that had dotted the road before disappeared abruptly as she drove farther into the woods. The condition of the road deteriorated as well, and for a few minutes she was convinced there couldn't possibly be any inhabited dwellings farther down. Soon the road would simply end, dwindling to a narrow path studded with meadow muffins.

But she was wrong. After a particularly sharp turn and a particularly deep pothole, a cabin came into view. Mercifully, so did Tanner's pickup. The cabin was about how she had imagined it—small, wooden, and square, with minimal decorating or landscaping effort. There did not even appear to be a driveway—Tanner's truck was parked haphazardly among the trees in front. Another car was parked alongside the road, two wheels driven up into knee-high weeds.

Leigh steered the Cavalier into place behind the extra car, frowning all the while. Who else was here? Her whole point in coming was to be alone with Tanner. She'd thought he felt the same way.

Walking where the trees were thicker and the weeds not quite so robust, Leigh trail-blazed her way slowly toward the front door. The cabin seemed sturdy enough, it just needed a little attention. Perhaps a lot of attention.

As she got nearer to the cabin and heard no signs of life within, Leigh began to worry. Where was Tanner? She had expected him to come meet her—he couldn't possibly have not heard her car, since there was nothing else to be heard in the middle of nowhere. The front door of the cabin stood open a few inches, but the windows were dark and he was nowhere to be seen. Leigh felt a twinge of nervousness, and backtracked to confirm that she'd seen the right pickup. She walked close enough to look in the cab. Yes, it was Tanner's. Not too many pickups in Pennsylvania had Auburn University tote bags in the front seat. So where had he gone?

She made her way back up to the front porch and called out hesitantly. "Mike? It's Leigh. Are you here?"

The only answer was an odd huffing sound, as if

someone was having trouble breathing. Leigh ran the last few steps to the door and darted inside. Her own breath stopped cold.

Tanner lay kneeling on the floor in the middle of the dark, crowded room, his back toward Leigh. His body shook with sobs as he rocked back and forth, holding something in his arms. She stepped forward involuntarily until she could see what he was clasping so desperately.

Stretching out on the floor away from him was a figure dressed in a lime T-shirt, plaid polyester shorts, and comfortable shoes. Leigh bent down to see the woman's face, and regretted it immediately. The shiny heap of short platinum hair could not hide the pale face, the shocked, staring eyes. And nothing could hide the dark red stain that spread on the hardwood floor beneath her.

Leigh stepped back. She had seen enough dead creatures to know there was no point in taking a pulse. Furthermore, her recent experience had given her a new instinct for self-preservation. Hands firmly at her sides, she stood quietly, watching Tanner.

"She's dead," Tanner moaned between sobs. "I loved her, and now she's dead." His words were difficult to understand—he spoke as if to himself, giving no indication that Leigh was in the room. He continued to rock on his knees, holding the woman's upper body in his arms, repeating the same muffled phrases. As he rocked, Leigh could see that the woman's back was soaked with blood. Had she been shot?

Leigh looked at him as she would at a wounded animal. She wanted desperately to comfort him, but there was nothing she could do. Stacey Tanner was dead.

Chapter 11

Leigh did not stay long. A week ago she would have pulled him away, got him a glass of water, tried to calm him down. Then maybe she would have thought about Stacey, and notifying the authorities. She certainly wouldn't have worried about what the police would think.

Not now. Leigh fought down her shock at the sight of another body and began to run her brain in the same autopilot, crisis-management mode she used with emergencies at her father's clinic. First: triage. Stacey was dead and that was that. As for Tanner, his emotional state was distressing, but she knew he would get a grip on himself eventually. She pulled a dusty wool blanket from its resting place over the back of a chair and wrapped it around Tanner's shoulders. There was no point in trying to pry him away from Stacey—he would only resist. She couldn't do anything else for him, at least medically. In any event, the shock would be temporary. His other problem might not be. Whatever had happened to Stacey, he had come in on the wrong end of it, and as the "feuding ex-husband" he had a good chance of topping the suspect list.

She wanted to help him. Was Stacey already dead when he got here? How long had he been like this?

Could he prove when he'd arrived? Was the body already stiff?

She shivered. The last question would have to go unanswered. In fact, they all would. He was in no state to discuss his situation rationally. Leigh took a deep breath and looked around. Could she help him? There didn't appear to be a gun lying about, or any other weapon for that matter. Was there anything else that might incriminate him? Should she claim they'd arrived in tandem?

An image of Maura Polanski—complete with her sternest tone—popped into Leigh's mind with a vengeance. *Touch one thing, Koslow, and I swear to God I'll deck you.*

Yes, Leigh considered glumly. That's exactly what Maura would say. And exactly what Maura would do. She bent down and took another pitying look at Tanner. His eyes were swollen, his face pale. "Why did you leave me, Stacey?" he mumbled softly. "Why?"

Leigh straightened up. Tanner's problems were beyond her. For once, she was going to do the intelligent thing. She was going to get the hell out of there.

She bumped the door with her shoulder and walked out, proud that she hadn't accidentally touched anything inside. She ran straight to her car, heedless of the weeds she was trampling, and took off. How far down was the next cabin? Two miles? Three? It was at least ten to the nearest pay phone. Should she go straight there, or stop at the nearest cabin?

The last question was answered for her when she realized that, like Tanner's cabin, the nearest two dwellings had no phone lines. She had driven about eight miles when she saw the first series of telephone poles, heading to the small cluster of trailers where she had stopped before. The boy was still playing in the yard, along with two other small children and the exuberant rotty. The grandmother was nowhere to be seen. Leigh pulled her Cavalier off onto the road's nearly nonexistent shoulder. The children at first ignored her, but the young rottweiler found the visitor quite fascinating.

She rolled her window down partway as the puppyish but solid creature rushed at the car, barking madly. "Hey there, pup," she said soothingly. The rotty stopped barking, put his paws up on the car door, and panted through the crack in the window. He seemed all right, but she'd been crossed by too many rotties to trust one she didn't know. The grandmother appeared on the trailer's makeshift front porch, looking at Leigh suspiciously. "Excuse me," Leigh called out. "There's been some trouble up the road. Could you please call the police?"

The woman scrutinized her company. "Anybody hurt?" she yelled.

Leigh nodded grimly.

"An ambulance too, then?" the woman asked matter-of-factly. Leigh nodded again. The woman turned slowly and disappeared into the house.

Ten excruciating minutes passed. After an initial period of staring at her through the car windows, the children and dog had returned to their games. The woman herself had merely emerged, given Leigh a confirmatory nod that the job had been done, and gone back inside.

Leigh slumped down in the seat, wondering if anything in her life could get much worse. What had happened to Stacey? Why was she at the cabin? Tanner would never have asked her to meet him there. Not when he knew Leigh was coming. But Stacey hadn't been there alone. Someone had been there with her. And that someone had killed her.

When a car from the Butler County Sheriff's Department finally pulled up the road, Leigh rolled down her other window and waved, anxious that her location not be overlooked. "There's been some trouble at the Tanner cabin," she explained. "I think a woman is dead."

She led the deputy sheriff down the pathetic road, the Cavalier moaning at the repeat agony. An ambulance soon appeared as well, and the threesome progressed steadily. When they reached the cabin, none bothered to find parking spots, but merely stopped in the road. Leigh breathed a sigh of relief at seeing Tanner's truck in place. If he had taken off, they'd both be in trouble.

She got out of her car, but nodded meekly when the deputy ordered her to stay outside the cabin. They couldn't get her back in there if they tried. Two state police cars soon joined the crowd, and Leigh tried to calm her nerves. Frank worked for the city squad; this was Butler County. With luck, the detectives up here could see beyond what hit them in the face.

She remained obediently by the Cavalier while a woman in uniform questioned her, then searched both her and her car. For what? A gun, perhaps? Right. Like she could pack heat for ten minutes without shooting herself in the foot.

Minutes seemed like hours as she leaned against the car waiting for something to happen, the phrases Tanner had uttered reverberating in her mind. *I loved you. Why did you leave me?* She shook her head to dismiss them, hoping Tanner was keeping his mouth shut now. The police would have to look beyond the obvious, all right. Way beyond.

Finally, a stretcher was carried out the front door and loaded into the ambulance. She watched the door anxiously for signs of Tanner. The paramedics were probably working on him too—shock was a medical condition, after all. But what were the police doing?

She got her answer all too soon. A trio of uniforms

stepped out the door, Tanner wedged in between them. He was pale as a ghost, and not walking too steadily. The paramedics had fastened a clean blanket around his shoulders, and the officers were helping him down the porch steps. As they turned at the bottom, Leigh's heart sank. Of course they were helping him. It was hard to walk down steps with cuffs on.

"Just so you don't think I'm hiding anything," Leigh heard herself say as she faced her new interrogator in the state police barracks, "I'll tell you that I was falsely arrested in Pittsburgh this week and am out on bond."

The trooper's eyes widened. Joe Smitty was much more personable a detective than Frank, being in his early fifties and appearing to have some sense of humor behind his soft brown eyes and chubby cheeks. "Is that so?" he asked conversationally.

Leigh nodded.

"Falsely arrested for what?"

She sighed. "For the murder of an acquaintance."

The trooper's face lit up. "Of course! Leigh Koslow. I thought I'd heard your name before. The zoo murder. Nasty business. And they arrested *you*?" He smiled at her as if in collusion. "What do they know?"

Leigh smiled back. He was probably playing a confidence game with her, but she didn't care. He seemed genuinely nice, regardless. "I can't talk about that, unless I call my lawyer—"

"Of course you can't."

"—and I don't want to pay her any more than absolutely necessary," she finished.

Smitty laughed heartily. "No one would. I promise I won't ask you anything about that."

She smiled appreciatively. Katharine would probably kill her for talking about anything, but she had to tell what she knew at the scene, or else she would look guilty. Besides, she wasn't a suspect here. No one had even bothered to read her her rights before questioning.

"Miss Koslow," Smitty began, leaning back in his chair. The ambience was much nicer here too, Leigh thought. Padded chair, no glass spy walls. Next time she found a body, she would definitely try to do it in Smitty's jurisdiction. "Did you see or do anything unusual on your way to the cabin, particularly after you turned onto Barber Road?"

"I didn't meet any cars going the other way, if that's what you mean," Leigh said helpfully. "But I did almost hit a dog. And a little boy was entirely too close to the road too. They weren't being watched very carefully," she said reproachfully.

The trooper smiled slightly as he took notes. "Did you make any stops between there and the cabin?"

Leigh shook her head.

"And how long were you at the cabin?"

She considered. "Probably only about five minutes. It seemed longer at the time, but I really didn't do much except look around, put a blanket on the man in shock, and leave. But I explained all that before."

Smitty nodded, his smile widening as he finished his notes. "I'm happy to say, Miss Koslow, that your story checks out very nicely with that of Martha Rehn, the woman who put in the emergency call. And you're right, she does need to rein those kids in tighter. It's a good thing that road doesn't get much traffic."

Leigh agreed tacitly. She liked this man. He liked her too, that much was obvious. He seemed to know she wasn't capable of murder. So what was Frank's problem?

"One more thing, Miss Koslow, then I'll let you get back to those bozos in Allegheny County. Do you know anyone who drives an old blue Buick Century—the gas-guzzling kind from the late seventies?"

She searched her brain, but came up empty. "No. Why?"

"How about a tan Eldorado, same age?"

Leigh shook her head.

"Thanks for coming down," Smitty said amiably. He stretched out a hand and shook hers. "I hope you'll come back if we have any more questions."

"I'd be delighted," she answered, almost truthfully. Who knew? Maybe Smitty and Frank were golfing buddies and Smitty would put in a good word for her. She was just about to walk triumphantly out of the barracks when the opening was blocked by a familiar figure.

"Koslow," the woman sighed, relieved. "At least you're moving the right direction this time."

"How did you know I was here?" Leigh asked, impressed, as she and Maura leaned on the hood of the Cavalier out in the parking lot.

"A friend heard about it and called me," Maura answered vaguely. "I understand Mike Tanner's been arrested."

"Well of course he was arrested. Don't police always arrest the person who finds the body?"

Maura looked at her sternly. "You don't know what happened. You weren't there. At least I'm *hoping* you weren't."

"I wasn't." Leigh gave Maura the story in a capsule. She was clearly in debt to the rottweiler—if it hadn't run in front of her, she wouldn't have been able to prove her arrival time. And her arrival time was of no small consequence.

"Koslow," Maura said seriously, "you can yell and scream and defend this guy all you want, but if you ask me, it doesn't look good. You can't know for sure that he didn't kill his ex-wife. You said yourself they had a violent argument just yesterday—"

"It wasn't violent!" Leigh said quickly. "Not on Tanner's end anyway."

"She could have agitated him," Maura insisted. "Ex-spouses have a way of pushing each other's buttons. Tanner's been under a lot of stress lately."

"But he's not a violent person!" Leigh was suddenly weary of trying to understand Mike Tanner and his motives. She had come up to the cabin with the hope of straightening out how he felt about Carmen; now she didn't understand how he felt about Stacey either. *I loved you*, he had said. *Why did you leave me?*

And just who left who? She thought that Tanner had left Stacey. After all, why wouldn't he? The woman was a shrew from birth. Leigh had never liked her, and she couldn't believe he did either, not really. But there he had been in the cabin, crying, rocking her. Could it be? Did he *still* love her?

"What are you thinking, Koslow?"

Leigh shook her head. "I don't know what's going on in Tanner's head, no. But I know he's not a killer. If he were, Stacey would have been dead a long time ago."

"You seem awfully sure of yourself," Maura said carefully.

"I am. Now, if you'll excuse me, I'm going to go find him."

"No, you're not." Maura answered firmly. "Tanner has a busy day in front of him. You don't even know where he is—he could be in the hospital or the county jail."

"He's been falsely arrested!" Leigh cried indignantly. "He'll need a lawyer, and bail money."

Maura sighed. "Look, Koslow. You've got to stop taking personal responsibility for this man. You got the hots for him, fine. But you've got to think about your own situation. He's been arrested for murdering his ex and he may be guilty. He may have had something to do with Carmen's death too."

Leigh's eyes blazed. "That's crazy! I was with him that whole night, remember? I'm telling you, he didn't kill anybody."

"Then let him prove that. He's a big boy. He can get his own lawyer, hit up his own friends for bail. You've got to stay out of it. The fact is, anything and everything that ties you up closer with Tanner just makes you look guiltier."

Leigh took a deep, sulky breath. Maura was right. She was having enough trouble saving her own hide. If she wasn't careful, she could make things worse for both herself and Tanner.

"Fine," she said tiredly. "So what am I supposed to do now?"

"Talk to your lawyer," Maura answered firmly. "Tell her everything that happened today. And if you go to see Tanner later"—she lowered her voice for emphasis—"take your lawyer with you."

Leigh looked up at her friend. Maura had always been good at beating things into or out of one's head as needed. "Thanks for rushing up here," she said somewhat sheepishly. "I really didn't intend to make you rescue me at two police stations in one week."

Maura shrugged. "Par for the course, Koslow."

Leigh pulled into the parking lot at her apartment building with a heavy heart. She was free, but Tanner would be spending the night in jail. If, of course, he made it out of the hospital. It was wrong. Why should she get so lucky? Her cousin had jumped to pay her bail, and had the wherewithal to do it. Did Tanner have any rich friends or family? She doubted it. All she knew about his family was that they raised beef cattle in Alabama. And he'd never mentioned any close friends outside of the zoo. He was alone.

Leigh parked, opened the front door, and headed for the stairs. Not that she was a health nut, but the elevator was slow and she hated waiting, even if it meant walking up four flights. Suddenly remembering that she should be on the lookout for reporters, Leigh glanced around, but there was none to be seen. She began trooping up the stairs, but when her calves started aching by the second floor, she decided to take a temporary detour to Warren's. Maybe he had some of that great peach iced tea brewed up. Maybe he was even cooking dinner.

She knocked on his door, unconsciously licking her lips. When she heard female laughter from within, she started to retreat, but the door opened.

"Hey, Leigh!" Warren said cheerfully. He was wearing cycling shorts and a T-shirt, looking sweaty and flushed from exercise. Behind him on the couch sat an almost unrecognizable Katharine Bower, also in biking gear, and also sweaty and flushed. She was sipping a peach iced tea.

"I'm sorry," Leigh said unconvincingly. "Did I interrupt something?"

"Yes," Warren said, laughing. "In a few more moments I would have had Ms. Bower here turned into a first-class Democrat. She's lucky you dropped by."

"It'll never happen, Harmon," Katharine quipped, not looking as if she felt at all lucky.

"We've been biking up at Moraine State Park," Warren explained unnecessarily. "Great weather for it. Would you like some iced tea?"

Leigh shook her head. "I can't stay. I've got to—" *What? Call my lawyer? Right.* Her lawyer was obviously having a good time on a Saturday afternoon. She didn't need to hear Leigh's problems this second. "I've got to do some work for Hook. I'm behind, you know."

"Is that why you're back already?" Warren said casually, taking a seat on the couch next to Katharine.

"Kath said you were going to Tanner's cabin for the day."

Now she's "Kath," is she? "My lawyer and I will need to talk later," Leigh retorted. She wasn't telling her legal woes to anyone with good muscle tone. She would wait for the return of the real Katharine Bower, the one that was cool, composed, and uncomfortably dressed. Bidding the twosome a hasty farewell, she headed back to the stairwell to tackle two more flights. She was now not only depressed about Tanner, she was annoyed too. Why did her lawyer have to have a thing for Warren? Lawyers should be celibate, like priests, so that they could concentrate on their jobs. She pushed her key into the lock with a vengeance, opening her door.

I bet he fixes dinner for her too.

Maura Polanski hadn't left Butler when Leigh did, but had doubled back into the state police barracks. She had no trouble finding the employee break room in the basement, nor Sara Jean, who lounged inverted on the ragged couch, her long legs draped over its back.

"Polanski!" she effused, swinging her feet over with ease. "Long time, no see, woman!"

Maura smiled. Sara Jean was some sort of relative, or so they had always assumed. All they really knew was that they had both grown up in Avalon and tended to show up at the same reunions. Sara Jean stubbed out her cigarette in a candy wrapper and banked the wad off a NO SMOKING sign into the trash can. "Good aim," Maura praised.

Sara Jean shrugged. "Practice." She motioned for Maura to sit down. "So how're things in Avalon? Have they made you detective yet?"

Maura's teeth clenched slightly. "Not yet. Everything in Avalon is the same. Except Mom's worse."

Sara Jean shook her head sympathetically. "I know

what you're going through, believe me. It was rough with my granddad, but we got through it. You ever need a relief person, you call me, you hear?"

Maura nodded, then changed the subject. "Thanks for calling me about Leigh. I'm surprised you remembered her name."

Sara Jean laughed. "After all that mess in Avalon last summer? How could I forget? No, when I heard her name on the news, I knew it was your friend. So when I found out she was coming in here, I figured you'd want to know."

Maura smiled appreciatively. Sara Jean had a good heart, but hopelessly loose lips. How she had managed to secure a job as a police records clerk was a mystery, but Maura suspected it had something to do with her libido. "So what's up?" the policewoman prompted.

"Guy knifed his ex," Sara Jean said simply. "Got him plain as day. Blood all over him, moaning about how she'd left him. Classic." She reached into her pocket and lit another cigarette. "Classic," she repeated.

Maura sighed. "Do you know how long the woman had been dead when they found her?"

Sara Jean looked at the ceiling as she considered. "Seems like I heard she wasn't stiff yet when they picked her up."

Probably less than five hours.

"Your friend reported it," Sara Jean continued. "Sounds like she's got a thing for this guy. You think he did that woman at the zoo too?"

Maura winced slightly. "I hope not. Was there anything you heard about this case that didn't fit? I mean, that might make you think he *didn't* do it?"

Sara Jean shook her head. "They didn't find the knife, but he could've got rid of it easy enough."

"Anything else?"

Sara Jean shrugged. "They were asking about another car for a while—some woman down the road saw somebody shooting off like a bat out of hell earlier. But she didn't get a license or anything. It was probably just some drunk coming down from one of the hunting cabins."

Maura was quiet for a moment. "You remember what kind of car?"

Sara Jean shook her head. "I could look it up if you want."

Maura shook her head. Listening while Sara Jean shot her mouth off was one thing. Asking her to look in confidential files was another. "Thanks, cuz. You know my number, right?"

Sara Jean grinned. "You know I do."

Leigh paced around her apartment for exactly three minutes before heading back down to Warren's. She knocked on the door loudly.

"Come on in!" Warren yelled cheerfully. Leigh obliged. He and Katharine were still sitting next to each other on the couch, smiling as if they shared some private joke.

"Mike Tanner's ex-wife was murdered today," Leigh announced without preamble. "And the police think he did it."

Chapter 12

Katharine Bower's peach iced tea spewed forward about three feet, most of it over the *Wall Street Journal* on the coffee table. Warren leaped up to fetch a towel, glancing unkindly at Leigh as he went.

"Tanner did *what*?" Katharine cried.

"I didn't say Tanner did anything," Leigh said defensively. "Being arrested for murder doesn't make you guilty, you know."

"He's been arrested?" Katharine asked, choking a little.

She nodded.

Warren took a firm hold of Leigh's arm and maneuvered her into a chair. "Sit down and start talking." He handed one towel to Katharine and began salvaging the *Wall Street Journal* with another.

Leigh took a deep breath. She really didn't want to go through everything again, but what choice did she have? She had to tell Katharine, and Warren wasn't going anywhere. She squirmed uncomfortably and began, noting that her chair was wet.

Warren listened without comment; Katharine asked a million questions. But when Leigh had finished, the lawyer seemed pleased. "You did good," she said approvingly. "You could have sealed your own coffin with this one, but you used your head.

And almost hitting the dog was a hell of a nice break."

Leigh would have liked to bask in the moment, but she felt too bad about not helping Tanner. "Can't we do anything for Mike?" she asked plaintively.

"The good doctor can get his own damn lawyer," Warren said sharply. "Katharine's going to concentrate on saving your butt, remember?"

Assuming this would not be a good time to see if her lawyer could represent someone else on the same tab, Leigh kept her mouth shut.

"We need to talk to Tanner right away," Katharine said firmly. "I shouldn't have let you see him on your own in the first place, but what's done is done." She looked at her watch. "Hey, Warr—mind if I use your shower? Leigh and I can just take off from here."

Warren smiled. "Sure. Whatever you need. There are clean towels in the hall closet."

Leigh looked at him with disgust. If a friend asked to use her shower, she'd say yes too, but only after she spent twenty frantic minutes picking up personal items and blasting the shower with Tilex. And what was this "Warr" business?

Katharine grabbed her tote bag and headed for the bathroom, while Leigh headed for the kitchen and a glass of peach tea. As she returned with it, she noticed that Warren had settled back on the couch and was watching her. After a moment, he spoke. "Tanner could very well have done it, you know."

"He could not!" she responded testily, plopping herself into the chair opposite him. "You met him. Did he seem like a murderer?"

Warren studied her face. She hated it when he did that. This time, however, his mind-reading abilities worked to her advantage.

"No," he said finally, with a small sigh. "If you

really think he's innocent, I suppose I trust your judgment."

She smiled.

"Not about everything, mind you. You've obviously misjudged him in other ways, but I think you'd know if the man was violent."

"Tanner's a lamb," Leigh said, sipping her iced tea thirstily. "He can blow his top and yell, but he's not the type to hurt something weaker than he is. I can tell by the way he is with his patients." Her mind backtracked to Warren's other comment. "And what do you mean—misjudged in other ways?"

Warren looked at her again for a moment, then shook his head. "Look, Leigh. I hate to burst your bubble, but don't you think you could be a bit more objective about this guy?"

Her blood pressure rose. *"Meaning?"*

"Meaning that you're seeing the same idyllic hero you saw when you were a kid. He was unattainable then—a fantasy. Now he's interested in you, and you've convinced yourself it's destiny. But it's not, Leigh. It's still just a fantasy."

Leigh's eyes blazed. "You don't know anything about it."

"You told me about it!" he protested. "You were still obsessed with him in college—when we met. You joked about how you wanted a Southern man because *they* knew how to treat a girl."

"I did?" Leigh tried to sound ignorant, but she was starting to remember. For a few years after Tanner had left the Koslow Animal Clinic to start a prestigious zoo residency, she had carried around a rather large torch. She was sure Stacey would meet some beach bum in San Diego and take off for good. Then Tanner would come back to town . . .

"That was stupid kid's stuff," she said, blushing.

"I know it was," Warren said, more gently this

time. "What I'm trying to say is—it still is. Do you understand?"

Leigh turned away from him and drained the last of her iced tea. Sometimes, Warren was too damned perceptive for his own good.

Katharine insisted on doing the driving. Leigh didn't feel like arguing, but she did demand they visit a Wendy's drive-through on the way up. Lawyers might be able to work on negative calories, but advertising copywriters could not. She ate the chicken sandwich without enjoyment, watching out the windows as rain started pouring down from the darkening sky.

The ambience was perfect.

Tanner hadn't been in the jail long, having spent a fair amount of the afternoon at the Butler hospital. He sat across from them at a table, handcuffed, while a guard looked on. He looked almost as miserable as Leigh felt.

"Do you have a lawyer yet?" Katharine asked.

Tanner shook his head. He seemed older than his thirty-eight years, and very tired, but at least he was lucid again. "I thought I'd call my brother in Alabama and see if he can float me a loan. I'd use a public defender, but my salary may disqualify me. I don't have any savings. Most of what I had—"

He broke off in midsentence, but Leigh could guess the rest. "Most of what I had, Stacey got." The pain in his eyes was deep, far deeper than the anger she had seen when Stacey had confronted him at the zoo the day before. Leigh recalled an old expression about love and hate being two sides of the same coin. She watched him as he mechanically answered Katharine's gently worded questions, his eyes bloodshot and moist. He didn't seem to realize that the lawyer was there only to help Leigh; in fact, he didn't seem to notice Leigh at all.

The realization sunk into her brain with a dull ache. Tanner really had loved Stacey. He probably had never stopped loving her, insufferable witch that she was. Had he even wanted the divorce?

"Do you have any idea how long you were at the cabin before Leigh arrived?" Katharine asked.

Tanner looked at Leigh for a brief moment. "Were you at the cabin?" he asked tonelessly. "I didn't see you."

I'll bet not. "You were in shock."

He looked at her as if he didn't believe her, but made no comment. "I can see why they arrested me—I guess. I was there. But they've got to keep looking for the real—" he stumbled over his word choice. "The real person who did this. Stacey wasn't even supposed to be there. When I saw her car, I thought she'd come for the antique rifle. She probably did." He smiled slightly, as if even his ex-wife's avarice was now endearing. "But someone else was there, or someone else surprised her." His tone assumed a faraway quality. "A madman in the woods."

"You didn't see anybody else?" Katharine prodded him.

Tanner shook his head.

"Did you pass any cars on your way in?"

He jerked his head up and looked at her. "No, should I have? The detective asked me about cars, but I didn't know why."

Leigh sat up. "What cars?"

"He asked if I knew anyone who drove either a green Pinto or a tan Eldorado."

Leigh looked at Katharine meaningfully. "He asked me about a Blue Buick or a tan Eldorado." She turned to Tanner. "*Do* you know anyone who drives a tan Eldorado?"

He nodded. "I used to. One of the keepers. But she's gone now."

First excited at the prospect of a break, Leigh's joy was suddenly tainted with dread. She thought she knew whose name was coming next.

"Kristin Yates," he announced, nonplussed. "But I don't see how she could have anything to do with this. She's in Washington now. And even if she wasn't, she'd never do anything like this."

Leigh studied his sincere expression, and began to wonder if this Kristin Yates and the one she remembered were one and the same after all. The Kristin Yates she knew would have had a hard time reaching thirty without committing a felony. "Was this Kristin from the same high school as Carmen?" she asked Tanner.

He looked surprised by the question. "I don't know. They were old friends, though. Why?"

Leigh shook her head and shrugged.

Katharine asked Tanner several more questions, most of which he answered without hesitation. But on the subject of his personal relationship with Carmen, he was closemouthed. Katharine seemed to accept this stonewalling as expected, and when Leigh asked for a moment alone, the lawyer threw her an approving look and obliged.

Wary of the guard who hung just close enough to overhear, Leigh leaned over the table and lowered her voice. "I'm really sorry about this, Mike," she said honestly. "Believe me, I know exactly how you feel. But I'm going to beat this thing, and so are you."

He smiled, but not sincerely. It seemed more of a polite gesture.

"There's one thing I have to know, though. And I'm not asking for my own petty reasons. I'm asking for my own deadly serious reasons." She took a deep breath. "The prosecution's theory is based on the idea that you and Carmen were involved. And don't play semantics with me. You know what I mean. They think that the three of us were caught up in some love triangle, and that Carmen attacked me, or I attacked her, or some such nonsense. Then of course we nonchalantly hacked her up and fed her to the tigers."

Tanner winced, but Leigh pressed on. He could get squeamish—and she could throw up—later. "Everyone at the zoo has testified that you and Carmen were an item. I want to hear it from you. Were you?"

She stopped, sitting back in her chair and trying not to look as anxious as she felt. She didn't want to ask, and she didn't really want to know. But she had to do both. Warren had been right, blast him. She hadn't been looking at Tanner objectively, and if she didn't wake up soon she wouldn't be up just any creek, she'd be up the Niagara River.

Tanner avoided her eyes. She'd never seen him squirm before. Did he squirm before he lied, or before he told the truth?

He sighed, long and deep. "Look, Leigh. It was true what I said before. Carmen and I were friends. First and foremost. Maybe there was more there occasionally—maybe she wasn't as sure what she wanted. But I knew what I wanted. I didn't want to be tied down to another woman. Period."

The words washed over Leigh in a muddy drizzle. Evidently, her hero had studied hard at the Bill Clinton School of Semantics. She, however, was an alumnus of the School for Women Who Aren't Idiots. She hadn't believed Clinton then, and she didn't believe Tanner now.

"I see," she said simply. His definition of the word "friend" was now clear. A friend was someone he liked, but had no intention of ever committing to. Sex would not be precluded, of course. It was just another form of friendly recreation—like going to a movie.

She rose to leave. "Leigh?" he said hesitantly. "You believe me, don't you?"

Leigh looked at him sadly, painfully aware of his navy-blue jumpsuit and shackles. Being a prisoner was demoralizing, even if Butler County did have better fashion sense than Allegheny. She couldn't kick a man when he was down.

"Don't worry about what I think," she said, smiling. "Concentrate on getting yourself out of here. Try to figure out how Carmen's and Stacey's deaths could be connected—if they are connected. Can you do that?"

Tanner nodded.

"Good." Leigh smiled again. "If you come up with anything, call me. Or if they won't let you, have your lawyer call mine." She headed for the door, then turned around. "When you're out, we'll do dinner, OK? I'm buying."

She left him smiling, which was at least some small accomplishment. She wanted him to hang in there, to stay strong, to come out swinging. Because after she bought him the dinner she'd promised, she was going to beat the crap out of him.

Chapter 13

Katharine dropped Leigh off at the front door of her apartment building, and Leigh climbed immediately to Warren's floor. The thought of her empty apartment with its maniacally blinking answering machine held little appeal, and she suddenly felt very lonely.

She knocked on his door and he pulled it open partway, as he sometimes did when he had an important visitor. Leigh's heart sank.

"Hi," he said, a trace of sadness in his voice. "I've got company. Can you come back in about fifteen minutes?"

Leigh nodded glumly and mounted the last two flights to her own apartment. A neglected Mao Tse attacked her shins immediately, and Leigh swept the cat up and cradled her upside down. Mao Tse purred contentedly. She wouldn't let just anybody get away with that, but Leigh was privileged.

The answering machine announced a mere four messages, and Leigh was pleasantly surprised. Two were from her mother, announcing the specific location, menu, and agenda of tomorrow's family conference. The menu—her Aunt Lydie's famous lasagna—sounded great. But given the location and agenda, Leigh wasn't sure she could stomach even that delicacy.

Jeff Hulsey had also called—he said for Leigh not

to worry, that the whole incident could actually be good for Hook's business, provided she got off OK. Despite his impure motives, Leigh was cheered. He seemed to have no doubt (along with everyone else who knew her and had half a brain) that she was innocent. Character witnesses were allowed in criminal trials, weren't they?

Only one message was from a reporter, and there had been no reporters waiting outside. She smiled. It was a good trend. All messages disgorged, the machine rewound happily and beamed its stable light once more.

Leigh looked at her watch. It had been twelve minutes since she'd talked to Warren. That was close enough. She plopped Mao Tse down on the couch, and the Persian protested loudly. "Oh, all right," Leigh said, feeling guilty again. "You can come with me."

She plodded down the stairs, holding tight to the anxious Mao Tse. "Don't get out much, do you, girl?" Warren's door was open a bit, and as she came closer, it swung open the rest of the way to admit a well-dressed, portly gentleman with a briefcase. Leigh stepped back.

The man shook Warren's hand good-bye and took off down the hall away from Leigh. She crept forward slowly, her hands clamped tight on the struggling Mao Tse. Warren hadn't completely shut the door, so she walked on in.

"Is the coast clear?" she teased, shutting the door behind her.

Warren, who had collapsed into a recliner, didn't look up. "Yeah. Come on in."

She sat on the couch opposite him, and released Mao Tse onto the coffee table. The cat sniffed tentatively at the tea-soaked *Wall Street Journal*, then hopped down silently and began strolling toward the bedroom. Warren scowled. "I don't have a litter box, you know."

"Don't worry," Leigh said assuringly. "She'll make do."

Warren threw her a hard glance, and Leigh noticed that he didn't look so well. "How'd it go with Tanner?" he asked.

"Fine," she answered evasively. "Who just left?"

He sighed. "Myran Wiggin, chair of the Allegheny County Democratic Party. How's your talent for spin holding up these days?"

"Superb, as always," she answered proudly. No doubt it was a big reason Warren tolerated her friendship. But why did he need PR now? "Myran Wiggin the philanderer?" she asked. "What did he want?"

"He wanted to inform me of how having my fiancée convicted of first-degree murder is likely to affect my future."

For a happy few seconds, Leigh didn't get it. She was the only woman she knew facing first-degree murder charges, and she and Warren were just friends. Then the perpetual knot in her stomach twisted up another notch. They hadn't acted like friends last Thursday morning, had they? She felt slightly nauseous. The publicity was annoying, yes, but she hadn't really thought about the fallout to her friends. She had certainly never considered herself a political liability to Warren.

The wheels in her brain churned. A seat on the new county council was Warren's dream—at least his most immediate one. He couldn't lose it because of her. "But Barbara Wiggin didn't have any reason to think we were engaged!" she cried. "Just tell them it was a one-night stand. Myran should appreciate that!"

Warren shook his head sadly. "It's too late. I sort of misled Barbara, you see."

Leigh remembered when Warren had whispered into Mrs. Wiggin's ear. The shocked woman had visibly relaxed afterward. "You told her we were engaged?"

He sighed again. "I didn't lie to her. I just implied we were heading that direction, and she thought what she wanted to think."

Leigh wondered what Warren could have implied that wouldn't be a lie. He wasn't the type to twist words. The Bill Clinton School of Semantics would have thrown him out in a day. "NOT TRYING HARD ENOUGH," his report card would say. "REFUSES TO COMPROMISE PRINCIPLES." It was a hard line to toe in politics, and it would probably be his downfall. But Leigh couldn't help but be proud of him.

Looking into his sad eyes, she was miserable. "I'm sorry," she said sincerely.

Warren sat up. "Don't apologize. None of this is your fault. You didn't ask to be falsely arrested and you didn't ask to participate in the charade for Barbara. That was my bright idea."

"I can tell the Wiggins that we broke it off," she offered. "I can tell them that you found out about my sordid past and dumped me."

He gave a melancholy laugh. "You don't *have* a sordid past, my dear, remember? You didn't do anything wrong. You keep forgetting that."

Oh. Right.

He shook his head. "There's no reason to be apologetic here. You're going to be cleared. In the meantime, I'm not going to avoid being seen with you just because Babs has been blabbing around that you're my fiancée. She can admit she was mistaken—she knows I never actually said we were engaged."

"She'd do that?" Leigh asked hopefully.

"If Myran tells her to, she will." He laughed a little. "This has all increased my net worth in Myran's eyes, if you can believe it. The idea of dallying with a murder suspect seems to intrigue the old guy."

Leigh's dislike of Myran Wiggin intensified. "So Barbara will tell everyone that I'm just a girlfriend, that you're not that serious about me?"

"Something like that."

She nodded approvingly. "That will work. No one will care nearly as much as if they thought we were engaged."

"Probably not."

Leigh relaxed a little. All she had to do was avoid being seen anywhere with Warren—whether he liked it or not—and she would no longer be mistaken for even a girlfriend. Everything would be OK.

She suddenly felt very tired. "I'm going to crash," she announced.

"Big family conference tomorrow?" Warren asked with a grin.

Leigh scowled. "Don't taunt me, or I'll drag you along. My mother would love it."

"Frances has already invited Maura," he said, imitating envy. "She's going to be a guest panelist, I hear."

Leigh cringed. The terms she jokingly used to describe family get-togethers were a bit of an exaggeration, but her mother was definitely getting more systematic with the process. Family conferences used to be a simple matter of bad advice given over dinner. Now there was a whole damn program.

"I'll need my sleep." She started toward the door, and suddenly wondered how Warren would be spending the rest of the weekend. She turned around. "So, you and 'Kath' have any more plans?"

He looked at her with undisguised amusement. "Not yet. Shall I call you if we do?"

She narrowed her eyes. "Don't be ridiculous. It's none of my business. Even if she is too old for you."

Warren smiled, but didn't respond. Leigh opened the door.

"Oh, Leigh," he said playfully.

"Yes?" She was oddly happy he was calling her back. Perhaps he didn't have plans with Katharine. The emotion, and the thought, surprised her. And what did it matter if he did? He'd had girlfriends before. None serious, of course. But Katharine was different. She was smart, and she seemed to make him laugh, though Leigh couldn't fathom why. What if they got serious? Would she and Warren still be able to pal around, or would it be Christmas cards and an occasional dinner with him and the missus?

"Haven't you forgotten something?" he asked.

She considered. She seemed to be forgetting a lot of things lately. She hadn't really said good-bye, but then, she rarely did. Did he want her to?

"Leigh!" he said, laughing. "Just get this wretched cat of yours, will you?"

Church was bad enough. Leigh was too cognizant of the stares all around her to pay any attention to Reverend Albers's discourse on intolerance. They were people she'd grown up with, and they meant well. But this kind of spotlight was not to her liking. She suffered through a morning of shaking hands, accepting hugs, and assuring people she was fine only to move on to an even more humiliating event.

"Family conference" was a term first used jokingly by the younger set. Frances didn't get the joke, but she liked the name, so it stuck. Frances had inherited the role of family-reunion orchestrator, and it was well accepted that the power had gone to her head. Under her regime, reunions weren't just for fun any-more—they were a mission. When Frances wanted the family to get together, the family got together.

First came the personalized invitation. Either a call or, time permitting, a handwritten note. The next step was the visit. Frances had once driven to Erie to con-vince a cousin that it did not, as he had insisted, take over four hours to get from his apartment to the

Koslows' dinner table. After everyone accepted the fact that coming to family conferences was considerably less annoying than being pestered by Frances, attendance was good.

It wasn't always a bad thing. Family conferences had helped one of the cousins out of bankruptcy, and provided round-the-clock companions for Leigh's grandmother after her apartment was broken into. But brainstorming to help a relative was one thing. Being the victim of honor was another.

When Leigh arrived at the Koslow homestead, most of the crowd had already gathered. It was her mother's family, naturally. Although Leigh's Grampa Koslow had been a genuine Pittsburgh steelworker, there were no other Koslows left in the area, and her grandmother's people were all Kentuckians.

The Mortons, however, were ubiquitous in western Pennsylvania. Frances and Lydie had been two of six Morton children, and there were many more Mortons on other branches of the tree. "Leigh, dear," said a thin, older woman with hair of an absurdly uniform dark brown. "Frannie told us it wasn't true, and of course we believe her. Even if this girl was the one who got you in so much trouble a while back."

Leigh smiled painfully. It wasn't enough that her mother found it necessary to clarify her innocence. Now she was elaborating on possible motives. *Oh, yes. This would be fun.*

She moved stiffly through the throngs of relatives, accepting sympathy and resisting specific offers of crisis counseling, phone harassment, and aromatherapy. She was about to lose her tenuous hold on pleasantness when a large-boned woman with a modified beehive swept her off center stage and started walking with her toward the back door.

"You looked like you needed some fresh air." The woman smiled in her typical half sincere, half tongue-in-cheek manner.

Leigh smiled back. "Thanks, Aunt Bess." Bess Cogley was one of Leigh's mother's siblings, and like Lydie, bore a resemblance to Frances that was only skin deep. Bess was a radical independent, hence the beehive. She had it because she liked it. It was only "modified" because she'd had to switch hairdressers when arthritis forced her original to retire. "Nobody does beehives like Ruth Ann," she had bemoaned.

Bess directed Leigh out onto the patio, where Cara was nursing her infant son in one of the deck chairs.

"You stay out here and relax awhile," Bess said kindly, squeezing Leigh's shoulder. "It's safe as long as Cara's nursing out here. None of them would chance it—they might see something scandalous, you know." She looked at Leigh with twinkling eyes, winked at Cara, and went back inside.

Cara laughed. "Aunt Bess is a gem, isn't she?"

Leigh nodded.

Her cousin's tone was light, but she looked worried. "How are you holding up? I've been calling you, but I keep getting that stupid machine. I don't believe you pay any attention to those messages, by the way."

Leigh smiled. Cara knew her well, which was no surprise. They had grown up side by side—more like sisters than cousins. "I'm coping," she answered. She stepped forward and admired her guzzling "nephew." "How's little Mathias? Seems happy to me."

"Oh, he is." Cara beamed. "He's sleeping through the night now. At two months old. Do you believe it? Most breast-fed babies take much longer."

Leigh could believe it. She knew from before Mathias's birth that he would be perfect, just like his mom. Cara didn't look a pound heavier than before she'd gotten pregnant, except for a little extra voluptuousness in the chest area. As if she needed it. The petite, strawberry-blond Cara had always been a vision. She was also smart. And before she had started on the mommy track, she had been a graphic artist of considerable acclaim. But now the professional look had been replaced by the earth-mother aura, complete with flowing tie-died garb and sandals over socks. Cara never did anything halfway.

"I'm sorry I haven't been by to see you," Cara apologized. "I wanted to go to the hearing with Gil, but Matt has me on an hour's leash."

Leigh waved away the apology. "Don't sweat it. You're busy. There's nothing you can do, anyway. You've already done too much by posting my bail."

"Don't be ridiculous," Cara reproached. "You had to have bail, and it's not hurting us any. What's the use of having money around if you can't use it for a good cause?"

Leigh had no response to that. Cara was one of the most matter-of-fact nouveau riche she knew. Of course, she didn't know that many. Cara and Gil had made their fortune themselves, why couldn't they spend it however they wanted?

"I promised myself I wouldn't ask you anything about your case today," Cara said proudly, though not without a lamenting undertone. "And I won't. But when you're ready to talk, I'm ready to cook. How about my homemade spaghetti sauce, with strawberry cheesecake?"

Leigh laughed. "Have you been taking Morton lessons? Feed them, and they will talk?"

"Whatever works," Cara grinned. "You *know* I'm dying here."

Leigh did know. Her cousin was exhibiting remarkable self-restraint, in fact. And someday, Leigh would tell her all about the fun and excitement of being arrested on murder charges. But for now, she was sick of talking about it.

Mathias Luke March detached and yawned. Leigh smiled at him. It was nice to be around someone who didn't wonder if you really had chopped a woman's legs off. "Could I hold him?" she asked.

Cara rose and placed the warm bundle in Leigh's arms. Mathias didn't seem disturbed by the switch, but contentedly nuzzled deeper into his blanket. "He's such a doll," the new aunt beamed.

"Thank you," Cara answered proudly. "He looks just like his dad, I think. And he's tall for his age already. Part of that is nutrition, you know."

Leigh's bore-o-sensor started chiming. All the signs were there. As much as she loved to be around Cara and her nephew, if she was forced to endure one more lecture about the health benefits and unparalleled rapture of breast-feeding, she was going to get her tubes tied.

"Where is Gil, anyway?" she asked quickly, pouncing hopefully on Cara's second favorite topic.

"On a day trip to Chicago."

Leigh looked up accusingly. "He swore he wasn't going to be doing any more business travel till Matt was six months old!"

Cara smiled slyly. "He's not."

Leigh rolled her eyes with begrudging respect for her cousin-in-law. He had risked Frances's wrath to avoid the Mortons. Good for him. If only she were so brave.

"Leigh, I know these family gatherings aren't always too productive, from the standpoint of real help," Cara began apologetically. "But the Mortons mean well. And if there's anything else I can do—"

"There isn't," Leigh answered quickly, feeling self-conscious again. "Not unless you know what really happened to Carmen Koslow."

"Sorry," Cara said softly. Then her eyes began to shine. "But I do remember her. Not as well as you do—I don't think I ever really talked to her. But I do remember the stories you told me."

Leigh's eyebrows rose. "I told you Carmen's stories?'' Cara had been two years behind Leigh in school, and to say that Leigh had been overprotective would be an understatement.

"A watered-down, censored version, I'm sure," Cara said, laughing. "But I remember them well. Especially the boyfriend with the sanitation department. Carmen was quite selective about her men, as I recall. They had to be tall and skinny, with no butt."

Leigh's eyes widened. Of course! *Tall, skinny, no butt.* It was Carmen's mating maxim. How could she have forgotten? An image of Tanner fleeted across her mind, but she squelched it.

"And then there was the parole officer, and the gym teacher at the middle school—"

"Cara, dear?" a grating voice intervened. "Are you finished feeding the baby? The lasagna's ready and we're waiting for you and Leigh." Frances smiled sweetly.

Cara and Leigh nodded and headed back inside. "I'm lucky I got to feed the baby on the patio," Cara whispered as they went. "I thought maybe Frances would stick me in the half bath."

Leigh snickered. "Consider it your ticket to solitude," she whispered back. "And mine. Ten bucks says Mom wouldn't let anyone set foot on that patio until your shirt was down."

Cara laughed. "I bet you're right. And hey—if things get bad after dinner, just tug on your ear. Mathias will suddenly be starving."

Leigh smiled. Between Cara and her Aunt Bess, she might survive the family conference after all.

It was a close call. Despite the fortification wrought by two large pieces of Aunt Lydie's to-die-for lasagna, Leigh had a tough time with the "debriefing" part of the program. Her mother had half the facts wrong, and her delivery indicated she'd been watching entirely too much television. Leigh begrudgingly clarified a minimum outline of her case, after which the formal "solutions" part of the program began. Of course, virtually every relative with an idea had been unable to resist spilling it before dinner, so here the program sagged a little. Leigh took advantage of the lag by explaining what an excellent job her lawyer was doing, and on a suitable parting line, Mathias got hungry.

She was recovering in her apartment when Maura stopped by. "I'm sorry I couldn't get to your folks' house," the policewoman apologized. "I was really looking forward to that lasagna too."

"Well, today's your lucky day," Leigh answered tiredly. "I've got some leftover in the fridge. Help yourself."

It was dinnertime, but Leigh wasn't hungry. The post–family conference depression still lingered, and the lasagna she'd already consumed would last well into the evening.

Maura wasted no time loading a large helping into Leigh's microwave. "Ick," she protested. "Don't you ever clean this thing?"

Leigh didn't respond. She was lost in thought. "Maura," she asked. "What do I do next? I mean, I have to do *something*."

"You can talk to me," Maura answered matter-of-factly. "There are a lot of things about this case I still don't understand."

"Like what?"

"Like why the police only found two legs and an arm. Where is the rest of the body, and why did the killer take it with them?"

It was the last thing Leigh wanted to think about. Pondering in the abstract about who might have wanted to kill Carmen was one thing. Reliving the horrors of what she'd seen in the tiger run was another.

"And what about Stacey Tanner?" Maura continued. "Are the two murders connected? Frank already thinks you were working with somebody—otherwise there's no way the rest of the body could have disappeared. I'm sure he suspects Tanner. They don't have evidence against you for Stacey's death, just like they've got nothing on Tanner for Carmen's. But don't think they're not working on it."

Leigh sighed and stretched out prone on the couch. Maura rotated the plate of lasagna, then continued. "I want you to tell me everything you know about Carmen. If we're lucky, maybe we can figure out what might be going on here."

Leigh was highly skeptical, but Maura's calm confidence was comforting. "It's like this," she began. "Carmen had no conscience whatsoever. As far as she was concerned the world was a hopelessly rotten place, and she had every right to do whatever she had to do to get along in it. She used people, especially men. Women bored her. For whatever reason, she was possessive of Tanner. He liked certain things about her. Somewhere along the way, he and Stacey divorced."

"Stop there," Maura instructed, checking to see if the lasagna was done. "Are you saying Tanner was involved with Carmen?"

Leigh ground her teeth. "Evidently."

"And when did you find this out?"

"Last night," Leigh answered, wishing Maura would show some mercy. "But I suspected all along." *I just couldn't face it.*

"Well, that explains it!" Maura said happily, pulling out the plate of lasagna and diving into it on the way to the table.

"Explains what?" Leigh asked irritably.

"Why Frank didn't believe your story."

Leigh sat up enough to glare at her friend. Maura had the most annoying habit of talking in teasers—

she really should be in advertising. "Explanation, please?"

Maura downed a few hearty mouthfuls of lasagna before answering. She wasn't trying to be dramatic, she just had uncanny timing. "You're right," she said, pointing at the lasagna with her fork. "Primo." Then, before Leigh could explode, she began explaining.

"Your story isn't that far out. Most anyone who found a body under those conditions would freak. Picking up the knife was a stretch, but it was understandable. And yet from the very beginning, Frank suspected you."

"Frank doesn't like me."

"Probably not. But only because he's a misogynist and you like to bait him."

"*I do not*—"

Maura waved away the protest. "The point is, Frank is a good detective. He knows how to keep his personal feelings out of his work, or so I hear."

As Maura paused for another large mouthful of lasagna, Leigh sat quietly and glared. She was in no mood to hear praise for Detective Gerald Frank.

Maura went on. "I can see now what must have happened in your interrogation. You were telegraphing guilt all over the place."

Leigh's brow furrowed. "I was what?"

"You felt guilty. Not about having killed Carmen, but about your feelings for Tanner. You suspected he was involved with Carmen and you were afraid if the police knew how you felt about him, they'd think you killed her out of jealousy."

"That's ridiculous."

"Sure it is. Aren't most people's subconscious thoughts? Or maybe it was more than that. Maybe you felt guilty about Tanner regardless of Carmen. Maybe the sixteen-year-old in you still considered him a married man."

Leigh had had enough ten-cent psychology. She rose and went to the refrigerator for a drink. It was empty. She sat back down.

"Look, Koslow," Maura continued. "I'm not trying to get you upset. I'm just trying to explain what might have happened in the interrogation room. If you felt guilty, for whatever reason, Frank would sense that. Maybe you hesitated before answering, maybe you fidgeted—whatever. But it explains a lot."

Leigh sighed and turned away. It was true, she did feel guilty. About everything. She hadn't done anything wrong, but she still felt guilty. It was a curse.

"So what do we do now? Go back and tell Frank he misread my body language? I'm sure he's open to that."

Maura grinned. "Probably not. Let's concentrate on the real killer. Who do you think did it?"

The question caught Leigh off guard. She didn't know, and even though it was her ticket to salvation, a part of her didn't want to know. "Tanner thinks it was a professional hit," she offered, explaining.

Maura seemed skeptical. "It's a bit too labor intensive to fit that profile," she said thoughtfully. "Besides, there's the matter of the bone saw being taken from the hospital. And the fact that this person managed to wander around the zoo without being seen, or at least without raising suspicion. I think it was an inside job."

Leigh could see the logic, but it led her down a path she didn't want to take. She knew—or at least had met briefly—almost everyone at the zoo. She preferred not to have any of them be a murderer.

"Do you know if Carmen had any enemies at the zoo?" Maura asked.

Leigh scoffed. "A lot of people hated her, but for different reasons, I think."

"You'll need to figure out those reasons, then. Your lawyer should have copies of their statements, but likely as not, what's written down won't tell the whole story. When's your next meeting?"

"Tomorrow morning," Leigh answered regretfully. She would like to spend one day thinking about something else, but it wasn't meant to be. She had already called off from Hook for the next few days—one could hardly fend off murder charges one minute and write pizza slogans the next.

"I told your lawyer I'd be happy to do some investigating for you," Maura offered. "But don't advertise the fact. It could be viewed as a conflict of interest, even though I'm not on the city force. Ms. Bower wouldn't even consider it if Warren hadn't put in a good word for me."

Leigh smiled. It was nice to have your friends pulling for you behind your back. Carmen didn't have any friends, or so Lisa Moran had said. The closest thing she'd had was Kristin. Kristin with the Eldorado.

"Maura," Leigh began thoughtfully, "I'm not sure why, but the trooper asked both Tanner and me if we knew anyone who drove a tan Eldorado. Tanner said a keeper named Kristin Yates did—but a few weeks ago she left to take a job at the zoo in D.C. Kristin was supposed to be Carmen's closest friend, but another keeper told me they had a falling out over a man." A man. And she had credited Carmen with some mysterious love interest. Mysterious, ha! Ten bucks said it was Tanner.

"I don't know what the car had to do with Stacey's murder," Leigh continued, "but Kristin's worth checking into, don't you think?"

Maura nodded.

Chapter 14

Instead of reporting to work Monday morning, Leigh reported to her lawyer's office. She hoped the change would not become a habit. Katharine seemed unusually chipper, and Leigh wondered idly where Warren had been last evening. She had a hard time concentrating on Katharine's tedious summary of recent events, though she did gather that false prosecution in Butler County was unlikely. Katharine's enthusiasm for Leigh's case seemed boundless, though her cheery disposition seemed independent of its current outlook. "You have no alibi," the lawyer said happily. "But there are other angles we can attack. First and foremost, we've got to highlight the weaknesses in the prosecution's case. Lucky for us, there are plenty. Secondly, we've got to prepare a defense theory. Thanks to your friend the cop—we've already got a head start."

Leigh shivered a little at her memory of last evening's conversation with Maura. Someone on the cabin road (perhaps the rottweiler grandmother) had seen a car speeding away from the cabin long before Leigh—and presumably even Tanner—had arrived. If the car was in fact a tan Eldorado, Kristin Yates might no longer be safely in D.C.

Horse-faced Kristin. No female had inspired such fear in Leigh before or since that fated day in eighth-

grade biology. Leigh hadn't meant to splash formaldehyde on Kristin's new Calvin Kleins, even if she
was pretty sure—given Kristin's economic situation—that the jeans were hot. Kristin had threatened
bodily injury, even going so far as to announce a
time and place. But nuisances like Leigh were a low
priority for the likes of Kristin Yates, and the threat
had soon been forgotten.

Just to be on the safe side, however, Leigh had
stayed out of Kristin's way for the four and a half
years until graduation, and it was a policy she had
every intention of continuing now.

"We'll need some serious investigative work done
on this Kristin Yates," Katharine said pleasantly,
"and on Dena Johnson too, of course."

Dena Johnson. The name switched Leigh's mind
instantly from fear to anger, but it took a moment
for her to figure out why. *Of course!* The Dena of "I
saw Leigh Koslow in the tiger run just before the
murder" fame. So much had happened since yesterday morning, she'd almost forgotten her mysterious
accuser. "The enemy I didn't know I had. How flat-
tering," Leigh said morosely. "Why would she lie?"

"People have different reasons," Katharine said
with a lighthearted shrug. "You can't assume she's
the killer. She may be protecting someone else, or she
may have even made an honest mistake. Sometimes
people tell police what they think they want to hear.
Do you know if she was an enemy of Carmen's?"

"I can't even remember what she looks like!" Leigh
said with frustration. "Tanner introduced me to so
many people at that stupid cookout, and I'm terrible
with faces. Whoever she is, I bet she didn't get a very
good look at me, either. It was dark most of the time.
And I'm pretty sure I didn't meet anyone named
Dena earlier in the week."

Katharine typed away. "The darkness angle is
good. But remember, you were the new girl, the belle

of the ball, if you will. It would be normal for her to pay more attention to you than vice versa."

Leigh got that sick feeling in her stomach again. The belle of the ball, indeed. More like Tanner's latest plaything. *Come on, everybody, let's see how gullible this one is!*

"We'll need to get the other zookeepers talking if we're going to get anywhere," Katharine instructed. "But you've got to be very careful what you say to them yourself. If they feel the least bit threatened by you and your questions, they could complain to the authorities and get your bail revoked."

"But I work there!" Leigh insisted, though she wasn't sure if she still did. Her boss was in jail. What would she be able to do, anyway? "I'm sure I can still talk to Lisa Moran—and maybe a few others. I've already talked to them since I became a suspect, and it didn't scare them then."

Katharine looked at her skeptically. "It's your call. If you think you can get good information out of someone without intimidating them, it might be worth a try. But the decision is yours. Don't say I didn't warn you."

"But if I don't talk to them, who will?"

"I will, your friend Maura might, or another private investigator."

Leigh shook her head. "Lisa Moran at least knows more than she's saying, but I don't think she'd tell you or a six-foot policewoman she's never met before. She'll talk to me, though. I think she feels sorry for me."

Katharine repeated her previous warnings, then launched into a long list of motions to be prepared and information to be requested. Leigh appreciated the lawyer's efforts to keep her informed, but boring was boring, and legal jargon was well down in the excruciating range. She squirmed in her seat and wondered how much she was being charged by the word.

"That's all for now," Katharine said finally. "I'll keep you informed, and you'll do likewise. Oh, and one other thing—could you give this to Warren when you see him?"

Leigh accepted a small cardboard box, closed loosely with clear tape. She waited for an explanation, but none came. "Sure," she answered. "No problem." She tucked the package under her arm and carried it out to her car. A package for Warren, eh? She wondered, jaw muscles idly clenching, if he had left something at Katharine's place last night. She threw the package in the car's backseat and took off. Warren Harmon could buy another damn toothbrush. She had work to do.

She approached the zoo's gates that afternoon in a sweatshirt and jeans, covering most of her face with a visor. Paying to get in rankled, but it was worth five bucks to escape the scrutiny of the security guards. In her uniform she'd be recognized, and she wasn't sure what the result would be. It seemed unlikely that she still had a job, and she had no intention of being "escorted" out again.

She passed through the gates without incident, and headed up the hill toward Asian Country, where Lisa Moran had last been "floating." She had just managed to steel herself for another tiger encounter when she spied her prey cleaning up after the camels on hoof-stock row. The zoo was conveniently uncrowded, allowing her to slip unnoticed behind the employee lines.

She crept through the double wooden gate and emerged beside the Dumpster pile—a massive conglomeration of exotic animal feces—just as Lisa Moran arrived with another wheelbarrow's worth. Lisa didn't recognize her at first, then laughed. "Hey!

They let you out, eh? Congratulations." She dumped the wheelbarrow over the ripe pile, jiggling to release the last clinging contents. "So, why are you sneaking around here? Leo out to get you?"

Clearly, Lisa was not intimidated. Leigh relaxed. "I just wanted to talk to you," she began, following along as Lisa rolled the empty wheelbarrow back toward the camel run. Better just to spit it out. "The other day, were you by any chance trying to warn me about Tanner?"

Lisa assumed a puzzled expression. "No. If you think Tanner really whacked his ex, you're crazy. Not that it wouldn't be justified, from what I've heard."

Leigh shook her head. Word traveled fast. "No, I didn't mean warning me he was violent. I mean— warning me about his past. About Carmen."

Lisa stopped to open the camel's gate and pushed the wheelbarrow through. "If you want to talk—help. There's another rake in the shed."

Leigh located a rake and scoop shovel and carefully opened and closed the gate behind her. The smallest camel, a pale dromedary, promptly walked over for a sniff, plastering Leigh's shoulder with saliva.

"Zada!" Lisa chastised. "Leave her alone!" She walked over and gave the camel's large head a shove. "Sorry about that. She and Zealah are bottle babies. They're the worst, you know. The others will leave you alone."

Leigh surveyed the rest of the camels, hoping that Zealah wasn't one of the larger ones. She stayed close to Lisa, dutifully raking up the tiny balls that littered the ground by the thousands.

"I don't interfere with people's love lives," Lisa began sanctimoniously. "But Carmen Koslow was kind of a special case. I did try to warn you about her, when you first came, but you didn't pay attention."

Leigh sighed. She was beginning to accept the fact that where Tanner was concerned, she had been hearing only what she wanted to hear.

"It's like this. As far as Carmen was concerned, Dr. Mike was hers. As far as he was concerned, he wasn't anybody's. After the divorce, I'm told he openly flirted with just about everybody here, right under Carmen's nose. She acted like she didn't care, but whenever he got serious about somebody, she freaked."

The image of Carmen "freaking" was not a pleasant one. "Was Carmen the reason for the divorce?"

"I didn't work here then," Lisa said regretfully. "But I don't really think so. Everybody says Stacey just got tired of him. She was a real social climber, and he wasn't climbing fast enough. I think she wanted him to start his own clinic. You know, pump up Fifi and Fido with wormer and rake in the big bucks."

Leigh took issue with this definition of private practive, but chose to let it go. "So Carmen was afterward?"

"No. Carmen was always. She went after him on day one. I don't think his wife noticed, or cared. At least not until the divorce settlement."

So much for Tanner being the love of Stacey's life, Leigh thought ruefully. She went back to an earlier question. "What do you mean about Carmen freaking? She was never possessive when I knew her. I mean, she used men—she wasn't dependent on them."

Lisa shook her head. "Tanner was different. She really had a thing for him. God knows why. I mean, he's hot and all, but geez. He'd treat her like dirt and she'd go asking for more. It wasn't—like—a monogamous relationship, on either end. It was weird. Carmen would seem OK with him seeing somebody else, and then she'd go and hang out at the other woman's area and scare the crap out of her. I'd only been here a week before she started stalking me. Smiled and acted nice, but just hung around, watching me. Gave me the creeps."

A sudden memory chilled Leigh to the bone. Carmen, those first two days of work. So effusive, so nice. So *happy* to see Leigh again. She had taken her to the Asia section, showed her around, told her all the animals' names. Asked questions about what Leigh was doing. Seemed to care. Leigh had thought Carmen was just trying to be nice to an old schoolmate. But Carmen had kept coming to the hospital, for one reason after another. She always seemed to be around. And Tanner had treated Leigh like a queen. Right under Carmen's nose.

"She was doing it to you too, wasn't she?" Lisa asked.

Leigh tried to erase the glazed expression from her eyes. "Maybe," she answered.

Lisa laughed. "Sure she was. Right off the bat too. I did try to warn you. You should appreciate it. Nobody warned me when I got here, they just sat back and watched the show. After Carmen got killed, I figured you didn't have anything to worry about anymore, so why bring it up? You seemed to be enjoying yourself." She smiled coyly.

Rarely had Leigh felt like such a complete idiot. So, Tanner had put the moves on Lisa too. Another time, another "new girl."

Not feeling so chatty anymore, Leigh hastily finished up her portion of the raking and excused herself. She had one more person to talk to, and then she didn't care if she never set foot in this accursed zoo again.

Dena Johnson worked in the bird house with Tonya. Leigh knew Tonya only barely and Dena not at all, but she desperately wanted to face her accuser. After all, the mysterious Dena's testimony had probably been the last nail in her case's coffin. She rounded goat mountain and headed for the outside trail, but as she passed the reptile house, a fuzzy redhead appeared in her peripheral vision. She looked up to see Art Faigen ducking out of sight behind the building's back corner. What was his problem? He wasn't scared of her, was he?

Remembering Katharine's warnings about intimidating people, Leigh started to get cold feet. Dena was a wild card. She had lied once—what would stop her from complaining about harassment and getting Leigh's bail revoked?

She stopped walking. Confrontation and revenge were nice, but life with your own toilet was better. She did an about-face and headed back down the path, but had only gone a few steps when a sticklike figure called to her from behind the elephant barn. She sucked in her breath. It was Tish Holly. Amazon woman.

Tish waved her over. "Koslow! Back here!"

After Leigh's mind waged a short battle between curiosity and irrational fear, her feet carried her to the elephant barn. She crept hesitantly through the open back door and into a storage area, where her hostess was lounging on a bale of hay.

Leigh tried to determine exactly what it was about Tish that scared the hell out of her, but she wasn't sure. Undoubtedly it was some combination of the other woman's hostile aura and imposing physical appearance. Tish was a little taller than Maura, but as lean as a strip of fake bacon, with long, slender arms and a boyish figure. She peered at Leigh through small, narrow eyes, oddly mismatched with her broad forehead and jutting lower jaw. The perpetually scowling face cracked a thin smile, revealing an incomplete assortment of crooked, neglected teeth. "Have a seat. There's something I want to tell you."

Leigh made a cursory inspection of the barn, subconsciously noting all possible exits. Tish guffawed. "You scared of me, Koslow?"

There seemed to be no point in lying. "Yes," she answered.

Tish laughed again. "That's OK. Most people are. Suits me." She lit up a cigarette and offered one to Leigh, who politely refused. "Good girl, aren't you? You look it. I don't know how the cops can be so dense."

Leigh looked at her quizzically.

"Do I think you did it?" Tish offered. "Hell, no. Why should you? For a playboy like Tanner? Huh-uh. You're too smart for that."

Leigh began to relax. Tish seemed pretty smart herself. "Thanks for the vote of confidence," she said sincerely. "What did you want to tell me?"

Tish took a long drag on her cigarette before answering. "I think I might know who did kill Carmen. But I'm not sure, and I'm not getting fired over it. Now you, you've got to be looking to get yourself off. I figured you could check it out."

Fear forgotten, Leigh took a seat on the next hay bale. "You have proof?"

"I said no," Tish replied irritably. "Proof is your problem. I'm just planting the seed, and I'm not admitting any of this, got it? You tell anybody and I'll call you a liar."

Leigh got the picture. She nodded encouragement.

"You knew Carmen already, right?" Tish began.

Leigh nodded.

"Then you know she wasn't right. She was one seriously messed-up chick. There was, like, this power thing going on. She wanted to be able to control everybody, because she didn't trust anybody. She'd find out what your weakness was and hold it over your head. But in a nice way, always with a smile."

Leigh remembered better than she wanted to, but

she didn't say anything. Tish wanted to talk and she wasn't going to derail her.

"She liked having control over the animals too. She liked messing with the dangerous ones—it gave her a thrill or something. I'm not talking about moving the tigers from one pen to the other, either. I'm talking crazy stuff. Like going in with the leopards. She'd run from one gate to the other just to see what they'd do. Sometimes she'd even wave her arms to get them interested. She went in with the tigers all the time. Lost a shoe once climbing up the chain link when one took after her."

Leigh looked at Tish in amazement. "Why?"

"Who the hell knows? I said she wasn't right." Tish pounded out the last half of her cigarette in a callused palm. "Worst thing was, sometimes she'd leave the gate open behind her, so she could get out quick, then she'd go in and start messing around. One time one of the tigers made a break for it, and if I hadn't been close enough to slam the gate, he'd have been gone."

Leigh swallowed. "Couldn't she get fired for that?"

Tish snorted, then smiled a little. "Not Miss Carmen. Miss Carmen didn't have to worry about nothing like that."

As little as Leigh was beginning to think of Tanner, she couldn't believe he'd employ a keeper who was such a loose cannon. Then it occurred to her that Tanner wasn't really Carmen's boss. Who was?

Tall, skinny, no butt. The decade-old words rang in her ears. It was a stretch, but the man in question could certainly fit the bill. He was ugly as sin and as stooped as an eighty-year-old, but he was tall and skinny. And although she hated to admit that she'd noticed, the man had no butt.

"Leo Martin?" Leigh asked tentatively.

Tish smirked, and touched a finger to her nose.

Leigh drew in a deep breath. "Carmen and Leo Martin. He's married, isn't he?"

"Very. Wife's got money too. Pretty much bought him his job. He didn't get it for his looks, you know."

Or his public relations skills, Leigh thought. The pieces suddenly fit. She looked up at Tish. "You think Carmen had something on him, don't you? Threatened to expose their affair?"

"I told you, she was into power games."

"And so he—" She stopped. Leo Martin, a cold-blooded killer? She looked into Tish's eyes, searching for confirmation.

Tish shrugged. "I can't see ol' Leo getting his hands messy, but that don't mean jack. You talk about motive—he's got one." She got up and opened a gate that led farther inside the barn. Leigh followed.

"Why are you telling me this?" Leigh asked. "Do you have something against him?"

Tish turned and scowled at her. "You leave me out of this. You tell anybody I said all this and you'll be begging to get back in jail."

Leigh forced a smile and took a step backward. "Don't worry. I can keep my mouth shut."

Tish turned on the hose and began to rinse down an empty stall. Gathering that she was being dismissed, Leigh left the way she had come and walked around the side of the barn back to the main road. She had taken only two steps when Leo Martin blocked her path.

Chapter 15

"You shouldn't be here." The words were hissed, rather than spoken, around the side of a nearly spent cigar. Leo Martin bent his already stooped frame a little farther, putting Leigh at eye level with his liver-spotted hook nose.

She stepped back, as Leo seemed to have little regard for the rules of personal space. "I work here," she said defiantly, trying to sound as though she believed it.

"Not anymore, you don't. You're suspended. Didn't Tanner tell you?" Leo pulled the cigar butt out of his mouth and dropped it on the road. "No, of course he didn't. He was too busy whacking his ex."

Leigh fumed. She was no longer officially defending Tanner, but she'd defend Jack the Ripper against this Neanderthal. "Tanner didn't kill anyone and neither did I. Somebody at the zoo did, though, and when it comes out who, your butt's going to fry."

She regretted the words as soon as they were out, and hoped with every fiber of her being that Tish wasn't eavesdropping. The distant hum of a water hose instantly reassured her. Women like Tish gave her nightmares. Self-obsessed bullies like Leo, however, were merely irritating.

He stared at her as if with enough hostility he

could melt her down to a puddle on the asphalt. "You don't know what the hell you're talking about. We didn't have any problems until you showed up, missy. Now I've got a dead keeper and a vet behind bars." He raised a finger and shook it firmly in Leigh's face. "You get your butt out of here now and I don't ever want to see it here again. You understand?"

Leigh considered her options. To save face, she had to get the man off balance somehow. Inspired, she simply sat down on the road, Indian style. It took the fun out of getting in someone's face when you had to crouch to do it. "My butt rather likes it here," she lied. "And after the charges against me are dropped, I think I'll do a little investigating into Carmen Koslow's way with animals. I think the public might be interested to know how the big cats around here get their exercise. By the way, did I tell you I write for the *Pittsburgh Post?*"

It was partially true. She had once written a free-lance piece for the *Post,* and there was at least a one-in-a-thousand chance they'd buy another. She leaned back casually, her palms on the pavement.

Leigh was now at eye level with Leo Martin's knees, which shook with rage. She waited for his next move, which she was reasonably sure would not be a kick, since even a bully like Leo knew what constituted assault. Besides, a few happy zoo patrons had just appeared around the bend. Leigh smirked.

"Get out," Leo hissed. "I'm sending security."

Lame parting line concluded, Leo blustered away from the approaching sightseers. Leigh rose and smiled at them warmly. "Nice day, isn't it?"

She passed them at a normal pace, then headed for the main gates at a faster clip. Let security come. She wasn't going to be here.

Maura Polanski's shift ended at 3:00 P.M., and she quickly slogged home to relieve her Aunt Charlotte from the Mary Polanski day watch. She was exhausted. She couldn't remember the last night she had slept more than a few hours in a row, and as much as she hated to admit it, the strain was wearing on her. She would have a rough night tonight as well—it was also her turn on the Mary Polanski night watch. Not that she wasn't roused multiple times when it wasn't her turn. Her aunts were both frail; her mom was strong as an ox.

But she had work to do. She had promised to do some incognito investigating for Leigh's lawyer, and she always kept her promises. With her mother dozing peacefully upstairs and Charlotte returning to the other side of the duplex to do the same, Maura sat down at the Polanskis' cluttered dining-room table/desk and collected the rolled paper that her dusty fax machine had disgorged. The fax didn't get much business—it and the already outdated Packard Bell computer had been her father's toys—and his last major purchases. Though hardly state of the art, next to the harvest gold carpet and rabbit-eared television, they were anachronisms.

She unrolled the paper, which as expected contained Carmen Koslow's credit history. Tanner had told Leigh that the keeper was deeply in debt, but apparently Tanner told lots of women lots of things. Maura had wanted to see for herself.

In this case, the good doctor wasn't lying. Carmen had moved around a lot, but at least some of her debts were keeping up with her. She owed an impressive sum for a woman of her means, and Maura strongly suspected—given the illegal gambling on Carmen's rap sheet—that this report wasn't telling the whole story. Oddly enough, the report contained no mention of payments for Carmen's relatively new car—which brought up some interesting questions. Like where it had come from.

Maura tapped her fingers on the wooden table.

Carmen's criminal record, though far from pristine, wasn't bad for an alleged psychopath. Possession and shoplifting early on, the gambling, a myriad of traffic violations. No grand theft, no fraud, no violent crimes. If Carmen really was a psychopath, she either had her aggressive side firmly under control, or she had been damned clever about covering her tracks.

Maura shook her head and rubbed her temples. A smart psychopath was a police officer's nightmare. They lied fluently and liberally, and—like Carmen— often met premature, violent ends. What had she done this time that was worth killing over? People who drove nice cars while destitute could be expected to have friends in low places, but if Carmen was killed for her monetary sins, why hadn't the perp taken her keys and car?

Deciding that a Mountain Dew would hit the spot, Maura rose and headed for the refrigerator. When Katharine Bower had asked her opinion on whether Carmen's death might have been a professional hit, she'd said "possible, but unlikely." Nothing she'd seen since had changed her mind. Dismemberment was both labor intensive and time consuming, and professionals preferred to do things the easy way. This murderer was willing to take some risks.

She chugged the Mountain Dew, crushed the can in her hand, and launched it toward the recyclable bag hanging off the pantry door. The can hit the bag's sagging rim and bounced off. Maura ignored it and headed back to the dining room.

Leigh was lucky she had announced her presence at the tiger shed that night, giving the killer time to make a getaway. It was about the only thing Leigh had been lucky about, except for Warren's help in getting a decent lawyer. Katharine had been very professional, with the exception, of course, of letting a cop help out on the case. But that lapse was excusable.

Maura settled back down at the table and pored over her copies of the witness reports. No—this was no professional hit. It could have been an act of cold, calculated vengeance, or the sudden impulse of a perp with poor emotional control. Either way, it was a crime that Leigh Koslow, neurotic as she was, couldn't possibly commit. So who could?

Maura's money was on the zoo crowd. The murderer knew about the "secret" entrance, and apparently all one needed to roam around the zoo after hours was a uniform. Then there was the bone saw. Two people had left prints on it—Leigh and Doris Sanders, the full-time vet tech. Both had legitimate, job-related reasons to have done so. The kicker was that the saw somehow got to the tiger shed and was used for its grim purpose without acquiring any more prints. Unless a third party independently (and for unfathomable reasons) moved it from the hospital while wearing gloves, it had to have been collected by the murderer. And only a zoo employee would have known where to look for it.

She picked up the phone, ready for her second assignment. Finding out anything, and everything, about Kristin Yates.

By the time Leigh had made her way back to Ross Township, she had worked herself up into a grand funk. Though besting Leo Martin had been momentarily amusing, Lisa Moran's words were festering in her ears like tinnitus after a rock concert.

He openly flirted with just about everybody here, right under Carmen's nose. I'd only been here a week before she started stalking me.

Why on earth had she ever thought Mike Tanner was anything more than a two-bit, boot-wearing, live-for-the-moment good ol' boy? She had been trying to turn her first crush into destiny—laying her heart on the line for poetic justice.

Idiot!

She had just gotten out and slammed her car door shut—with no small amount of force—when she spied Katharine's package lying in the backseat. For Warren.

Leigh scowled. Why couldn't Katharine deliver it herself? It wasn't like she wouldn't be back. Still, seeing an excuse to slam the car door again, Leigh retrieved the package. Warren should be home by now, provided he didn't have a dinner date.

She trudged toward the apartment's rear entrance, since true to the pattern of her day, there were no parking spots in front. The door was locked, which she was pleased to see. Half the time she came this way the door was propped open, inviting anyone and everyone to come on in and browse around. She shouldn't complain—at least none of the reporters had stumbled on to the option. Not yet, anyway.

She made her way through the lower hallway and climbed the steps to the second floor near Warren's place. *Did* he have a dinner date? The idea vexed her.

She, Warren, and Maura had been inseparable in their college days, and even for several years after. Eventually real life had intervened and they had all gotten busier, especially Warren. But in the last few months, since Leigh had moved into his apartment building, she'd gotten spoiled. It was nice to have a friend readily available to make microwave popcorn or loan you a can of tamales. Not that Warren was always home. Like most people with a political bent, he had an active social life. But his dates never stayed over, and he never stayed out all night. At least, she didn't think he did. Had he come home last night? She wasn't sure.

She lifted the package to her ear and shook it. Would he hate her if she opened it?

Probably.

She sighed and approached his door. It was none

of her business. Even if Katharine was too old for him. And even if lawyers made lousy wives. She had read that somewhere, hadn't she? Warren didn't need a lawyer. Certainly not her lawyer. Furthermore, Warren didn't need a wife. A wife would throw a serious wrench in her ability to obtain quesadillas.

She knocked on the door, and it opened promptly. "So," she began, her funk returning at the sight of him, "you're home."

"Is there somewhere else I'm supposed to be?" he asked indifferently.

She narrowed her eyes at him. "I thought you might be having dinner with Katharine."

He looked mildly amused. "Evidently I'm not. What's your problem?"

"My problem?" she asked innocently, still squinting.

Warren sighed and returned to his couch, which was littered with stacks of legal-looking papers. He moved most of them to the coffee table, sat down, and invited Leigh to do the same.

"So, what has some man done now?"

Leigh's eyes narrowed farther. "I beg your pardon?" she asked.

"Don't give me that nonsense," he said firmly. "I know that look. You're not worked up in this state because I failed to go to dinner with your lawyer. Some male did something annoying and now I'm scum of the earth like all the rest. So, let's have it. What did we men do this time?"

Leigh exhaled loudly and plopped down on the couch, package still in hand. She couldn't look at him. If her eyes got any narrower she wouldn't be able to see.

"You were right," she said finally.

"Of course I was," he agreed. "What was I right about?"

She exhaled again. "About Tanner."

A pause followed. "Oh—that. I'm sorry, Leigh."

"I should have known," she continued. "I can usually pick out his type a mile off. What's wrong with me?"

"Nothing's wrong with you. You're a good judge of character, in general. If you'd met Tanner for the first time last week, you'd have had his number in a minute. You're just sentimentally disabled, that's all."

Leigh smirked. Her cousin Cara had once told her that sentimentality was her Achilles' heel. Cara knew how to take advantage of it, too.

"Besides," Warren continued. "We all make character misjudgments from time to time. You should see this new staffer I hired for the Register of Wills office last month. I thought she was professional and efficient. Now she takes four smoke breaks an hour and dots her i's with smiley faces."

Leigh laughed, then turned thoughtful again. "You said I'm a good judge of character. So that means I have good taste in men, right?"

Warren laughed out loud. "Hell, no."

"I beg your pardon?" she snapped.

"You have lousy taste in men. You always have."

She sat up, causing the package to slide onto the coffee table—and a few papers to slide off it. "And how the hell should you know?"

Warren smiled and leaned back on the couch. "Well, let's see. First there was your tutoring charge. 'Turf' something, I believe his name was. He would have been the love of your life, as I recall, except that he couldn't read his name off his jersey."

"He was sweet."

"Uh-huh. He looked like a drawing on the cover of a romance novel. Had about as much depth too."

Leigh said nothing.

"And then there was 'Hillel-on-the-Harley.' How realistic was that?"

"He was a philosopher."

"He peddled pot at the middle school."

"He did not!"

"And of course there was that exchange student who was some sort of royalty in the Middle East—"

"I never even went out with him!"

"No, but you tried. Wonder what you were looking for there?"

Leigh humphed. "And your point is?"

Warren took a breath and looked at her. "Haven't you ever asked yourself why you're attracted exclusively to men who aren't right for you?"

She looked at him and scowled. They had had this discussion before. "I have my criteria."

"Uh-huh. And they're right out of the Big Book of Fairy Tales. Handsome, swashbuckling, able to leap tall buildings in a single bound. Jousting ability might still be in there too. Am I close?"

Leigh crossed her arms over her chest. She really didn't have any criteria. She always just figured she'd know a good thing when she saw it. But that plan didn't seem to be working out too well.

"If I'm waiting for a knight in shining armor," she said defensively, "that's my business."

"Wait for whomever you want," Warren answered wearily. "But as far as I can tell, your current criteria are good at only one thing—screening out anyone you might actually be happy with." He moved off the couch and collected the papers Leigh had knocked onto the floor, then sighed and looked at her thoughtfully. "Maybe that *is* what you really want. Have you ever thought about that?"

The words hung in the air for a moment, then Leigh rose. She was done with the topic, as of now. Her eyes rested on the package, and she picked it up and plunked it into Warren's hands. "From your latest, Mr. Harmon. Katharine asked me to give this to you."

Warren looked at the package and smiled. "Did she? How nice." He rose and put it on the kitchen counter.

"Aren't you going to open it?" Leigh asked. He hadn't even shaken it.

"Sure I will," he answered. "Just as soon as you leave."

Leigh's face reddened. It really wasn't any of her business, was it? Sure it was. She tried again. "I figured you must have left something important over at her place, so I thought I'd get it to you as soon as possible."

Warren's face assumed the tight look it got whenever he was trying to hide a grin. "That was very thoughtful of you, Leigh."

She waited another few seconds, then sighed and said good-bye. Get him talking about her problems, and he'd lecture for hours. Try to get something interesting out of him, and he'd clam up. It figured.

Maura looked at the phone with chagrin. She didn't like private investigation—too much deception. She didn't like lying and she wasn't good at it. But getting the information she needed without lying was no small challenge.

The phone rang twice before it was answered by an unenthusiastic personnel secretary. "National Zoo HR. This is Rhonda, may I help you?"

"Yes, I hope you can," she said, using the maternal tone she reserved for delivering bad news. "I'm trying to get in touch with one of your employees. I'm afraid that a close friend of hers here in Pittsburgh has died."

"You talking about Kristin Yates?" the secretary offered.

Maura's spirits rose. This would be easy after all. The woman hadn't even bothered to ask her name.

"Yes, that's her. Is she aware of her friend's death, then?"

"Don't know," the woman answered tiredly. "She's not here."

Maura plowed on. "Oh? She quit?"

The woman sniffed. "She never started. She was supposed to start last week, but she called off sick. Then she called again and asked if she could wait till next week to start."

"Do you remember what day she called last?"

The woman sighed. "Thursday or Friday, I don't remember. Look, who are you, anyway? I already went through this once. Are you a Pittsburgh cop?"

"I'm with the Avalon, PA, police department," Maura answered honestly. She wasn't supposed to be misrepresenting herself as a cop, but in this case, she'd be misrepresenting herself to deny it. "Thank you. You've been quite helpful."

The woman hung up without ceremony. "Yeah, whatever."

Maura returned the phone to its cradle and drummed her fingers on the receiver. So, Kristin Yates hadn't shown up for work yet. Perhaps she wasn't in D.C. at all. Perhaps she never had been.

Chapter 16

As she always did when in Avalon, Leigh drove past the Koslow Animal Clinic just to see what was going on. It was a little past seven, and the evening clients were starting to pile up. An older man approached the door, leading a medium-sized mutt on a rope leash and carrying a small paper bag. Leigh smiled. It was Mr. Coleman. He looked a lot older and had gotten a new dog, but she'd know him anywhere. No matter what his dog's problem was, he always brought a little sample, just in case. One Christmas, he'd even tied a bow on the bag.

She passed the clinic and drove on to Maura's house, feeling a little queasy. Maura had wanted to talk to her about the case, and she hadn't sounded particularly happy. When she opened the door, she didn't look particularly happy either.

"Hey, Koslow. Thanks for coming. Sorry to make you drive out, but I couldn't leave Mom, and I didn't want to get into this over the phone."

Leigh waved off the apology. "It's my nightmare, why shouldn't I be the one to do the driving? Besides, you look beat."

"Beat" was an understatement. Maura looked like death warmed over. The bags under her eyes had merged with her apple cheeks, which were considerably paler than they should have been. Her eyes themselves were bloodshot, and her lids looked heavy. Worst of all, Maura was slouching, which was particularly unusual. She had always been proud of her height.

"I'm OK," she answered vaguely, motioning for Leigh to have a seat at the table. "Do you want something to drink?"

"No," Leigh insisted, sitting. "But if I do I'll get it myself. When was the last time you got a good night's sleep?"

"I don't know," Maura said dismissively, picking up some papers from the desk. "Look, I called you out here because I think you ought to know that Kristin Yates never started her job at the zoo in D.C. Most likely, she's been here in Pittsburgh the whole time."

Leigh's earlier nausea returned with a vengeance.

"You said that Kristin was the scary type and that you'd known her in high school," Maura continued. "Anything more you can tell me?"

Leigh took a deep breath, the horse-faced image looming large in her mind. "I first met her in middle school, actually, but I never really knew her that well." She described the formaldehyde incident. "In retrospect, I don't think Kristin was ever out to get me. I doubt she knew who I was then, and almost certainly wouldn't recognize me now. But she was part of a tough group of girls that most of us went out of our way to avoid."

"A gang?"

"Nothing that organized. The membership came and went. Carmen hung out with them sometimes, but Carmen was more of a lone wolf. Kristin was the ringleader, the one they all gathered around outside in the smoking area. I used to watch them out the windows as I was walking down the back staircase. Kristin was the queen of mean. She'd sit on the concrete block wall out there, puffing away. The others would form a semicircle around her, most of them standing, making wild gestures. I used to try to guess what they were talking about." *I used to wonder if they were talking about me.*

Leigh didn't add the last part. Maura already thought she was paranoid. "I don't know everything Kristin was really into, but I know she and her cronies beat up a few girls. There were also a lot of things stolen at the school, though Carmen had a hand in that too, I'm sure. Outside of school—who knows. She was probably into drugs, maybe she hung out with older men. I don't know."

"What about her relationship with Carmen?" Maura asked.

"Carmen didn't talk about her a lot." *But I used to try to get her to.* Leigh remembered well the nagging fear she'd carried for years. She had always wanted to know what Kristin was doing—sort of like keeping tabs on the enemy. In a way, she supposed that was part of what drove her to stay on Carmen's good side. An ally among Kristin's friends couldn't hurt. Unfortunately, Carmen wasn't anyone's ally.

"I think Kristin wanted Carmen to be her friend," Leigh explained. "The other girls she had in her pocket, but Carmen was a challenge. Carmen could have had her own circle of admirers gathering round, but she never sat still long enough. Carmen was sophisticated and worldly in a way even the toughest of the tough couldn't mimic. She was independent. She didn't need anybody. She didn't care."

"That does sound like an antisocial personality," Maura commented.

"When Lisa Moran told me that Kristin was Carmen's only friend, I wasn't surprised. Kristin wanted that. But I doubt Carmen looked at Kristin the same way."

Maura nodded. "And the grown-up Kristin? Did the other keepers talk much about her?"

Leigh frowned. "They talked about her like she was normal. Easy to work with, career-oriented even. I find that hard to believe."

Maura shrugged. "Maturity can change people, if their behavior is halfway normal. Simple intimidation and adolescent power games are one thing. If she was torturing cats, that's another story."

Leigh shivered. In high school, she wouldn't have put anything past Kristin. But it was possible that she might have exaggerated the evilness of her foe— just a little. On the other hand, if it was Kristin's car that was seen leaving Tanner's cabin . . .

"Do you think Kristin killed Carmen and Stacey?" Leigh asked suddenly.

Maura looked thoughtful, but shook her head. "I can't say. We don't know for sure that the murders are related, much less done by the same person. You know of a motive?"

"It could be anything," Leigh said tiredly. "Carmen was capable of anything. She managed to alienate, offend, or enrage almost everyone she knew at one time or another. Kristin was supposedly her only friend. But even friends have limits, right? And as for Stacey, I'm surprised she lived as long as she did. She was a whiny, weasely, money-grubbing, self-centered pain in the ass."

"Do your case a favor, Koslow," Maura said with a grin. "Don't volunteer your opinion of Stacey to the police, OK?"

Leigh stifled the next comment she'd planned to make, and changed gears. "I do know of a motive someone else might have, at least for Carmen's murder," she began, and recounted her meetings with Tish and Leo Martin.

Maura listened intently. "Have you told Katharine about this?"

Leigh hadn't had a chance yet. Maura pressed her to do so, explaining that the more alternative scenarios the defense could present, the greater their chance of inspiring reasonable doubt. She finished her speech with a yawn.

"I'd better take off," Leigh said quickly, looking at her watch. "You need your sleep."

Maura gave a sideways smile. "No sleep for me tonight, Koslow. Mom should be up any minute."

Leigh's eyebrows rose. "Up?"

"Yep," Maura answered matter-of-factly. "I told you her day-night cycle is off, remember?"

Leigh did. "But you and your aunts are spelling each other, right?"

"Yes," Maura answered, sounding grateful. "They're doing all they can."

Leigh knew Maura well enough to interpret the statement correctly. Maura had been up at night, every night. No wonder she looked like hell.

Leigh dug around in the pocket of her jeans and produced her keys, then peeled off two. "Here," she said, handing them to Maura.

"Here what?" the policewoman asked, puzzled.

"Chez Koslow is open for business, free of charge. There's no Jacuzzi, but lucky for you I just changed the sheets, and there might even be fresh milk in the fridge."

Maura smiled sadly. "Thanks, Koslow. But you know I can't leave Mom."

"And why not?" Leigh protested. "I'm no registered nurse, but I can keep your mom company and make sure she doesn't wander. She and I go way back, you know. It'll be like a slumber party. Just point me toward the coffee, and I'm set."

Maura wavered, and Leigh pressed.

"I do owe your mother my life, remember? Or at least a limb or two. Besides, I have nothing to do tomorrow but sleep. I'm taking some time off from Hook, and zoo security has orders to shoot me on sight. So get out of here already."

Maura swallowed. "I should at least stay with you, just in case—"

"Forget it," Leigh said firmly. "You need a change of scenery." *And to sleep without one eye open and both ears craned for the slightest sound.* "Go."

The policewoman hesitated only a moment, then reached out and took the keys. "Thanks, Koslow," she said wearily.

Leigh smiled.

Maura awoke the next morning to the sound of her watch alarm, telling her that if she went directly from her bed to the shower to the street—eating a Pop-Tart or two on the way—she could just make it to the station on time. Unfortunately, that particularly timing pattern only worked when she lived three blocks from the station. To make it from Leigh's Ross apartment, the shower would have to go.

She shook her head to clear the cobwebs, but they were amazingly thick. Her watch assured her it was morning; her body disagreed. Not that she hadn't slept—she had collapsed onto Leigh's bed around 8:30 P.M. and hadn't moved since. But with her accumulated sleep debt, such a stretch was just a teaser.

She dragged her backpack into the bathroom and emerged ten minutes later with a fresh uniform and clean teeth. The promised milk was waiting in the refrigerator, and she downed a glass hungrily. The Pop-Tarts she'd have to pick up on the way. Ready to head out, she went to the bar counter to collect the keys she'd tossed there last night.

They weren't there. She walked around the bar, looking at the kitchen floor on the other side. Nothing.

Her brow furrowed. She had tossed them on the counter—she was certain of that. The cat could have moved them, assuming her imperial highness had ever come out from under the bed. Did cats play with keys?

Maura searched fruitlessly around the floor of the apartment, her wariness increasing. Finally she walked to the door and bent down to examine the pattern of light filtering through the crack between the door and its frame. The dead bolt wasn't locked.

Had she been so groggy she'd forgotten to lock it? No—locking doors at night was second nature to her, if more to keep her mother in than strangers out. She had locked it. She was sure of it.

She pulled a handkerchief from her pocket and carefully opened the door. Pulling it into the room, she examined the outside of the dead bolt and sighed. There were scratches around the keyhole— fresh ones. The apartment had been broken into.

She turned and surveyed Leigh's living area and kitchen, but hadn't a clue what it had looked like last night. Had she even turned the kitchen light on? Nothing appeared to be out of place—no open cabinets, no overturned drawers. She knew of nothing that was missing except the keys, but if something else had been taken, she wouldn't be able to tell.

Damn! Had she slept that soundly? By all accounts, yes. At home she'd slept lightly, forcing herself to listen for signs of trouble. But last night, in different surroundings, she'd been blissfully able to turn her brain off. Once out she was way out—it wouldn't have surprised her if she'd slept through her own alarm.

She looked out into the hallway, but knew it was a pointless action. Whoever the intruder had been, he or she was long gone. She closed the door and trudged over to the telephone. There was no point in minimizing the break-in. It could be simple vandalism, but where Leigh Koslow was concerned, nothing was ever simple. In the last week alone she'd gotten arrested for one murder and narrowly escaped

charges on another. The intruder could be someone
involved in the murders—or a distant relative trying
to hide snuff in the toilet tank. With Koslow, one
never knew.

The Ross Township police arrived promptly, and
Maura began a calm explanation. She was about halfway through it when an extra—and uninvited—branch
of law enforcement pulled in. Detective Gerald Frank
walked through the open door with a look of surprise—and annoyance. "Leuthold!" He interrupted
the older of the two officers talking to Maura with a
none-too-pleased tone. "What the hell's going on
here?"

Sergeant Leuthold, who did not seem unduly disturbed by the detective's outburst, answered pleasantly. "Had a break-in last night. What's up with
you guys?"

Frank's gaze passed over Maura without interest.
She was just another uniform in the crowd. "Search
warrant," he growled. "Where's Leigh Koslow?"

Maura rose from the couch where she and Sergeant
Leuthold had been sitting. "She's at my house. I'm
Maura Polanski, Avalon PD."

"What's she doing there?" Frank demanded sourly.

"Taking care of my mother. She hasn't been here
all night—I stayed here."

"You two friends?" he asked caustically.

"Since college."

Frank's dark eyes bounced from Maura to Sergeant
Leuthold and back. "You were staying here—and
someone broke in?"

"Right."

"Did you see them?"

"No."

"Anything taken?"

"The apartment keys. Past that, I wouldn't know."

Frank's gaze was penetrating enough to bore holes

in her head. "How do you know Miss Koslow herself didn't pick the locks?"

Maura returned an unfaltering, studying gaze. He was sharp all right. If he was even halfway honest, he'd eventually see his mistakes where Koslow was concerned. He just needed a little help.

"I don't know that she didn't, Detective. I told you, I was asleep."

Frank's eyes narrowed, and Maura knew she'd scored a point. As she had guessed, this man respected objectiveness above blind loyalty.

"Have you contacted her about the break-in?" he asked.

"No," Maura answered, "not yet."

He stepped closer to her. "And why not?"

Maura didn't hesitate. "Because I didn't want her coming over here until after the officers had had a look around." *Freaking out and messing up evidence.*

Frank stepped back, the softening in his gaze assuring Maura that she was on the right track. His mouth slowly curved up, and he chuckled. "Sounds like you know her pretty well."

Maura smiled slightly, but didn't respond. Sergeant Leuthold jumped back in. "What you looking for, Detective?"

Frank hesitated slightly before answering. "Miss Koslow's been arrested for murder, and her boyfriend's under arrest up in Butler for another one. An anonymous tipster would have us believe that Miss Koslow was involved in both." He stole a sideways glance at Maura before finishing. "But you know how it is with anonymous tipsters. Sometimes they have their own agenda."

Exhausted, but driven by anxiety, Leigh took the steps to her apartment two at a time. It had been an excruciatingly long night. Mary Polanksi was worse—much worse. Her lucid periods had become few and far between, and she had a hard time remembering where the bathroom was, much less who Leigh was and what she was doing there. Mary had always been a fascinating woman to talk to, but now her dialogue simply repeated itself on a five-minute cycle. By 3:00 A.M., Leigh had become a master at derailing the topic train and switching it to a new track, but the effort was taxing. Mary had tried to go outside for a walk at least twice every hour, and had only slept briefly between 4:00 and 6:00 A.M. Leigh slept even less, and at 7:30 A.M. had wearily relinquished her duties to Maura's Aunt Judith.

The experience had left her with a strong sense of duty where her friend's family was concerned. They all had to face facts. Maura and her elderly aunts simply could not keep this up—it would destroy their health, and it was only going to get worse. They would either have to hire live-in help, or investigate an Alzheimer's care home. Left to her own sense of loyalty and responsibility, Maura would care for her mother until she dropped—literally. Somehow Leigh had to convince Maura that her own needs mattered too.

She had headed for the Avalon police station with hopes of launching into the needed discussion right away, but was hit head-on with another disturbing revelation. According to the desk clerk, Maura was late for work because the apartment she'd been staying in had been broken into.

Peachy.

Leigh leaped up the last flight of stairs and jogged down to her door, which she jerked open while still in motion. She skidded to a halt and burst in on a sea of uniforms. "Maura!" she called out breathlessly. "Are you OK? What happened?"

"I'm fine, Koslow," Maura answered.

The only non-uniform in the room turned to look

at Leigh. Her face fell. All she needed now was her number-one nemesis.

"Good morning, Miss Koslow," Frank said with a smile. "We were wondering when you'd show up."

Leigh rankled at his obvious sarcasm, and returned in kind. "It appears I wasn't invited to the party. Rather rude, don't you think?"

Frank's upper lip lifted enough to show teeth—but only on one side. "Officer Polanski here says you spent the night at her house in Avalon. That true?"

Leigh nodded.

Sergeant Leuthold stepped forward and introduced himself. "Could you tell us if anything is missing?" he asked politely.

Eager to show Frank how cooperative she was with officials who had social skills, Leigh jumped to the task. She examined the apartment from head to toe, and honestly could not see where anything had been disturbed, much less taken.

Frank, who had hovered over her like a vulture the entire time, seemed to be getting impatient. "Check your tools and cutlery. Anything you have that might be used as a weapon."

Leigh hadn't a clue what he was driving at, but continued with the good-girl act and reasoned that the only potential weapons she owned were her kitchen knives and her scissors. She looked at them again—all seemed present and accounted for.

Frank gave her a tired, frustrated glance and instructed another officer to produce a zippered bag. "Have you ever seen this item before, Miss Koslow?"

Leigh peered through the plastic at a nasty-looking knife with a long, serrated blade seated in a brown plastic handle. The blade was spotted with a dry, reddish-brown residue, and she recoiled instinctively. "No," she said firmly. "I don't think I've ever seen this particular knife before. It certainly isn't mine."

Frank exhaled loudly and ran fingers through his

remaining hair. "You'll have to wait outside until these men finish up," he barked, then abruptly left the apartment.

Leigh walked quickly to Maura's side. "What the hell was that? And why is he even here? Doesn't he have enough false evidence against me?"

Maura shook her head purposefully and led Leigh out into the hall. Frank was nowhere to be seen. "Watch what you say around these guys, OK?" she chastised.

"Fine. Answer me!" Leigh insisted. She was agitated beyond repair, though she couldn't help but be encouraged by the lights in the back of Maura's eyes.

"This may not be such a bad thing after all," Maura began in a whisper. "I'm not sure, but it looks like somebody just made a big mistake. And it looks like you got a hell of a break."

Leigh's own eyes lit up. She didn't understand anything that was happening, but a break sounded good. "What?"

"I'm just guessing, but here's my take. Someone broke in to leave you a gift, then phoned the police to make sure they knew you had it."

"Had what?" Leigh demanded loudly.

Maura put her finger to her mouth, then answered in another whisper. "The knife that killed Stacey Tanner."

Chapter 17

Leigh realized her mouth was open, and shut it. "The knife that killed Stacey Tanner? I thought she was shot."

"Did Tanner tell you that?" Maura asked.

"No. I mean, he might have said something about it when Katharine and I talked to him, but I don't remember specifically. I guess I just assumed."

"Based on what?"

Leigh shrugged. "There was blood all over her back, but no knife sticking out—no weapon anywhere. I just figured she'd been shot from a distance and that the killer had left with the gun. It did happen on hunting land, you know."

"The killer couldn't have left with a knife?"

Leigh exhaled in frustration. "I suppose so, I just never really thought about it. What does it matter?"

Maura still looked relatively happy. "It might matter to your defense—and Tanner's. If your statements showed you thought the victim was shot when in fact she was stabbed, it supports your innocence."

Leigh smiled. *All hail ignorance.*

When Katharine Bower called Leigh to her office at noon, she had several new stacks of paper with which to torture her client. Though one would think that even minute details of one's own murder case would manage to intrigue, Katharine's lengthy discourses left Leigh wishing for a pillow. Leigh wanted to talk about the planted knife, but Katharine was too methodical for that. They progressed in an ordered manner—and ad nauseum—through various items, actions, and motions before Stacey Tanner's murder was mentioned. When the subject did come up, it took a moment for Leigh to rouse to full consciousness.

"Did you say that Tanner's out?" she asked incredulously. "As of when?"

Katharine looked at Leigh over the top of her glasses, lips pursed. Though it was none of Katharine's business who Leigh did and did not want to see, Leigh clarified her intentions. "I'm not involved with him, if you care. That's over. I just wondered how he got out so quick, that's all."

Katharine did not appear convinced. "Quick? He was in two nights. You were in about five minutes, as you recall. He was released on bail Monday afternoon, and he now has a private attorney."

"Where did he get the money?" Leigh said without thinking.

Katharine looked at her impatiently. "I'm *your* lawyer, not Tanner's accountant. Besides, what does it matter? You're not involved with him anymore, remember?"

Leigh's mind drifted. Tanner was out. Tanner who kept insisting he had no money. Had this mysterious brother in Alabama come through, or was that a lie too? He hadn't come to see her—evidently his life was now too complicated for the employee-of-the-month game. Had Leo fired him as well? If not, was he back at the zoo now? *Where had he been last night?*

"Leigh!" Katharine commanded.

"What?" she snapped, irritated at losing her train of thought, such as it was.

"Can you please pay attention? I was telling you

that I met with Tanner's lawyer this morning. He's green, but I think he's competent. And he was willing to share information about Stacey's murder. An eyewitness confirmed your passing and return on Barber Road, and the timing was such that you couldn't possibly have been at the cabin more than a minute or two. Another plus: the medical examiner's report placed the time of Stacey's death at at least an hour before you got there."

"Then Tanner should be off the hook too," Leigh said hopefully.

"Why? You don't know when he got there, do you?"

She thought about it. She assumed he had arrived just before she did, but she didn't know that for a fact. "No," she answered glumly.

Katharine's attention turned back to the report.

"Stacey was stabbed once in the upper back. The blade penetrated the left lung and nicked the left pulmonary artery, causing massive hemorrhage and death within minutes. Yet in your statement you used the word 'shot.' Excellent. Ignorance is bliss. Tanner wasn't so lucky. He seemed to know she was stabbed, even though no murder weapon was found near the body."

Leigh swallowed. Whoever killed Stacey must have taken the knife with them. Why? Had they known they would be framing someone?

"Leigh," Katharine said seriously, taking off her glasses. "What the appearance of the knife in your apartment means is that you are no longer merely a victim of circumstances. You are being deliberately set up."

A chill crept down Leigh's back and didn't fizzle until it reached her socks. The concept was no surprise, but hearing Katharine say it brought the facts into alarming focus.

"Dena Johnson's statement about seeing you at the

tiger run the night Carmen was murdered may be part of the plan, and it may not. Either way, this woman knows something. Unfortunately, she has repeatedly refused to meet with me, and has said in no uncertain terms that she does not want to see you. I talked with Maura Polanski shortly before you came in—she's going to see what she can get out of Dena this afternoon. Let's keep our fingers crossed."

Maura confronting Dena? Leigh couldn't quite picture it. Maura without her uniform was a fish out of water. But then, one never knew what Maura Polanski was capable of.

"If you'd been in your own apartment last night," Katharine continued soberly, "you might very well be back in the county jail today. Your friend's quick thinking is a big boon to our case. I talked to Frank this morning, and although he wouldn't admit it to me, I could tell he thinks the knife business was a frame job."

Katharine leaned forward at her desk. "As I said, I'm working on a pretrial motion to have the charges against you dropped. If our luck holds with these pathetic framing efforts, I think we've got a shot."

Leigh smiled broadly. So, there was light in the tunnel after all.

Maura walked up the hill past Goat Mountain, trying to remember where the bird house was. It had been years since her last visit to the Riverview Park Zoo. A sign soon guided her in the right direction, and she picked up her pace. She was tired, but thanks to last night's sleepover, not exhausted. And thankfully, she had two days off before starting the night shift again.

She was dressed in street clothes, since her role as private investigator forbade her to act as a cop. Her task, according to Katharine, was to find out why Dena Johnson had lied about seeing Leigh the night of the murder. Not an impossible task, given an ordinary police interrogation. A tremendously complicated one, given no real authority and a moral dilemma about lying.

She recognized the bird house when it came into sight, and decided that it hadn't changed much. It was still a relatively plain, concrete-block building with glass skylights, connected by screened walkways to a large outdoor aviary. Several women with strollers were heading through the main door into the building, and Maura tagged along after them.

Being inconspicuous was a challenge, which was one more reason she preferred police work over the private sector. As a cop, her physique was a definite plus. As a private investigator, it was a disaster waiting to happen.

She toured the building slowly, walking patiently behind the women as they pointed out brightly colored birds to their assortment of infants and toddlers. Maura looked too, but not at the birds so much as the building's layout. She knew that Dena worked here, along with another keeper named Tonya. So where did the staff hang out?

The path spiraled through the building in a lazy S, terminating in the entrance to the outdoor aviary. As the women and strollers plowed on, Maura peeled off from the group and slipped out an unlocked screened door marked EMPLOYEES ONLY. The staff area was clearly at the rear left of the building, and probably had its own outside entrance.

She skirted around the bird house's back corner, and much to her delight, found the expected door standing open several inches. Hearing voices, she moved closer quietly.

"I couldn't believe they had the nerve to charge six dollars for parking!" a female voice complained. "And nothing but a mud field! Like tickets don't cost enough already, you know?"

Another female voice agreed. "Tell me about it. Last concert I went to, we sat for *two hours* before we even got to the highway!"

"Crazy," the first voice said. "That place needs paved or something. You know, with lanes and all."

Her strategy decided, Maura crept back around the building and went in the door she had come out of. She walked along the S path until she came to an unmarked door, then paused and knocked.

The door was soon opened by a short, pudgy woman with close-cropped blond hair, who looked at Maura with oversized, vacuous blue eyes. "Can I help you?"

"I hope so," Maura said pleasantly, reading DENA JOHNSON off her nametag. "My name is Maura Polanski. I'm working as a private investigator for Leigh Koslow's attorney."

Dena's wide eyes stretched wider, then narrowed. "I can't help you," she said flatly. "And you shouldn't be knocking on this door. This is a staff-only area."

Maura forged ahead without pause. "I was wondering if you could help me find an ex-employee named Kristin Yates. She's our prime suspect now, you know."

The bird keeper's eyes widened as far as her mascara-laden lids would allow, her jaw dropping slightly in concert. "I don't know anything!" she said, her voice shaking. "Now leave me alone or I'll call security."

"No, ma'am," Maura said cheerfully. "That won't be necessary. I'll go. Thank you for your time."

Dena Johnson shut the door quickly as Maura turned and headed back toward the front entrance. Once out of sight, she doubled back, went out the back door, and snuck around the outside of the building again.

Eureka. The outer door to the staff area was still

open. Maura crept close carefully, craning her ears. She needn't have bothered—the volume of the voices inside had doubled.

"What do you think she meant, Kristin is the prime suspect?" Dena sounded on the verge of hysteria. "She couldn't be! Leigh Koslow was already arrested!"

"She was lying," the second voice answered. "She works for Leigh, doesn't she?"

"But why ask me about Kristin?" Dena railed. "Why should they think I know anything about Kristin?"

"They probably found out you were friends. Don't sweat it."

"Do you think they know Kristin was here that night?"

The second voice sighed in exasperation. "Calm down, will you! How could they know? Nobody saw her but you and me. If they had, they would have said something."

There was a pause, during which someone seemed to be pacing. "Maybe she meant Kristin was a suspect about Tanner's ex," Dena said hopefully. "Do you think that's it?"

"How should I know? Stop that!" Maura heard a dull thwack, and the pacing stopped.

"I can't help it, Tonya!" Dena whined. "I don't want Kristin to get in trouble, I mean, especially not now, with the baby coming and all. But no way am I getting my butt fried over this!"

"You won't."

"I could!"

"It's your word against hers."

"Whose?"

"Leigh Koslow's, dimwit!"

"Stop calling me that!" Dena screeched. "You're not the one that could go to jail for—" She faltered. "What do they call it when you lie to a judge or whatever?"

"Are you going to obsess about this all afternoon?" Tonya barked, ignoring the question. "Or are you going to do the finches?"

Maura stood frozen in position until the sound of the inside door opening and closing indicated the show was over. She smiled to herself, crept back around to the outdoor aviary, and completed her tour. "Perjury, my dears," she said softly to the darting swallows overhead. "The word is perjury."

For the first time ever, Leigh had left Katharine's office in a good mood. So good, she had spent the next few hours hanging around Station Square, and had even indulged in a double dip of caramel turtle fudge in a sugar cone. Fortified, calorically and emotionally, she set out for Tanner's house.

Why Tanner chose to live so far from the zoo was a mystery. The drive was inconvenient enough that he often slept over at the zoo hospital, yet he showed no desire to move closer in. Leigh took her map of Allegheny County out of the glove compartment and located the road she'd heard Tanner mention, which was in Findlay Township, past the airport. It was a long road. What was his house number? She pulled over at a pay phone and looked in the white pages. "Tanner M C, Beaudoin Rd Fndly Twp." *Thanks.* She started to close the book when she noticed another entry farther down. "Tanner S P, Beaudoin Rd Fndly Twp."

She slammed the book shut. Mystery solved. Stacey lived in Findlay Township too. Or at least she had. Just how obsessed was Tanner with his ex?

She got back in her Cavalier and headed toward the airport. She was going to find Tanner's house if she had to scour the entire road. He said he was renting . . . was he renting from Stacey? Surely not. Obsession or no, she'd charge him a fortune. More likely she still lived in what had been their house, and he had rented his place to be near to her after the divorce.

The thought made Leigh mildly nauseated. She had heard about the power of first loves—but please. If she'd married her first love she'd be living in some commune in California, eating organic tofu and growing marijuana in a Chia pet.

Beaudoin Road was unimpressive. Rural, with a blend of old and new houses dotting its sides only sporadically. Leigh drove from the midway point down to one end and back, checking every driveway for Tanner's truck. It was a wild goose chase, really. He could have his truck in a garage, or he could simply not be home. But she didn't mind the risk. It was October, the foliage was at its peak, and she was in the mood for a drive. And a confrontation.

She was almost to the end of the second half of the road when she spotted it. Tanner's truck. She had no doubts this time. She pulled off the road and onto the gravel driveway. The house was a newer one— a red brick ranch with a satellite dish. Her eyes narrowed. How could Tanner afford a place like this? It hardly looked like your typical bachelor rental.

Her heart sped up a bit as she approached the front door, but she willed it to slow down again. She was *not* going to find any bodies inside. That would be like getting struck by lightning three times, and remarkable things like that simply didn't happen to ordinary people like her.

She stepped onto the concrete porch and pressed the doorbell. A hanging basket of geraniums caught her attention, and her heart sped back up again. Tanner, into gardening? She was in the wrong place.

Before she could bolt, the door opened. "Leigh?" Tanner asked, clearly amazed. "What are you doing here?"

She looked at his bloodshot eyes and rumpled clothes, and felt mildly sorry for him. But only mildly. Though he didn't appear inebriated, the odor of beer lingered pungently on his breath, and the room behind him looked dark and smelled stale.

"Come in," he said automatically, moving quickly to open up the window shades and turn on a few lamps. "I didn't know you knew where this place was."

"I didn't," she answered. "I was just in the mood for a drive, so I thought I'd check it out. I knew you lived on Beaudoin Road, and I saw your truck."

"Oh," he said flatly.

"I heard you got out on bail yesterday," Leigh said cheerfully, trying to lighten the oppressive mood. "I'm glad. Did your brother come through?"

Tanner smiled. "Yep. Wynn was great about it. Even got me a lawyer. Not as fancy as yours, but he'll do."

Leigh picked up on an implied criticism, but chose to ignore it. Tanner was being cordial, but the endearing charm he had shown at the zoo was no longer there. She supposed she was no longer a plausible playmate. She was more like a partner in misery.

"I came by because I wanted to talk to you," she began, sinking onto a surprisingly expensive-looking couch. "I know that my lawyer and your lawyer are working together now, but there are still some things I want to hear from you. You know there's virtually no chance that Stacey's murder and Carmen's weren't related."

He nodded.

"You also know that whoever killed Stacey planted the murder weapon in my apartment last night."

Tanner nodded again.

Leigh was surprised by his lack of animation. "Well? What do you think is going on?"

Tanner sighed and dropped into a recliner. "Someone's killing the women I care about, that's what."

She looked into his reddened blue eyes and saw a kind of grief she hadn't expected. One murdered lover, and Tanner could bounce back. Two was pushing it. Especially when one was the love of his life.

"But the knife being planted is good news, really," she went on, wanting to see his eyes twinkle again, just a bit. How could she continue righteous indignation against a broken man? "The police suspect that the knife was a plant. That's got to help your case too."

Tanner scoffed. "Tell that to my lawyer. He thinks the police suspect me of planting the knife."

Leigh's eyes widened. "But you were in j—" She stopped, heart sinking. "No, you weren't in jail. You got out yesterday afternoon, didn't you?"

He nodded. "With plenty of time to go back to the cabin, retrieve the knife from wherever I hid it that the police couldn't find it, and take it to your place."

"That's stupid," Leigh argued. "Where could you possibly have hidden it?"

"Don't ask me," Tanner said tiredly. "I'm sure they'll think of somewhere."

A spark of anger ignited. "You're not just giving up, are you?" she demanded.

He shrugged. "Why not? Two of my best friends are dead, I'm facing prison time, and I don't even have a job to go to. You got a better suggestion?"

"Yeah," Leigh said caustically. "Stop feeling sorry for yourself, get your butt in gear, and *do* something about it! You can't bring Stacey or Carmen back, but you can keep yourself out of prison, and you can get your job back."

"Leo told me I was suspended indefinitely. Unless and until I was acquitted."

"Leo Martin is an ass. If I have my way, he'll be the one out of a job himself before too long."

Tanner's eyebrows rose. "Oh?"

"I can't get into the details," Leigh said quickly,

wishing she could keep her mouth shut once in a while. "But suffice to say, I don't think the board would like what I've found out about him. Not to mention the fact that he stinks as a director. The man needs some serious public relations adjustments."

She wasn't sure, but she thought that for just a second, Tanner's eyes twinkled. "You go, girl," he said, breaking into a ghost of a grin.

"*You're* the one who needs to go," Leigh continued. "Carmen's death wasn't a paid hit. You should be thinking about other motives, other possible killers. And then you should be passing them on to me." She paused. "These cases are one, you know. If we find the real killer, we'll both be free."

His eyes flashed with something that could be interpreted as either inspiration—or desperation. "I already know who did it," he said evenly.

Chapter 18

Leigh stared at Tanner dumbly for a moment. "You *what?*"

"I know who did it," he repeated defensively. "It had to be."

She waited a quarter second, then nudged. "Are you going to tell me or am I going to have to get physical?"

He sniffed, then looked away from her. "I don't have any proof, but it had to be Kristin Yates. Saturday afternoon wasn't the only time that woman on Barber Road saw a tan Eldorado. She'd seen it a couple of times in the days before. That was Kristin's car—it had to be. How many tan Eldorados can there be in western Pennsylvania?" The words were firm, but his tone was unconvincing. He paused, and began fidgeting with an ash tray. "I can't imagine why Kristin would have killed Carmen. They were friends. But it all makes sense otherwise. She knew about the cabin, she could have been hiding out there. Stacey probably ran into her up there and they got into it. Maybe Stacey figured it out, and that's why—"

He didn't finish the sentence, but hurtled the ashtray like a Frisbee. It hit the backrest of a nearby chair and bounced softly onto the seat cushion below.

"It just all makes sense. More than anything else, anyway."

Leigh hated her mind for fixating on certain things, but she seemed to have little control over it. "How did Kristin know about the cabin?"

Tanner shrugged. "She'd been there."

"And how would she have gotten in?"

"Everybody knows where I hide the damn key," he said bitterly. "I might as well hang it on the door."

Leigh took a deep breath. She was *not* going to get upset about this. She wasn't. "Everybody?" she said, choking slightly on the word. "So you have wild parties up there, eh?"

Tanner fell into the trap. "No, but I take—" He stopped too late and covered poorly. "A lot of my friends have been out there at one time or another. A bunch of people from the zoo. You know."

She did. Carmen, Kristin, maybe Lisa Moran. Who else? Tonya? Dena the mystery woman? Leo Martin? She let herself smile at the thought. *There, that's better.*

"There were all kinds of prints all over the cabin," Tanner continued. "Which doesn't help me at all. If the knife that was planted in your apartment was my hunting knife, it probably has my prints on it. That doesn't help me either." He sighed. "But I told my lawyer I think Kristin did it. He's going to go with it."

For a man who might have figured out a way to beat murder charges, Tanner was surprisingly unenthusiastic. Leigh studied him for a moment. "You think Kristin killed Carmen over money?"

His head jerked back, almost as if he were stifling a laugh. "I doubt that."

"Then what?" Leigh persisted.

Tanner's voiced turned irritable. "I told you, I *don't know.*"

Leigh looked into his eyes, which were as close to hostile as she'd seen—at least when they were look-

ing at her. Of course, she could do hostility pretty
well herself.

"Well, *think about it!*" she snapped. "You don't
suppose jealousy could have played a role here?"

Tanner looked half angry, half embarrassed. He
said nothing.

She was trying to remain objective, but the idea of
Tanner with a woman who had once threatened to
beat her up rankled big-time. "Horse-faced Kristin?"
she said, voice rising. "It's not enough to go through
every other female keeper, you have to get it on with
horse-faced Kristin?"

Much to her annoyance, Tanner grinned. "She does
look kind of like a horse, doesn't she?"

Leigh chose to rein in her anger, funneling it back
into its rightful place—veiled disgust. She no longer
cared about the extent of Tanner's depravity where
women were concerned. But she did still care about
wringing the truth out of him. She was tired of
pussyfooting. "Someone at the zoo told me that you
and Kristin talked about getting married," she said
automatically.

"They said *what*?" Tanner jumped up to the edge
of his chair, his voice escalating to a yell. "Who the
hell said that?"

Leigh stared at him a moment, trying to figure out
the next step in this impromptu lying game. The
comment had come totally out of left field, but evidently she'd hit a nerve. *Onward.*

"I thought that's what they said," she replied uncertainly, thinking fast. "Maybe they were talking
about Carmen. I don't remember."

Tanner glared at her, his bright blue eyes fiery.
"I never said I'd marry anybody, you understand?
Carmen lived in a fantasy world—she thought what
she wanted to think. As for Kristin, she'd be dreaming. She wasn't anything to me."

Leigh could believe the last part, at least from his

perspective. The other women he'd pursued had at least something going for them . . . if not Carmen's animalistic seductiveness, then petiteness, pretty hair, or a sense of humor. (The latter category she had created for herself.) Kristin had nothing. She was average in height and average in weight, with dull light-brown hair and a particularly unattractive face. "So, why did you invite her to your cabin?" Leigh asked shamelessly.

Tanner looked flustered. He changed the subject. "It doesn't matter. The point is, she killed Carmen and she killed Stacey. Maybe she had some weird thing for me, I don't know. But if she did, it was one-sided. I never encouraged her. And if I find her, so help me I'll—"

He cut off the phrase, and Leigh was glad. She wasn't afraid of him, but the beer on his breath and the hostility in his eyes were far from endearing. It was interesting that he couldn't bring himself to admit to her who he had or hadn't been involved with, even though they both knew her status as girlfriend-to-be was over. Way over. Perhaps it was some Southern chivalry thing, or perhaps he was just a no-guts weasel. Either way, Leigh was quite certain he *had* been involved with both Kristin and Carmen. And come to think of it, she could remember one reason why an oversexed cowboy such as himself might have a weakness for horse-faced Kristin. There were two reasons, really. And they'd been prominent ever since Kristin hit puberty.

"Well, apparently Kristin *thought* she was going to marry you," Leigh said deviously, launching off into uncharted waters. "I bet that's why she wanted to kill Carmen and Stacey." She took a breath. "After all, everyone knew how you'd never really gotten over Stacey, despite what was going on with Carmen."

Leigh waited for a protest, but none came. "I think

you might as well be honest with the police about that," she said with a sigh. "It could help your case, you know." *And mine.*

Tanner ran both hands roughly over his face, then got up and went into the kitchen. He returned with another beer and sat down. Leigh noticed he didn't offer her one. She hated beer, but that wasn't the point.

"Look, Leigh," he said calmly, his anger suddenly replaced with weariness. "I know you're facing murder charges too, but you're barking up the wrong tree. Women don't go around killing each other over men like me. I don't believe it. There must have been something else going on. And Kristin wasn't the type anyway. She had a better head on her shoulders than half the other keepers. I don't believe she killed either of them."

Now he was openly contradicting himself. "You just said you knew that she *did* do it!" Leigh said with annoyance.

He threw back his head and groaned. "I know! I know! I did tell the lawyer that. I wish it was her. I keep trying to convince myself it was her. But I just don't believe it. Something else happened."

"Like what?"

"*I don't know,*" he said slowly, pounding out every word.

"Well neither do I!" she railed. "And this isn't getting us anywhere. Look, Mike. I didn't know these women. I knew girls. The Kristin I knew would have killed her own mother, so you tell me she's the one and I'm happy as a clam. But if you really did know Kristin, and I presume you did, biblical sense and all, and you don't think she's a murderess, then maybe the lawyers are wasting their time. And we don't *have* much time!"

Tanner looked at her thoughtfully. "What about you?"

"What about me?"

"You're so quick to assume the murders are all about me. What if *you're* the link?"

Leigh stared at him, uncomprehending. "Say what?"

"You start working at the zoo, and two women you've never liked die violent deaths."

She bristled and started to interrupt, but he stopped her.

"I'm not saying you killed them. But what if someone killed them on your behalf?"

Leigh stared at him as if he'd gone mad. She supposed he could be drunk, at the very least. "That's the dumbest thing I ever heard. You mean like in *Strangers on a Train*?" She scoffed. "I assure you, I never gave any hit man a list of my rivals. Furthermore, they weren't my rivals. I didn't even know you and Carmen were involved until after she died." Leigh wondered if he knew about the possession incident. How could he? "And as for Stacey—"

Tanner suddenly laughed. "You always hated her. Even when you were a teenager."

What's not to hate? Stifling the words on her lips, she took a deep breath. Had her dislike of Stacey always been so obvious? "There's no link through me." She said firmly. "That's nonsense. Maybe there's no connection with either of us. Maybe there's no connection at all. But let's get real—that's pretty unlikely. We've got one murder at the zoo and one at your cabin. You're involved. Kristin Yates is my new prime suspect number one, and if you have some *real* reason to think someone else did it, you'd better tell me now."

Maddeningly, Tanner just shrugged.

Leigh gave up. The more he drank, the less help he would become. He'd admitted a few things she already knew, and confirmed a few she suspected. But he didn't really think Kristin Yates was a murderess, and that bothered her. She rather liked seeing evidence pile up against the old schoolyard bully. Between the tan Eldorado at the scene of Stacey's murder and the knife frame-up, Kristin made for a credible defense theory. If the woman was innocent, it would be hard to convince the prosecutors that she did it. But then, Leigh thought wryly, stranger things had happened.

"You sit here and drink," she said sarcastically. "I'm going to keep trying to get my butt off the hook. And yours too, if you act nice. I'm glad you told your lawyer you suspect Kristin, because as far as I'm concerned, she's guilty. If you decide otherwise, give me a call."

Tanner said nothing, and Leigh walked herself out, giving the hanging plant a shove as she marched off the porch. Satellite dish, nice furniture. How could she have been so dense?

She got into her car with a sigh of disgust. This wasn't Tanner's rental—assuming he had one. This was Stacey's house. The house they'd lived in together. The home where his heart was.

It was dinnertime. Leigh's stomach was quite certain, despite her dispiriting run-in with Tanner. For the first time in days, things were looking up. The guilty party was going to be caught, and she was going to be free. She had already planned her vindication—it would involve another freelance article for the *Post*, and a certain amount of public humiliation for one Detective Gerald Frank.

She smiled as she pulled into the drive-in lane of a combination KFC/Taco Bell. The merger was a strange business decision, but one which she—as an avid lover of both tacos and buffalo wings—fully appreciated. She and Warren had practically kept the place in business by themselves. At the latter thought, she ordered two sampler combos to go. It occurred to her that Warren hadn't said anything yesterday about his political problems, and she had forgotten to ask. What kind of friend was she, anyway?

She arrived at the door to his apartment the same time he did. "Hi, honey! I'm home!" she said playfully, waving the cardboard boxes under his nose.

Warren smiled tiredly. "What's the occasion?"

"An apology. For being obsessed with my own problems. Your table or mine?"

Warren's table was closer, and within three minutes they were eating at it. "Are you sure there isn't anything I can do about Myran?" she offered. "I could say that we're really not involved seriously, that I'm secretly married to someone else, but I can't resist you because you're such a great lover. Wouldn't that push all the right buttons?"

He laughed. "I'll thank you to stay as far away from Myran Wiggin as possible. Everything will be fine."

Leigh smirked. "Well, if Wiggin thinks more of you because you're involved with a murderess, he's soon to be disappointed." She filled Warren in on the details of the knife planting and her growing certainty that Kristin Yates had killed both women.

"You need a good sliding dead bolt," he said when he got a chance. "There are ways around them too, but it can't hurt. Are you OK with sleeping there tonight?"

The question at first seemed odd, then gave rise to a creeping fear. Leigh hadn't given much thought to the fact that her apartment had been breached so easily. When she had arrived this morning, she was much more annoyed at having a sea of policemen, and in particular Detective Gerald Frank, rooting around in her stuff; the original intruder was more theoretical. It occurred to her now that this original intruder—almost certainly Kristin Yates—was still very much out and about. And had probably taken her keys for a reason.

A knock on Warren's door interrupted her thoughts, but only for a second. *Kristin*. She had gone out of her way to frame Leigh for Stacey's murder. Why? Tanner had been arrested; Kristin wasn't even a suspect. Could it be that a prison term for Tanner didn't jibe with her plans? Or, surely much, much, less likely, that she enjoyed watching Leigh squirm?

"Good evening, Miss Koslow," said a familiar voice that did nothing to lessen her chill. "Sorry to interrupt your dinner, but it's important that we talk. I've been looking for you all afternoon."

"Oh," she said offhandedly, stuffing in her last bite of taco. "How inconvenient for you."

Frank's superficial smile seemed tightened with resolve. "I'm not here to spar, Ms. Koslow. I'm here to make sure that whoever killed Carmen Koslow gets what's coming to them."

Leigh swallowed the mouthful and looked straight into Frank's beady black eyes. Maybe she was being overly optimistic, but she could almost believe he meant that.

"Have a seat," she offered, slightly more pleasantly. "Sorry, but the takeout's gone."

He sat in the chair where Warren directed him, but refused all offers of food or drink. A wise habit, Leigh figured, when dining with one's arrestees.

"I don't believe Leigh should be speaking with you without her attorney present," Warren said firmly. "If you intend to ask her any questions, I'll give Ms. Bower a call."

Frank waved his hand dismissively. "Call whomever you want. I can wait." He smiled pleasantly at Leigh. At least, he probably thought his smile was pleasant. She would liken it to a crocodile's.

"What is it you want, Frank?" she said impatiently. The idea of his smiling at her for the half hour it would take Katharine to arrive was not appealing.

"I told you already," he answered, still smiling. "I want justice."

She smirked, still unconvinced. "Isn't that a little too 'Joe Friday' for you, Detective?"

He didn't answer, but the smile faded, which made her a little more comfortable. "The knife we recovered from your apartment this morning came back clean," he said simply.

"Clean?" she repeated, eyebrows raised. "You mean, no prints at all?"

"That's right."

"Leigh!" Warren interrupted quickly, hanging up the phone. "Katharine will be here shortly. Until then, let me do the talking, OK?"

"The blade was stained with blood matching that of Stacey Tanner," Frank continued. "Yet the handle had been wiped clean. Odd, don't you think, to wipe down the handle and not the blade?"

"Not at all," Warren answered quickly, cutting Leigh off with a fierce warning glance. "Not if you're trying to frame someone. Keep the blood, lose the prints—especially if they're yours."

Frank looked at Warren. "My thoughts exactly, Mr. Harmon. Except that the person in possession of the knife needn't be the killer. The person in possession of the knife could, in fact, be someone close to the killer. Someone who wanted to prevent the killer from being convicted—quite possibly by taking the knife and removing his prints, then planting it elsewhere."

It took a second for Leigh to digest Frank's suggestion, but it took less than a second her for to make up her mind.

"Get out, Frank," she said coldly. Ignoring both Warren's verbal and nonverbal reprimands, she rose and pointed to the door. "I thought for a moment you were starting to see the light, but obviously I was wrong. You've got no right coming in here just to fish for more evidence against me. You want to question me again, you make me go to the bureau, *with* my lawyer. You were invited in here; now you're uninvited. Good-bye."

Frank's dark eyes looked her up and down, and for a brief moment, a ghost of the crocodile smile returned. He wasn't as angry as he should be, Leigh thought as she glared at him. In fact, he seemed almost amused. No matter, she decided, her own gaze hardening. He was leaving without whatever it was he came for.

The detective didn't resist, but got up from the table, nodded to them both, and walked out the door. Warren looked at Leigh with a mixture of frustration and annoyance. "I really wish you hadn't done that," he said tightly.

"I refuse to apologize for being to rude to the man who's currently ruining my life," Leigh defended. "He came here under false pretenses."

Warren studied her. "You think you know why he came here?"

"Of course. To hassle me about the knife. To trick me into thinking he believed it was planted, to get my guard down, then get me to trip up. I never even thought about being accused of taking the knife to protect Tanner." Now that she did think about it, the theory made a certain kind of sense. No—no, it didn't either.

"That's nuts," she thought out loud. "The police in Butler county searched me and my car. How could I have taken the knife away from the cabin? And who would have called in that anonymous tip? Not me, and not Tanner, who I was presumably trying to help. That scenario's far more cockeyed than the real killer planting the knife on me."

"I agree," said Warren thoughtfully. "Yet Frank suggested it to you. Why?"

"I told you, to get me to trip up," she said disgustedly.

"Or to gauge your reaction," Warren argued. "If you *had* taken the knife yourself, or known about it, you might have acted nervous or scared. You would hesitate to talk to him. But you didn't, because you were hoping that he was coming around. But when he starting accusing you again, you got angry. Not scared—angry."

"You're giving him far too much credit," Leigh sighed. "If he could read me that well, he never would have arrested me in the first place."

"Maura says you acted guilty after Carmen's murder, that you were—to use her words—'messed up in the head' because of how you felt about Tanner. Maybe he misread you before, but now he's getting a clearer picture."

Leigh sighed again. "Harmon, you're too much of a bloody optimist. Frank is a misogynist. And he's not that smart." She glanced at the phone. "Don't you want to try Katharine again? Maybe you can catch her before she leaves."

He shook his head, his eyes lost in thought. "I'd like to see her, actually," he said distantly.

Inexplicably annoyed, Leigh threw away the trash from her dinner and prepared to leave. "Fine. You and Katharine have a nice evening. But remember, it's a school night."

When she opened the door, Warren snapped out of his reverie. "Are you sure you want to stay in your apartment tonight? You can sleep here if you want, until you get a better dead bolt."

Leigh imagined herself tossing and turning on Warren's lumpy sofa bed, and declined. "Thanks, but I'll be fine. The locks have been changed, and the manager assured me there'll be no more door-propping. When Katharine gets here, you can tell her I've got news for her tomorrow, about a little talk I had with Tanner. Right now, I'm going to sleep, an activity I missed out on last night. Which reminds me, we've got to do something about Maura's mom."

Warren nodded. "I know. Mo can't go on like she has been."

"Have you talked to her about a personal care home or something?"

He nodded. "She's found one in McCandless that she could live with—they have a special wing just for Alzheimer's patients, and it has an excellent reputation."

"But?"

"But it's expensive, and aside from the Alzheimer's, Mary is healthy as a horse." Warren sighed. "Which is great, except that she could easily outlive Maura's ability to pay for her care. I've been over the Polanskis' finances, and there's only so much to draw on."

"The house?" Leigh said hopefully.

"It's paid for," he answered, "but it's not worth much, and Maura's dad had been letting her aunts live there for free, so if the house were sold the two of them would be forced to pay rent somewhere else—as would Maura."

Leigh sighed. "There's got to be a way."

"I'm working on it," Warren said reassuringly. "Don't worry about Mary tonight, OK? Get some sleep. And remember—the offer stands. You can even have the bed if you want. I'll take the couch."

His concern touched her, but she declined again. Katharine Bower was already on her way over, and Leigh wasn't up for any more legal wrangling tonight. Nor did she care to be a third wheel. She had just started out the door again when a thought occurred to her.

"Hey, Warren?"

"Yes?"

"Did Katharine happen to tell you what the problem is between her and Frank?"

He smiled wryly. "I think that's mainly Frank's doing. Apparently, Katharine cut her legal teeth on some divorce cases."

Leigh's shoulders slumped. "Please don't tell me she represented Frank's ex-wife."

"OK," Warren obliged, "I won't tell you."

Chapter 19

Leigh traipsed up the stairs, stuck her new key in her new lock, and detached a yellow sticky note from her door.

> Leigh, your mother sent me. You're welcome to come home for a while. Call tonight either way. Dad.

She smiled. Dear old Dad. He had a way with words—or lack thereof. She knew the real translation.

> Leigh, your mother has been calling your apartment every five minutes since she heard about the break-in, and I can't get her any more Valium without losing my DEA license. She sent me over to drag you back home using any force necessary. If you don't want to come that's fine with me, but you'd better call soon or I'll be sleeping at the clinic again. Dad.

She opened the door on an apartment that looked fine, but didn't feel right. There was a certain aura of violation that came with a break-in, the feeling that your stuff was somehow not yours anymore. She walked through the whole apartment quickly, opening closets and peering under the bed. Satisfied that the only other mammalian occupant was a sleeping

Mao Tse, she locked the new knob and bolt. Had the cat been fully alert, she would almost certainly be complaining about the irregular schedule Leigh had been keeping. But Mao had a thing about being awake for more than four consecutive hours, and the morning had been a rough one.

Leigh took a deep breath and tried to relax. They would be fine here. Why shouldn't they? Kristen had wanted to frame her, but that deed was accomplished. She wouldn't be dumb enough to come back now. Tomorrow Leigh would buy another dead bolt—or some other pickproof contraption. In the meantime, perhaps a small barricade? One sofa, an end table, and a Niagara Falls souvenir bell later, she felt better.

Her answering machine had collected five more messages, and she listened to them dutifully. One from Frank, two from her mother (where was a fast-forward button when you needed it?), one from Katharine setting up their next appointment, and one from Jeff Hulsey asking if she could make it to the office early tomorrow afternoon.

Deciding that Katharine and Jeff could have their wishes and that Frank could go to hell, she picked up the phone, plastered a fake smile on her face for mental preparation, and dialed home.

She was back at the zoo, cleaning up after the bison. It was cold, and wisps of steam rose from the gargantuan brown patties. The wheelbarrow was full, and so heavy she could barely move it. Someone was blocking her way out the gate.

"Move," she yelled, agitated. "Can't you see this is heavy? Get out of the way!"

The figure reached out a booted foot and kicked the handles out of Leigh's hands. Foul-smelling sludge sloshed out of the wheelbarrow, splashing over her face and arms. She looked up, furious.

Horse-faced Kristin looked down at Leigh from an impressive height, her thin lips curled. "You got my shoes dirty," she said sinisterly. "Nobody gets my shoes dirty."

A rising panic spread over Leigh, and she abandoned the wheelbarrow and started running. The zoo hospital was in sight, but no matter how hard she ran, she couldn't seem to reach it. Her knees were weak, her legs heavy. Every footstep seemed glued to wet ground.

"Where you running, girl?" came a voice inches from her ear. Kristin didn't even sound tired. The pursuer wasn't running, she was floating. Floating right over Leigh's shoulder. "Gonna see your boyfriend?"

"*He's not my boyfriend!*" Leigh yelled vehemently, stopping and whirling around. She couldn't see Kristin anymore, but she knew she was there.

"Damn right he's not," came another voice. Leigh strained her eyes to see through the heavy fog. She was still sinking into the wet ground, up to her knees now.

"He's mine. And he always will be." Carmen stepped out into clearer air, raven hair billowing around her lithe form. "You understand that don't you, Leigh?"

Leigh nodded frantically. "You can have him, you hear me! Take him! Just go away, both of you. Go away and leave me alone!"

Carmen tilted her head, an endearing mannerism Leigh had forgotten she remembered. "I like you, Leigh Koslow. You make me laugh. You think maybe we're cousins or something?"

As Carmen spoke the last words, a flash of metal shone over her shoulder and a giant saw blade cut across her shoulders.

"Take that!" said Kristin, now towering like a giant. Carmen's head rolled toward Leigh, entangling itself in the mass of black hair. Leigh tried to recoil, but couldn't move. The cold wetness of the ground was seeping around her waist, crawling up toward her armpits.

"It won't do you any good to run," said Carmen's head, looking at her sympathetically as it leaned against her ribs. "She'll find you, you know."

Leigh sat straight up in bed, her breath coming fast. She lunged over to turn on her bedside lamp.

It was her room, it was fine, and she was only dreaming. It was just a nightmare. A dumb nightmare.

Her breathing slowed, but only a little. She had known it was a dream while it was happening—she usually did. But that didn't mean the fear wasn't real. Or that it would go away easily. She reached for Mao Tse, who whined plaintively at being disturbed from her place on the other pillow, but soon mellowed and began to purr.

It was 1:54 A.M. Only a few hours since she'd fallen asleep. There were plenty more to go till morning. She sat bolt upright, trying to rationalize away the lingering fear. Kristin was not coming back. Why should she? She wasn't out to get Leigh. She had killed Carmen because . . . because why? Over Tanner? Over money? Over some other personal argument?

It was a hard sell. Cat fighting was one thing. Dismemberment was another. Why would Kristin throw Carmen to the tigers? Poetic justice? Was Kristin even bright enough to understand poetic justice? Leigh doubted it. And Stacey . . . did she kill Stacey because Tanner still loved her? Did Stacey accidentally intrude into Kristin's hideout, or had Kristin lured her there? And if Kristin really loved Tanner, why wasn't she trying to be with him?

Or maybe she was. Maybe framing Leigh was just

an attempt to get Tanner off the hook. If that was the case, Leigh wasn't in any real danger now, right?

Right. Kristin was a perfectly rational human being who had no intention of hurting anyone. Stacey had probably backed up onto the knife accidentally and Carmen had asked to be fed to the tigers because the zoo was out of cat chow. Leigh was perfectly safe. It wasn't like Kristin knew where she lived. Or how to pick locks.

Leigh had thought enough. Now she started moving. Mao Tse squawked in protest as she was swept up and out of the bed, her middle clutched in a vise-like grip. Cat in hand, Leigh threw a robe over her sweats, pushed aside her barricade with one arm and a hip, and locked the door behind her. Within seconds, she was knocking on Warren's door.

It took a while, but eventually footsteps pounded inside, followed by a pause—undoubtedly for a look through the peephole. The door swung open to reveal a wide-eyed Warren, looking GQ as usual in department-store pajamas. "Leigh! What's happened?" He pulled her inside, walking backward toward the phone as he spoke. "Did someone try to break in again?"

She shook her head, embarrassed.

"Then what?" he said, stopping.

She didn't answer for a moment. She had gotten him up in the middle of the night and scared him to death—for nothing. Why was she here?

Because she was petrified, that's why. She dropped a grateful Mao Tse onto a chair and avoided Warren's gaze. *How embarrassing.* "I'm sorry. I shouldn't have come down. It's just—I just had a nightmare, that's all."

Warren let out a sigh of relief. "Oh. You had me worried there for a moment."

"I know," she said miserably. "I'm sorry."

"Stop apologizing," Warren said as cheerfully as

one could at 2:00 A.M. "I told you you were welcome to stay here. I kind of meant all night—but that's alright. You want the couch or the bed?"

"The couch," Leigh said quickly. "I don't want to put you out. I probably won't sleep much anyway."

He looked at her thoughtfully. "What was the dream about?"

She tried to put it into words in her head. *Well, I was scooping bison poop, and Kristin was there, and there was this fog . . .* "It was just stupid stuff," she said dismissively. "Quicksand and decapitated heads—the usual."

Warren didn't look convinced. "It might help to say it out loud. The stupider it sounds, the easier it may be to forget."

Leigh shook her head. She knew exactly how stupid the dream was—and she still wasn't going back to her apartment.

Warren dumped a pillow and blanket on the couch, took Leigh's keys out of her hand, and headed for the door.

"Where are you going?" she asked, startled.

He laughed. "I wish I could say I was riding off on my white horse to slay your dragon, but you know I'm not the athletic type. Don't worry, I'll be back in two minutes."

He was back in three. Leigh sat tensely on the edge of the couch as the door reopened and he slid around it, carrying a large plastic pan. Her brow furrowed. "Why did you bring that down?" she asked.

He narrowed his eyes at her and set down the litter box. "You may not care squat for my belongings, but I'm rather attached to them. Now, the door is locked, and nobody knows you're here. If you don't mind, I'm going back to bed. I have a horrific schedule tomorrow."

"Thanks, Warren," Leigh said humbly.

"Thanks, nothing," he said with a smirk. "You're making breakfast."

Stirring milk into a powdered mix was just within the bounds of Leigh's culinary capabilities, and she proudly waved the warm blueberry muffins under Warren's nose.

"Excellent," he said with a smile. "I could get used to this. You have nightmares often?"

In the light of day Leigh's dream seemed quite surreal, and her fear inexcusable. But Warren was sick of hearing her apologize, so she made reparations by cleaning up both her dishes and his—a definite break in tradition. An impressed Warren headed off to work, and she headed back to the specter of her apartment. Staying just long enough to re-settle Mao Tse and get dressed, she headed back to the office of Katharine Bower, attorney-at-law. This time Maura was going to be there too, and Leigh was anxious to know if her volunteer investigator had learned anything new. She was also anxious to see Katharine Bower, who, she remembered with a smile, had not been at Warren's last night.

"Kristin Yates killed them both," she announced with a flourish as she plopped into one of Katharine's leather chairs. "I'm sure of it."

Katharine and Maura exchanged glances. "What makes you so sure?" Katharine asked. Leigh summarized her last, depressing meeting with Tanner, finishing with an impassioned editorial. "I don't believe Kristin killed Carmen over Tanner, though. I think there was something else going on that we don't know about."

"Quite possibly," Katharine agreed, and asked Maura to repeat the conversation she'd heard at the bird house.

"So," Leigh responded sullenly. "Tonya and Dena

both saw Kristin at the zoo that night. A *pregnant* Kristin."

"We can't know that for sure," Maura cautioned. "Dena just said 'with the baby coming,' she didn't say whose baby, or where it was coming from."

Leigh was unconvinced, but didn't say so. If Kristin was pregnant, her unexpected return from D.C. made sense. And if "friend" Tanner was the father, so did her desire to confront Carmen. "So, Dena went out on a limb to protect Kristin," she mused. "I wonder if she knows Kristin was the killer. Do you think she's scared of her now?"

"She sounded scared all right," Maura retorted. "But not of Kristin. She's worried about perjury charges if all this goes to trial."

"It won't," Katharine interrupted. "I had a little talk with Frank last night."

Leigh's eyebrows rose. "After I threw him out?"

She nodded. "I'm not Frank's favorite person, as you know, so he wasn't exactly effusive. But I'm virtually certain that he's beginning to doubt your guilt. It appears that he's working with the state police to get the pond by Tanner's cabin dragged."

"Dragged?" Leigh repeated. She knew what dragged meant, but she had no idea there was a pond near Tanner's cabin. He had talked about fishing, but she assumed he meant going to a lake.

"I believe the police are thinking that whoever killed Carmen was using Tanner's cabin as a hideout. They removed the rest of the body from the zoo—probably in a car trunk—and drove to the cabin to dispose of it. Of course, they could have disposed of it anywhere along the way, but the pond would be a relatively easy target. I also learned from Tanner's lawyer that the wheelbarrow in the shed behind the cabin was spanking clean—in great contrast to everything else there. That may indicate the killer used it to haul the body, then cleaned it out."

"Did Tanner have a boat?" Maura asked Leigh.

Leigh shrugged, finding the question an odd one. "I don't know. I know he fished and hunted, that's all. I didn't really get a good look around the cabin."

"There's no mention of a boat in the report I have," Katharine answered, flipping papers, "but that doesn't mean anything. Why?"

Maura sat back in her chair, brow furrowed. "It's probably not important. Leigh, you said Tanner was the outdoors type. What about Kristin?"

"I don't know anything about Kristin's hobbies," she answered. "But I know she grew up around West View, somewhere near Carmen. It's hard to picture either one of them pitching a tent or cleaning fish, if that's what you mean. They were definitely urban types."

Katharine, who seemed a little miffed at losing control of the conversation, broke in. She explained her plan to get the charges against Leigh dropped, which included pushing the police to locate and question Kristin Yates. There was no credible evidence to connect Kristin directly to Carmen's murder, and the link with Stacey's murder was tenuous at best. Furthermore, suspects had already been arrested in both cases. But looking at the whole picture, Kristin's rating as a suspect—or at least an accomplice—wasn't too shabby. The police had known all along that Leigh couldn't possibly have removed Carmen's body from the zoo herself; somebody had driven away with it. And not in her car or Tanner's truck, either.

"If we can break down either Tonya or Dena," Katharine hypothesized, "we can place Kristin at the zoo the night of the murder. I think I can trip Dena up pretty easily—thanks to Officer Polanski's information gathering. With the prosecution's star witness debunked and another plausible suspect in the picture, I think we've got a shot here. A good shot."

Leigh smiled. Things weren't looking so bad, at

least from the standpoint of her going to prison. Now if she could just stop her growing fear of a freely roaming homicidal Kristin, things would be perfect.

Maura excused herself from the meeting and left abruptly, before Leigh could ask her about her mother. The policewoman had been wearing plainclothes, which probably meant this was her "weekend." Perhaps they could get together with Warren for dinner. The subject of Mary Polanski had to be addressed sooner or later, preferably sooner.

The meeting adjourned fairly quickly, with Katharine heading off to another court appearance. Leigh started to drive to the North Side and Hook, Inc., but remembered that she had forgotten her files. She had thrown them in the car when she left Hook on Friday, planning to do a little extra work over the weekend. She had gotten arrested instead. They were now sitting in a neat stack on her desk in the bedroom, untouched. That's probably what Jeff Hulsey had called her about.

She pulled her car over to the right lane of the Fort Duquesne bridge, moving away from Three Rivers' Stadium and onto 279. After sitting through a few hundred stoplights on McKnight Road, she was home. Such as it was.

She ran into her apartment just long enough to grab her files and check on Mao Tse, who was sleeping peacefully on top of the refrigerator. She collected her mail from the box downstairs and returned to her car, flipping through bills and offers of credit cards she already had. The last letter in the pile stopped her.

It was a plain personal envelope, addressed in ink in a child's hand, and postmarked from her own post office. Her brow furrowed. She had a few Morton relatives of elementary age running about, but why would any of them be writing her a letter? She tore open the seal and lifted out a crumpled piece of white copy paper, written on in bold block print.

To whom it may consern,

I can't go on with what I've done—I killed two women to get my man but he doesn't want me. Its better if I end it now.

Leigh read the sloppy writing with confusion, skimming anxiously down to the signature. She looked at it with disbelief.

Sincerely,
Leigh Koslow

She stood frozen in the parking lot, her fingers turning white where they clutched the vile note. She crumpled it back into the envelope, hurried back to her car, and threw it on the passenger seat. Hands on the steering wheel, she sat.

Mind games. Somebody was playing mind games. At least the knife was planted for a concrete purpose—to frame her for Stacey's murder. This fake "suicide" note could only be meant to mess up her head. Kristin couldn't very well expect her to kill herself and use it.

Could she?

Leigh started up the car, but realized she couldn't remember where she'd been going. So she sat instead with the engine idling, her fingers clenching the wheel tightly.

It's better if I end it now. She was all for ending it, but not the way the author was hinting at. Somebody wanted her to take the rap for both murders. The implication was that she should just confess and go quietly. It would be ever so helpful for the real killer. Were they nuts?

Dumb question.

Leigh unclenched her fingers and began drumming them on the dashboard. The knife had been planted to frame her—but that same action had the effect of getting Tanner off. Was that the real plan?

Kristin. It always came back to her. If the murderer was anyone else, there would be no point in doing anything, because they stood an excellent shot of getting away with it. But for Kristin, the hounds were closing in. And Kristin might very well have her own reasons for wanting Tanner to go free—at Leigh's expense.

Making a decision, Leigh put the Cavalier into drive and headed to East Liberty, and the Central Detectives Bureau. The letter would soon be Frank's problem. She just hoped he wasn't so dim he'd think she mailed it to herself.

The bureau wasn't as busy as usual, but then, it was still morning. Leigh walked boldly up to the desk and asked for Detective Frank. "He's not here," the clerk quipped, looking at her as if she should know better. "He's out on a call."

Leigh sighed. "How can I get in touch with him?" she asked.

An officer who had just walked behind the desk looked up at her. "You Leigh Koslow?" he asked, incredulous.

Leigh thought he looked vaguely familiar, but she'd seen a lot of uniforms in the last week. "Yes," she answered gratefully. "I'm looking for Detective Frank. It's important."

The officer still looked at her as though she were crazy. Perhaps people out on bail didn't often seek the company of the detective who'd locked them up. But then, most people were probably guilty.

"You want to tell me what this is about?" he said skeptically.

Leigh sighed. Some people made it really hard to do the right thing. "I got a letter—a threatening letter. It may be important to the case."

The officer smiled a little. An unpleasant, sneering smile. "You think you're in danger, Ms. Koslow?"

Leigh's blood boiled. "Evidently not," she said hotly. "According to this letter, I'm already dead."

Chapter 20

Maura headed north on Route 8, her mind deep in thought. Something about Carmen's murder had always bothered her. Any way you looked at it, it was no run-of-the-mill homicide. Someone had not only killed Carmen, but dismembered her body and threw it in with the tigers. Leigh had interrupted the process, and the killer had dragged the remainder of the body out behind the shed. The killer was probably still there, waiting in the darkness, while Leigh investigated. When she freaked out and left, they dragged the body the rest of the way to the parking lot, loaded it in some vehicle, and took off.

Why bother? Someone had gone to an incredible amount of effort to accomplish no obvious purpose. Why not just leave the rest of the body, especially with the risk of discovery so high? And why throw the limbs in with tigers in the first place? A person from outside the zoo might believe that the tigers would dispose of the body, if it were cut up into enough pieces. But the zoo suspects, according to Leigh, would have known better. And only the zoo suspects would have known where to look for the bone saw.

Perhaps the killer was a true lunatic, and wanted to keep the rest of the body for some twisted, unfathomable reason. But that MO hardly reckoned with the stab-and-run technique used on Stacey Tanner.

Besides, *Silence of the Lambs* weirdness, though highly publicized, was rare. And Maura Polanski was not one to chase zebras.

A more mundane reasoning had to be at play, but she couldn't come up with any, which irked her. Short of locating Kristin Yates, there was only one sure way she knew of to get some answers, and that was to find the rest of Carmen Koslow's body. And if the state police would cooperate, she just might.

Leigh sat in the waiting area of the bureau and fumed. The officer had contacted Detective Frank, who would presumably swing by in a few minutes. Could she hang around till he got there?

Sure. No problem. She loved hanging out in the place she'd been booked. Happy memories galore.

She took out the crumpled paper and read it over again. It didn't get any better. It was just as lame—just as sinister. *Sincerely, Leigh Koslow*. Right. Like anyone would believe that. She, for one, knew how to spell "concern." She also knew the difference between "it's" and "its." The question was, would Frank? Or would he think she'd created the letter herself in some pathetic attempt to make it *look* like she was being framed?

She sighed. Perhaps coming down had been a bad idea after all. Her arm was poised to drop the letter in the trash can when Frank's voice startled her from behind.

"Destroying evidence?"

She turned, her eyes menacing. "The statute of boredom had run out. I have better things to do with my time than hang around here waiting to help you solve your cases."

"Did I ask for help?" Frank said pleasantly. There was color in his cheeks; the cold apparently in remission.

"No," Leigh retorted. "But you should. Any idiot

could tell you you arrested the wrong person. Which
has been highly entertaining for all concerned, but
it doesn't stop the real killer from roaming around
planting knives and sending me lame threats."

Frank lifted one eyebrow. "May I?" he asked,
pointing to the letter still clutched in Leigh's hand.

She handed the letter over, and he took it in his
omnipresent white handkerchief. She hoped it was
clean this time. He carefully pulled out the letter and
unfolded it on the front desk. His expression didn't
change as he read it.

"When did you get this?"

"Just now. This morning. By regular mail."

"And what do you think it means, Ms. Koslow?"

"I think it means somebody wants me in jail," she
said more civilly, then swallowed. "Or dead."

"Tanner's cabin? Some of the guys are out there
right now. You should just go catch them—Smitty's
a good guy." Sara Jean dropped her cigarette butt
into her Coke can, then jumped. "Aw, shoot!" she
whined. "I thought I'd finished it off already!"

"Sara Jean," Maura interrupted calmly, "do you
know if they're dragging the pond?"

"I think so," Sara Jean answered distractedly, trying to fish out the cigarette butt with a pen. "Well,
crap. It's just breaking up in there." She flung the
can into the trash and turned her attention back to
Maura. "That Pittsburgh detective—Funk, I think—
was pushing for it. Trying to find the rest of that
body your friend kill—I mean, well, you know what
I mean." She smiled.

Maura smiled back, though not so broadly. So,
Frank was pushing to find the body. It was a lot of
money to spend, considering that the results weren't
likely to add much to the case against Leigh. Perhaps
Frank was coming around.

Her smile widened. She had known he would.

* * *

"So, I suppose you have a theory as to who wrote this?" Frank asked.

"Sure I do," Leigh answered. "It was Kristin Yates, the person who really killed Carmen. And Stacey Tanner. Now if you'll excuse me, I've done my civic duty—and I'm out of here." She brushed past him and headed for the door, but just as she reached it, his words made her stop.

"I don't think you killed her," he said matter-of-factly.

She turned. "You what?"

He folded his arms over his chest and looked her straight in the eye. "I said, I don't think you killed Carmen Koslow."

Her heart started to beat faster, but her brain stayed skeptical. "And why not?"

One corner of his mouth lifted slightly. "Instinct."

Leigh wasn't convinced. "Your instincts are awfully slow."

The other corner of Frank's mouth twitched, but he kept a straight face. "The initial evidence was pretty damning, and you had an attitude. You're still a pain in the ass, but now the evidence is pointing another direction."

She stepped closer to him. "And what direction might that be?" The pain-in-the-ass comment she would let slide. It was, after all, a common accusation.

He shook his head. "I've said enough already. We're going to get the real killer. You keep your nose clean and stay out of it. Understand?"

Leigh didn't say anything. She just turned and left. Once out of the building, she allowed herself a little hop. He *could* be taught.

With Sara Jean's convoluted directions, Maura had to turn around six times before locating Tanner's hunting cabin. The exact building wasn't hard to pick out, given the number of official vehicles sprinkled on its lawn. Maura approached cautiously, following the voices to the rear of the cabin. She had to do this right. There would be no second chance.

The pond was a fair size—too small for power boating, but certainly big enough to host a body in its murky depths. Like most natural ponds, the edges were shallow and sloped gradually—you couldn't just throw a body in and expect it to disappear. It would have to be dumped in the middle. Knowing this, the half-dozen workers in attendance were laboriously casting and dragging their chains and hooks across the pond's center, hoping to snag any large object that might be resting on the soft floor.

One man stood alone on the near bank, and as Maura approached him, he turned around. "Trooper Smitty?" she asked respectfully, identifying him immediately by Sara Jean's description of a middle-aged, redheaded Santa Claus.

He looked at the huge woman before him in surprise. They were, after all, in the middle of nowhere. "Yes? Who might you be?"

"Officer Maura Polanski," she said, extending her hand for a firm shake. "I'm with the Avalon PD. I don't mean to intrude, but I have a personal interest in this case because a friend of mine has been falsely accused, and I'd like to keep tabs on it."

He looked at her thoughtfully, withdrawing his hand in the slow, furtive way macho men tended to after experiencing the pain of a Polanski greeting. "Maura Polanski? I knew your daddy." He smiled, recovering. "Damn fine man. You're kin to Sara Jean Pruszynski, right?"

She nodded tentatively, not sure that was a plus.

"Leigh Koslow," he said thoughtfully, returning to the subject. "I met her. Not a murderer."

"I agree," Maura replied, relieved. "I'm hoping

that finding the rest of this body will help prove that."

Smitty nodded. "Maybe. If we find it. So far, not much turning up. It's sad, really. You'd like to give the dead woman's people a little more to bury."

The trooper's words struck a chord. Carmen had no "people," at least none that the police had been able to locate. What would happen to her body? Unless the main squeeze Tanner had a sudden attack of financial conscience, the limbs would probably end up in a pauper's grave.

The latter thought took hold, and Maura's eyes widened. Of course. It would have been possible. Wouldn't it? Her eyes took in the shed, where the wheelbarrow had supposedly been kept, roughly a hundred yards away from the pond. A small rowboat lay inverted at the pond's edge, propped up on pillars of concrete blocks.

"Was there any evidence of a missing block?" Maura asked.

Smitty looked at her respectfully. "You mean for a weight. No. We checked that. No empty spaces, no bare rectangles crawling with pill bugs. But it's rained pretty good since the murder, you know. We can't be sure another block wasn't lying around. Plus, there's other things could be used as weights."

Maura looked again at the rowboat. It was balanced about two feet off the ground. If the murderer had used it to carry the body out into deep water, they'd been considerate enough to put it back. "Are there shovels in the shed?" she asked.

Smitty's gaze turned to puzzlement. "Yes. Mind telling me what you're thinking?"

Maura studied him. Sara Jean was a nut, but her sense of character was keen. Smitty was clearly a good guy. "I'm thinking that the perp was probably a woman," she began. "A zookeeper. They spend a lot of time shoveling and hauling, so they have good upper body strength. But unless they're into boating, I doubt they'd want to pull that one off the pillars, dump a body and a weight in it, launch it, navigate out, dump the body without tipping, row back, and lift the boat back up again."

Smitty nodded slowly. "Maybe not if there was an easier way."

"For a zookeeper, there would be," Maura suggested. "With a wheelbarrow, a shovel, and a good back, the perp could have taken the body a good distance from the cabin and buried it."

Smitty's wide brow knitted. He scanned the woods around the pond. "We already checked the clear areas. No disturbed ground. Out there—you got roots. It'd be tough."

"There must be some kind of clearing farther out," Maura insisted.

He scratched his chin. "There's a path around the pond—at least half of it. Let's take a walk."

As bidden, Leigh returned to the offices of Hook, Inc., in the early afternoon. Working at Hook had always been more of a pleasure than a drudgery to her, but this time she couldn't deny a certain dread. On the phone, everybody had claimed they believed she was innocent. But did they really?

She opened the squeaking door and smiled at the new receptionist, who had done wonders with the pathetic lobby. Had it really only been five days since the arrest? Only a week since that horrible night her world had started spinning? It seemed like half a lifetime.

"Hello, Leigh," the woman said pleasantly. "We were hoping you'd make it in. Everybody's in Jeff's office."

Leigh took a deep breath, laid her stack of files in her office, and went to Jeff's door, which was closed. She knocked nervously.

"Come on in!" he called affably. She opened the door and did a double take. Jeff, Carl, and Alice were clustered around Jeff's desk, wearing makeshift paper party hats. A sheet cake took center stage.

"Happy bail!" they shouted, then broke into laughter. Their party hats, which were crafted out of legal-size copy paper and stuck to their hair with paper clips, said "Get out of jail free," "Beat the system," and "Half-million-dollar woman," respectively. The cake, which was decorated with broken chains in blue icing, said, "Anything for a party."

"I can't believe you guys," Leigh said incredulously, laughing. "Love the hats. Where's mine?"

Carl smirked and immediately produced a fourth cone-shaped hat, which simply read "Innocent." Leigh smiled broadly and hoped desperately that she could avoid the tear thing. "This was so nice of you guys. Thanks. It means a lot to me."

"Yeah, yeah, whatever," Alice said dismissively, "now cut the cake, will you? We've had to smell the damn thing all morning and it's driving me crazy."

Leigh obliged. Unexpected cake she was compelled to eat. What more could one ask for on a Wednesday afternoon?

Maura and Smitty skirted the lake on the overgrown path, looking back into the surrounding woods. Smitty shook his head. "Looks pretty thick. I haven't seen any brush beaten down."

Maura kept walking. "There might be a stream or two feeding in. The perp could have pushed the wheelbarrow up the bed, if it was dry enough."

When they had almost reached the far end of the pond, Maura found what she was looking for. A shallow stream, barely a trickle at the moment, left over from the weekend downpour. The bed was a little rocky, but not so bumpy that a wheelbarrow couldn't easily be maneuvered upstream. She turned and followed the stream away from the pond, Smitty at her heels.

After about twenty yards, she stopped. A small tree had fallen across the stream, rendering it impassable to anything over twelve inches high. She looked anxiously to either side, but Smitty was already ahead of her.

"Look here," he said with excitement. "You might just be on to something."

Maura looked where he was pointing, at the base of the fallen tree. She had no experience whatsoever at hunting or tracking, but even to her eyes, the trampling of the underbrush was obvious. The path made an arc around the log, then disappeared again in the streambed on the opposite side.

She and Smitty exchanged hopeful glances and plowed on, looking carefully for further signs of an exit from the streambed. Three minutes later, they both stopped cold. The stream made a sharp turn, leaving a shoulder of flat ground that probably flooded with heavy spring rains, then dried out in the summer. A week ago, the elbow of soil had probably been covered with weeds, but now only a few remained around its edges. In the center was a circle of raw, plowed-up earth.

Chapter 21

Suitably dosed up with sugar, fat, and caffeine, Leigh managed a productive afternoon of slogan-spinning. It felt good to be thinking about something that didn't matter, and she left the office with firm plans to start back to work full-time the next day. If they didn't have enough writing to do, she could always help Jeff with the marketing. It was her business, and she should never have let it take a back seat, even for a week and a half. Cash problem or no, trying to work a second job at the zoo had been a mistake. For a lot of reasons.

Reaching the parking lot, she plucked a circular off the windshield of her Cavalier. It advertised (in an amateurish fashion, she noted) a new restaurant down the street, and as she prepared to crumple it she noticed that it was different from the circulars adorning the other cars around her. Hers had writing on it. She squinted at the odd script.

Mr. Jankowski was gay.

Her brow furrowed. Was this a joke? Some kids goofing off with the flyers they were hired to distribute? She looked closer at the blue ink, and tensed as she recognized the shaky block print. It was the same as the letter she'd received that morning.

Kristin.

She drew in a breath, picturing a skinny blond

man with a soccer ball and a whistle. Mr. Jankowski, her eighth-grade gym teacher. All the girls had crushes on him because of his baby blue eyes and high cheekbones. The boys all thought he was gay. In retrospect, the boys were probably right.

Cara's voice bounced around in the back of her head. *And then there was the parole officer, and the gym teacher at the middle school—*

Of course. Jankowski was one of Carmen's many paramours, or so she had claimed at the tender age of thirteen. And now Kristin was saying he was gay?

Leigh exhaled in frustration. Why on earth should anyone care? She tossed the circular in the car and climbed in after it. Did the note really mean anything, or was it offered merely as proof of a shared adolescence?

She started up the Cavalier and drove off. Being deliberately baited irked her. She was already under arrest for one crime Kristin had committed. What more could the thankless witch possibly want? It wasn't Leigh's fault that Tanner had got arrested, and it wasn't her fault the frame job failed. But Tanner was out on bail nonetheless, and if he was really what Kristin wanted, what was stopping her from scooping him up and carrying him off to make one big happy family?

Leigh's mind pulled up a picture of Tanner sitting in the gloom of Stacey's house. Perhaps Kristin had already tried. Perhaps she had sought him out, and they had talked. If so, he hadn't told the police. And he hadn't bothered to get himself—or more importantly, Leigh—off the hook.

Impossible. No way would a self-absorbed philanderer like Tanner go to prison for a woman he thought looked like a horse—even if she was carrying his child. Kristin hadn't contacted him. Only Leigh.

Lucky, lucky, me. Why?

She didn't have time to finish the thought, because as she stared blankly ahead at the traffic light, she saw it. Just two cars up.

A tan Eldorado.

"Detective Frank's on his way," Smitty announced to the officials that had assembled at the pond's far edge. "Forensics here? Good. Let's see what we've got."

Maura hung back, not wanting to appear too conspicuous. This was the state police's show—and any further involvement on her part could only complicate matters. That said, she wasn't going anywhere. Not until she knew for sure.

She looked anxiously at the cabin, aware that it had no phone service. She needed to get in touch with Leigh, but it would have to wait.

The forensics team gathered its equipment and began to trek into the woods after Smitty. Maura took a seat on a fallen log at the pond's edge, piecing things together in her mind. There was a lot she still didn't understand, but she was pretty sure she had the gist of it. And that made her more than a little nervous for Leigh.

Over an hour had passed when the peace of the dense woods was shattered by a loud bang. Maura skirted the pond's edge in seconds and made her way around the edge of the cabin, gun drawn. Peering cautiously around the corner of the building and into the road, she was surprised to see only Detective Frank, kicking his flattened car tire with contempt and cursing fluently. She chuckled and replaced her gun.

"Damn country roads!" he swore as he strode toward Maura, who had stepped away from the building. "Pits like canyons and gravel like boulders.

Knew I should have kept a decent spare—" He stopped short on recognizing her.

"You involved in this, Polanksi?" he asked suspiciously.

"I came out when I heard the pond was being dragged," she answered calmly.

Frank's eyebrows rose a little, but his voice turned more amiable. "Why exactly did you want to be here? Lousy way to spend time off, if you ask me."

Maura studied him. He didn't completely trust her, but he respected her, it would seem. "I think that finding the rest of the body could clear Leigh Koslow. I'm anxious to see what Trooper Smitty turns up."

She turned and began walking, leading him down the trail around the pond. "And why should finding the rest of the body help Leigh Koslow?" he asked as they reached the streambed. His voice was mildly patronizing, but such subtle slights had no effect on Maura Polanski.

She opened her mouth to answer his question, but was interrupted by an echoing yell from Smitty. "Hi ho!"

Maura and Frank took a few paces up the stream. "What do you have?" Frank called out to Smitty as the latter appeared up ahead.

"Come see for yourself," Smitty answered grimly.

Frank moved forward quickly, and Maura followed at a discreet distance. She didn't want to be accused of screwing up the crime scene, but she needed to see the body—and as soon as possible.

She watched from behind as Frank reached the stream's elbow and looked down into the shallow grave. He uttered an expletive and wheeled around, his eyes training quickly on Maura. "You knew we'd find this—didn't you?" he said hotly, dark eyes blazing.

Maura, who was still not close enough to see,

quickly stepped forward and looked down. "No," she said calmly, shaking her head. "But I had a hunch."

The tan Eldorado took a wide, slow left turn. Leigh stared hard to get a glimpse of the driver, but saw only tinted windows. She turned left and followed the gas-guzzling old car. How many could there be in Pittsburgh? Could it be coincidence that this one was here, when she had just gotten that ridiculous message on her car?

She cursed under her breath. If only she could call the police . . . but naturally she had no cell phone. Unbeknownst to Hollywood, most average-income people still didn't. Nor could she pull over at a pay phone—she would lose the car in a minute, and on the North Side, it would be hard to find again. Too many ways to turn, too many alleys to duck into.

She kept up behind the car, which began turning at every corner. Left, left, left, left. Right, right, right, right. They were going in circles. The car seemed to know she was following, and was toying with her. Leigh's annoyance grew, but she hung on, trying fruitlessly to get a better view of the driver. Unfortunately, time was against her. It was already growing dark.

Around and around the Eldorado circled, moving to a new area now and then only to circle again. Leigh followed doggedly. Sooner or later the car would stop somewhere, or else the driver would tire of the chase and make a break for a major road. Either way, if Leigh could call quick enough, the police would have a decent chance of catching up.

The chase had gone on for half an hour when Leigh realized that they were making progress, however slowly, in a particular direction. They were headed for the zoo. And thanks to the circuitous route, they were headed for the zoo in darkness.

* * *

The phone in Leigh's apartment rang four times before the answering machine picked up, only to expel a beep so long Maura doubted there would be any tape left. Her quick pleas for Leigh to answer if she were in went unheeded, and Maura stopped the call in frustration.

"Any luck?" Frank asked, reclaiming his cell phone.

Maura shook her head. "I'll just have to find her."

"Well if you're going anywhere near Zone One, can I hitch a ride?" Frank asked, more in the manner of a command. "I haven't got time to beg for a spare and fix this tank of mine—I've got work to do."

She nodded, and Frank piled into the ancient Escort. "Besides," he said casually, buckling his seat belt, "we need to talk."

It seemed like ages before the tan Eldorado finally reached the zoo and headed up the winding side road toward the employee lot. Having had plenty of time to mull over potential options, Leigh was ready for action when the moment came. She watched with a sly smile as the Eldorado made a wide swing into the employee lot. Immediately, she revved the Cavalier into high gear and drove straight ahead.

As brief as her time on the zoo staff had been, her excursions as a tourist were numerous enough that she had a good idea where the phones were. And it just so happened that the closest and most accessible one was up on the top of the hill, between the vending shed and the rest rooms. It was also quite near what Tanner had once referred to as "the high road"—his own personal after-hours entry.

Leigh scanned the tree-lined fence and tried to estimate the location of the phone. When she thought she was close, she pulled two of the Cavalier's wheels off onto the narrow shoulder and parked—

hazard lights blinking. The last thing she needed tonight was a totaled car.

She grabbed a flashlight from her glove compartment and began to walk the fence line, shining the beam through until she found the back wall of the vending shed. Then she headed downhill, focusing her attention on the tree branches overhead.

She found "the high road" quickly, tucked the butt of the flashlight in a back pocket, and pretended she was ten again. Jumping up high enough to hook the old maple's lowest branch was easy. Getting her bottom half to the same level was another matter entirely. Cursing her weight distribution, she scrambled up only after five tries and several nasty bark burns. Once she was up, however, the rest was easy.

A series of horizontal branches took her up higher than the fence's barbed-wire cap, and one particularly large limb offered safe passage across it. She swung down easily on the other side, but her sense of victory was short-lived. Her feet had no sooner hit the ground than she realized the flaw in her plan.

Never in a million years could she jump back up to the branch she'd just let go of. The "high road" was one-way.

Hell.

She looked nervously around her at the darkness. She hated being in this place at night even before she'd found Carmen's body. How had she ended up here again?

Trying to push the paranoia out of her mind, she focused on the task at hand. She was going to get to the phone and let the police know that Kristin was in the zoo. With any luck, the terror monger of North Hills High would still be here when they arrived. Zoo security could get to her faster, but they probably wouldn't. All they would do would be to take Leigh in for trespassing—giving Kristin plenty of time to wise up and take off.

She found the vending shed, and sighed a breath of relief. The pay phone was still there beside it, and it appeared to be in working order. She stepped up into the old-fashioned booth and picked up the receiver, then stared blankly at the numbered buttons beneath. 911 would reach the local cops—but what could she tell them? That someone she was scared of was at the zoo? Kristin was probably wanted for questioning, but the city cops might not know about that, and there couldn't be a warrant out for Kristin's arrest—not with charges still pending against Leigh.

She had to call Frank.

A dial tone buzzed happily in her ear, but she paused again. She had no money. 911 calls were free, but this didn't count. Was her entire plan going down the drain for lack of a quarter? She was about to panic when her rational side caught up with her endorphins. It wasn't a problem—she knew her phone-card number—she could charge it.

Calm down.

She took a deep breath, then pushed 0. She would ask the operator to connect her with the city detectives, and Frank would come through. He had to. He owed her.

"Detective Frank isn't available at the moment," a receptionist at the bureau answered dryly. "Perhaps one of the other detectives could take your call?"

"Yes, fine," Leigh stammered impatiently, looking toward some bushes that her paranoid imagination seemed to think were moving a little. "Get anybody. Just do it quick, OK?" She shuffled her feet on the concrete base, irritated at the gaping holes that were now so apparent in her plan. Sure, this had been the closest phone, but what was she going to do now? She couldn't go out the way she came in, and security would have a fit when they saw her—it might even get her bail revoked. On the other hand, there was Kristin. Who was now, in all likelihood, on the same side of the fence as Leigh was.

The wait for another detective seemed to take ages, but at least the bushes weren't moving anymore. Or after all.

"Hello. Detective Fanelli here. What can I do for you?"

Leigh opened her mouth to speak, but no words came out. Instead a piercing crash assaulted her ears, and hundreds of glass shards rained over her arm and side.

Chapter 22

Maura's Escort reached the North Side of Pittsburgh about the same time she and Frank finished piecing together a credible theory. They were almost within sight of the zone station when a ringing sound radiated from under Frank's coat. With reluctance, he withdrew the cell phone clipped to his belt. "This had better not be another surprise," he said gruffly.

After punching in some numbers and barking out his name, Frank listened for a moment, then turned toward Maura. She watched in alarm as his pupils darted about nervously.

"You got a caller ID?" he asked someone brusquely. After another moment of listening, he spoke quickly. "We're near there now—send backup." He replaced the phone on his belt and turned to Maura. "Forget the station. We've got to get to the zoo. *Fast*."

At first, Leigh thought she'd been shot. The explosion had been sudden and loud, and to say it startled her would be an understatement. She burst out of the phone booth as if she were on fire, running madly toward she didn't know where. She didn't stop till she had reached the bear caves, where she whipped through the staff-only gate and crouched on the other side. Her breath was coming heavy, and she tried to calm it.

What had happened? One second she was about to tell the detective all, the next, she was taking a shower in glass. She looked down at her arms, and was surprised to note only a few shallow scratches. What had broken the booth window? She didn't remember hearing a gunshot, only the breaking glass. Had someone thrown something?

She stood up and looked cautiously around the side of the gate. Seeing and hearing no one, she crouched down again. Was she overreacting? If Kristen had come in the employee entrance, she couldn't possibly have found Leigh so fast. How would she know where to look? Perhaps the glass had broken because of— She searched for a creative explanation, but found none forthcoming.

Someone had thrown something. Maybe just to scare her, or—an even less comforting thought—to interrupt her call. So much for doing the police a favor. Now she was here with no way to contact them, and no defense against a murderess.

Think.

She realized she shouldn't really be alone. Security was supposed to patrol the zoo all night—"supposed to" being the operative phrase. She had never actually seen a guard patrolling. Word had it that "the patrol" was a loose circuit running between the ape house and the main security shack—which shared the distinction of having television sets.

Her options were somewhat limited. She could come out from her hiding place and start running—and screaming—until she attracted attention. But the bear caves weren't particularly close to either end of the security loop, and it could be a long time before she caught up with a guard—a long enough time for someone else to catch up with her. She could try to get back to her car—but that was risky too. The fence nearest to her was up on a rise, and quite visible. Not to mention that she'd have a difficult time keeping her mouth shut when the barbed wire at the top started drawing her blood.

Think. Think.

Perhaps her best option was to head for the nearest security hub—the main shack—but to do it quietly. Presumably, whoever had assaulted the phone booth had already lost track of her. If she stayed low, she had a good chance of avoiding detection till she got within screaming range of the shack.

She had just steeled herself to stand up and peer around the gate again when a sound stopped her. Soft footsteps, trekking slowly down the path.

She sucked in her breath, her heart beating madly against her breastbone. Who was it? It could be a security guard, and if it was, her problems were over. But could she dare look?

The footsteps stopped for a moment, and Leigh heard a whistle. It was a high, accomplished whistle, and the tune was hauntingly familiar. The words popped into her head with a grim irony. *Buffalo gals, won't you come out tonight?*

An old tune, and one she might not know, except that in the seventh-grade choir she'd been forced to sing it till she dropped. She liked singing, but she hated the school choir because— Her racing heart stopped for a moment. Because there were some rough girls in it that she was afraid of. Part of the Seville Elementary crowd. And Kristin had been one of them.

The footsteps started up again, and this time sounded as if they were coming closer. Leigh curled her body into as tight a ball as possible on the ground behind the gate, breathing between her knees as softly as she could. The footsteps stopped, and she lifted her head.

A woman's fingers appeared around the edge of the gate, pushing it slowly in. *And dance by the light of the moon.*

Leigh considered springing—at least she would have the advantage of surprise. But she had no idea what type of weapon her pursuer might be carrying—and she, in the meantime, had nothing. Her flashlight had long since fallen out of her pocket, and there was nothing on the ground—not even a rock.

Despite her poor odds, Leigh readied herself. She and Kristin were roughly the same size—if she could knock the other woman to the ground, she could tell pretty quickly if there was a weapon involved. Anything less than a heat-seeking machine gun, and Leigh would head out screaming.

She drew in a deep breath, but held it. The gate stopped moving in, and the hand was withdrawn. An eternity passed as the figure stood somewhere on the other side of the gate, not moving. Leigh thought about pushing the gate out quickly to knock the woman off balance, but she wasn't sure it swung out far enough—and if it fell short, she would be in big trouble.

So instead she did nothing, just listened to the occasional scuffling noise the woman's shoes made as she pivoted in place. Finally, Leigh heard her make a sighing noise, and the footsteps moved slowly away.

When the footsteps were so faint she could barely hear them, Leigh allowed herself a few deep breaths. She couldn't go back out on the main path—Kristin would be looking for the slightest movement. She'd have to slink around as best she could behind the exhibits, snaking her way slowly down to the security shack—no matter how long it took.

She tried to remember what the layout was like behind the bear caves, but she hadn't a clue. She'd had no cause to be there as an employee, and zoo visitors were never allowed in the tunnels.

When the footsteps became too distant to be heard, she uncurled herself and stood up. The staff area here was sparse—a Dumpster by the gate, and the tunnel entrance. There was nowhere else to go, except the same way Kristin had gone. Leigh looked over her shoulder and walked slowly toward the tunnel, which was blocked by an iron gate. For a moment she thought it was locked, but was surprised to find only a flip latch. She jerked the gate gently at first, but found it opened with ease, and without a squeak.

Wishing she had somehow managed to hold on to her flashlight, she slipped into the dark tunnel and began groping forward along the damp walls. A thin area of light shone up ahead, and as she neared it she realized it was the opening into the brown bear run. Between the moon and the single security spot mounted on the trail outside, there was just enough light streaming through the thick bars to expose another gate farther down. Both gates were secured with padlocks, of which she was glad. For while the near one led only to the empty outdoor run, the far one led to the indoor cave, and had brown bear fur poking through its base.

Leigh sucked in her breath again and moved quietly past the sleeping bear. All she needed now was to irritate him. He might make noise and attract attention, or—should he suddenly jump up and growl at her—she would.

She crept along past the bear without incident and managed to pass the polar bear and grizzly runs in like fashion. Last would be the sun bears, and then— if there was justice in the world—another unlocked tunnel opening. She tried to remember if there was another staff gate at the bottom end of the bear caves, but her memory failed her. All she could remember was the gift shop; if it did have a gate beside it, she had probably never noticed.

The sun bears were also in residence in their cave, lounging idly. At first Leigh thought they were asleep, but as she passed they opened their large brown eyes and stared at her suspiciously. Despite the thick bars, she felt a pang of panic at moving along in the dark tunnel within inches of their giant claws. But the sun bears' interest quickly fizzled, and as she crept slowly along the far wall, their eyes closed again. Leigh looked ahead with hope. One more bend in the tunnel, and she would be free. Kristin would have long since lost track of her, and she could easily sneak behind the gift shop, around the fence line behind the petting zoo, and on to the security shack.

Things were looking up.

She rounded the bend and headed happily toward the exit, which appeared, like its uphill mate, to have only a flip latch. Light filtered in from the security spot over the gift shop, and Leigh could see that the gate led out to yet another Dumpster. She opened it with enthusiasm, but slowed the motion when the gate creaked loudly. Easing out as best she could without moving the gate any more, she finally found herself in the open air.

She took a deep breath and shook out her arms. Her back ached from tensing, but relief was in sight. She started around the back of the gift shop, stopping cold as the soft voice reached her ears.

"Hello, Leigh."

Chapter 23

Leigh froze in her tracks, not daring to turn around. The signals she was getting from her brain didn't make sense, and it annoyed her. She couldn't have heard the voice she just heard.

Or could she?

The wheels in her head spun, and she swallowed hard. Yes, of course it was possible. It was, in fact, quite probable. And she should have guessed it before.

She took a deep breath and turned around, determined to face her pursuer without showing fear. How good a job she did, she couldn't know.

"Hello, Carmen."

"These are their cars all right," Frank barked to the uniformed team as he shone a flashlight first in Leigh's Cavalier, then in the tan Eldorado parked a ways behind it. "Why the hell aren't they at one of the gates?"

"Detective!" Maura called from the nearby fence line. "I think they went in here." She shone her flashlight over the maple tree to give him the gist, then headed back to the Escort, which was only a few yards away. She could pass a physical when she had to, but with her bulk, gymnastics was out of the question. She drove the car up under the tree, stepped onto the hood, and hoisted herself onto the lowest limb.

The uniformed officers followed, with Frank bringing up the rear. "Zoo security's been alerted," he announced when all four had swung down inside the fence. "Keep your eyes open. The perp may or may not be armed, but she's a psychopath, so watch your backs. Look for a female, five-seven or five-eight, medium build, with long black hair. And whatever the hell you do, don't get her mixed up with Leigh Koslow. She's five-six, also medium build, with shoulder-length brown hair."

The officers received the rest of their orders and started off, while Maura scoured the area around the pay phone with her flashlight. "No blood," she reported tonelessly. "No signs of a struggle. Just broken glass—and a rock."

Frank exhaled. "Let's start looking, then."

Maura nodded, and they set off.

"I guess you weren't expecting me, huh?"

Carmen Koslow leaned casually against the sloping wall by the tunnel exit, twisting her hair idly between her fingers. Only it wasn't the long raven hair she'd been so proud of. It was chopped off unevenly just above her shoulders, and appeared in the dim light to be a bizarre burnt-orange color.

"I know—it looks like crap," she said, following Leigh's eyes. " 'Cinnamon Silk,' my ass. I'm going to get the company that sells this junk, I swear to God I am. But the cut isn't bad, I mean, I had to do it myself. That's pretty hard. You ever tried it?"

Leigh stood as calmly as she could, watching. Carmen sounded just like she always did—chatty and friendly. It was as if they were doing lunch, not playing cat-and-mouse in a dark zoo.

"I'm glad you came," Carmen continued amiably.

"I need you to do me a favor. I've got to get to D.C., and I don't want the fuzz hassling me. OK?"

Leigh studied the perfectly friendly psychopath in front of her, and tried hard not to be lulled into a false sense of security. As far as she could tell, Carmen had no weapon—there wasn't anything in her hands, and there didn't appear to be anything on the ground beside her. But the spotlight above the gift shop cast a shadow over her left side, and Leigh couldn't be sure there was nothing in the pockets of her bulky jacket. So she stood still.

"I was hoping you'd just commit suicide or something," Carmen suggested matter-of-factly. "After all, you're facing a pretty hefty prison sentence. That would be great for everybody, because then Mike could get off."

Leigh had a response in mind, but stopped the words before they came out. She had to be careful what she said. There was a chance she might talk herself out of this—or at least get far enough away from Carmen to make a clean run for it. "Mike loves you," she said softly. It came off the top of her head, but she was running with it.

Carmen scoffed. "Like hell he does. He never loved anybody but the wench. But he and I are good together. I'm going to come back and see him now and then, and I don't want him in jail."

"Have you talked to him?" Leigh asked, not entirely sure where she was going with the question.

"Nah. I thought I'd wait till I got this fixed up," Carmen answered, gesturing toward her hair. "It makes me so damn mad—I should have just got a wig."

Leigh closed her eyes for a second to orient her thoughts. Carmen was being her old self—obsessing about her appearance, letting Leigh in on all her shallow little concerns. But this wasn't the same harmless Carmen who had made homeroom so interesting over a decade ago. This was the Carmen who had killed her own best friend, cut her body into pieces, and stolen her identity. Probably just to get out of debt.

"You think I look like her?" Carmen asked.

Leigh didn't need to ask who "her" was. "No," she answered carefully, "you're much prettier."

"Yeah, I know," Carmen said dryly. "Mike loves me, not Kristin. He never loved her. I'm glad she didn't get the chance to tell him."

Leigh didn't bother pointing out the inconsistencies in Carmen's claims. She had learned early on that doing so was pointless. Psychopaths never saw any inconsistencies. "Tell him what?" Leigh prompted. She thought—just for a moment—that she had heard something beyond the fence.

"About her being knocked up," Carmen answered, rolling her eyes. "What do you think?"

Leigh said nothing. There was no more noise. Perhaps it was her imagination. She preferred to think it was zoo security. Pretending to be surprised, she spoke as loud as she dared. "Kristin was *pregnant?*"

Carmen looked at her as if she had a screw loose. "She said she was. It ticked me off, actually. Mike wanted babies, but the wench wouldn't have any. I told him I would, but—well, anyway."

An image of the teenaged Carmen flashed back into Leigh's mind. The long absence sophomore year. Carmen had come to school looking pale and thin, and told everyone she'd had mono. Junior year, she told Leigh she'd really had an abortion, got infected, and was really messed up inside. That's why she didn't have to worry about birth control. Leigh hadn't believed a word of it at the time. But in retrospect, it made a sick kind of sense. If Kristin not only slept with Tanner but was going to give him the one thing Carmen couldn't—it would have made her furious. Really furious.

"This has been fun, Leigh," Carmen began, standing, "but we've got to get going." She dusted off the seat of her jeans and straightened her jacket. She still appeared to have no weapon.

Leigh remained still, and took another deep breath. *We?*

They both jerked as the full contingent of zoo lights switched on, illuminating the paths like a stadium. "What the hell—" Carmen began, wheeling around.

It was all the head start Leigh needed. She sprinted for the staff gate, which was the quickest way to whoever was out there.

"Leigh, no!" Carmen called, using the same harried tone a mother might to keep a child from mischief.

Leigh landed against the door with a bounce and pulled up on the latch with one motion. It didn't move.

"You're going to hurt your shoulder," Carmen chastised her. "Now stop that. Just come here, and this will all be over with real quick."

Whirling around, Leigh watched in horror as Carmen reached into her coat pocket and pulled out a clear plastic baggie containing what looked like a wet paper towel. "I was afraid you wouldn't want to come. God knows why—you've got nothing ahead of you here but prison. But you always were stubborn."

"You haven't told me where we're going," Leigh croaked, still trying hard to sound casual. "Maybe I will go."

Carmen tilted her head and smiled. "Never con a con, Leigh. You're dealing with one of the best. I always wanted to fake my own death, and it's been a blast. But I don't need the cops chasing after me thinking I'm Kristin. I could be arrested for my own murder—pretty wild, huh?"

Heavy footsteps pounded on the pavement outside the gate, and Leigh screamed. It was a loud scream, but a short one, as Carmen darted forward, whirled Leigh around, and pressed the paper towel over her nose and mouth.

Ether.

Knowing better than to inhale, or even try to pull off the cloth, Leigh opted for a quick elbow jab to the ribs, and was rewarded. Carmen shrieked, and the gate burst open to reveal a uniformed city cop. Seeing Carmen doubled over, he trained his gun promptly on Leigh.

"Not me, you idiot!" she yelled. "*She's* the murderer!"

"How dare you!" Carmen bleated, not missing a beat. "How dare you say that after what you did! You've killed two people, and one was supposed to be your friend!"

Leigh's jaw dropped open. The young officer stood helplessly, his gun wavering between the two. "On your knees! Both of you!"

But it was not to be. As Leigh complied, Carmen darted behind her. A strong arm encircled Leigh's neck, and a cool piece of steel lay flat against her throat.

A pocketknife. *Damn.*

"Take it easy," the officer cajoled. "Nobody needs to get hurt here."

"Nobody would have if you'd stayed out of it," Carmen chastised. "Now, here's what's going to happen. Leigh and I are going back into the tunnel, and you're not. Got it?"

Beads of sweat erupted on the young officer's forehead. Leigh could tell he was waiting anxiously for backup, as was she. They soon heard shouts, and the young officer answered them with relief. But Carmen wasn't waiting for more company. She dragged Leigh back into the tunnel, being none too careful with the knife blade on the way.

Leigh walked backward with Carmen as best she

could, wincing as the knife blade grated against her skin. It didn't appear to be all that sharp—but she wasn't taking any chances. If she tried to bolt, Carmen could easily take out a vein.

They were inside the tunnel again, and after moving beyond the first curve, they were out of sight of the officer—and his presumed backup. "Now see what you did, Leigh," Carmen said, just a hint of frustration entering her voice. "I can't drag you all the way through this tunnel. You're going to have to walk. So go on ahead of me. I have a gun too, you know."

Leigh didn't believe her, but what did it matter? When she felt Carmen let up pressure on the knife, she started ahead. Did Carmen really think the police were stupid enough to stand around at the bottom of the hill and wait for them to come back out? Of course there would be someone stationed at the other end.

She plodded forward rapidly, hoping to get well ahead of Carmen by the time they met up with their rescuers. But Carmen kept hold of Leigh's arm behind her back, the knife hovering near her ear. They were behind the polar bear run when Carmen jerked her roughly to a stop, placing the knife again at her throat.

"This has all gotten too complicated," Carmen said, the annoyance in her voice increasing. She looked down the tunnel in front of them, and Leigh's hopes fell. So, Carmen wasn't so dumb after all. She knew the police would be closing in. But what did she plan to do about it?

Leigh tried to think of a plan, but she was about tapped out, and her neck hurt like hell. "What are we supposed to do now?" she asked weakly.

Carmen sighed as she forced Leigh to kneel. "I don't think I can get you out of here. Sorry. You'll just have to stay and take the rap for me. Or for

Kristin, I should say." She smiled. "But it sure would help me out if you said all this tonight was a joke. You're going to jail anyway, it shouldn't matter to you. Just get them to stop looking for Kristin. They've got to cut that out or it will ruin everything."

Leigh tried to follow the convoluted logic. "You're going to D.C.?"

"Sure." Carmen smiled. "I have Kristin's job all ready and waiting for me. And now I have a little bit of money; I'd have more if she hadn't maxed out all her damn cards."

With her free hand, Carmen pulled something else from her pocket and began to fidget with it as she talked. "I have plans, you know. Being dead has taken a load off. I can start all over. And it's worked out for everybody. Especially for Mike. He won't have to support some brat now, and he can finally stop thinking about that wench of a wife of his."

"And what about Kristin?" Leigh blurted, feeling a little faint. "Is she happier now too, you think?"

"Probably," Carmen said seriously. "Mike would never have married her, and she wouldn't do well raising some kid on her own. She was just such a bitch that night, telling me Mike was going to marry her and she wasn't going to let him see me anymore. Right. She was asking for it, I swear. But I wasn't going to kill her. Really, I wasn't."

Leigh felt, rather than saw, someone approaching slowly from around the bend. Soon, she told herself. Soon. When they made their move, she was making hers. If Carmen was the least bit distracted, Leigh could pull away enough to get her throat clear of the knife. Then even if Carmen struck out at her, she wasn't likely to do serious damage.

"I just hit her once, with the shovel," Carmen rambled, still fiddling with something behind Leigh's back. "Then I got the idea, you know. Not the dying thing, I was already planning that, but then it hit me—here's my body!"

Leigh swallowed in preparation. She wasn't sure, but she thought that someone was closing in from behind them too.

Then, without warning, Carmen yelled so loudly that Leigh's ears rang with pain. "*Everybody freeze!* I want you both to take three steps back or the good girl gets sliced, got it?"

"No problem. Just stay calm." The familiar voice that retreated up the hall was, for the first time, quite comforting. It was Detective Frank.

"Both of you!" Carmen screamed again.

"Backing up now," the second voice said soothingly. *Maura.* How had they known to come here?

Carmen continued struggling with something, and soon Leigh heard a dull squeak. "It's been real, Leigh. Sorry you couldn't jump bail. It would have been fun for you. Just remember what I said. Either suicide or just confess, that should get the heat off Kristin. OK? You owe me you know, remember that."

Leigh was still trying to make sense of the words when she realized the knife was away from her throat. She lunged forward up the tunnel, colliding with Frank's feet as they rounded the bend. He bolted over her, the light in the tunnel suddenly dimming as he and Maura blocked the opening to the polar bear run.

Leigh stood up and wheeled around, hoping to see a subdued Carmen in thick handcuffs.

She didn't see Carmen at all.

It happened so quickly that neither Maura nor Frank had a chance of stopping it, even if they'd known how. Carmen the daredevil, a woman who seemed to lack any capacity for fear, was taking on one more challenge. She had unlocked the gate into the polar bear run, a convenient shortcut to freedom.

She had sprinted across exhibits before—all she would have to do would be to get to the moat. Then she, unlike the bears, could shinny up the vertical cable planted strategically on its far wall.

But the polar bears were restless. Strange sounds had been coming from their ordinarily quiet tunnel, and when an odd animal suddenly arrived in their midst and invited chase, they were more than willing to oblige.

Leigh joined Maura and Frank at the gate, but soon turned away. It was an unfair fight—two on one, 1,000-plus pounds against 125. The bullets Frank shot were too little, too late. One swipe of a colossal white paw knocked Carmen to the rocks, and two giant sets of jaws closed in.

The battle was over in seconds.

Chapter 24

"So who all's coming?" Leigh asked, loading two sacks of ice into her freezer. At first she had felt a little funny about having a celebration so soon after Carmen's death, but Warren had insisted that she needed closure, and after some thought, she had agreed.

"Your folks, Cara's gang, Katharine, and Maura all said they'd drop by," Warren answered, transferring two-liters from grocery sacks to Leigh's countertop. "Maura will have her mother with her, though, so they may not stay long."

"I'll send some food home with them if they miss it," Leigh smiled. "I'm so glad Maura's taking her mother to see Maplewood. I just hope Mary responds well. It's a miracle, her qualifying for that private funding."

"It's not that unusual a setup, if you can find it," Warren said matter-of-factly. "A few wealthy benefactors who've been touched by Alzheimer's can make all the difference to a family like the Polanskis."

Leigh's buzzer rang, and she was happy to admit her first guests a little early. Warren made Mary comfortable while Maura, who was beaming from ear to ear, gave Leigh a stellar report on Maplewood. "They knew exactly what they were doing," she gushed.

"They anticipated every question I had, and the whole place is just beautiful. Mom said she could sit for hours and listen to the little waterfall in the lounge, and they even have a greenhouse where residents keep up their own plots. Everything is very calm, very structured. It's exactly what Mom needs. And it's right on the bus line, so my aunts can visit anytime—"

Leigh grinned. She hadn't heard her friend gush so much in years. Only after Maura had finished a considerable testimony to Maplewood did she remember the purpose of the party. "Are you doing OK?" she asked. "That was a pretty gruesome scene last night, but I hope you're not still feeling guilty about Carmen's death. Because if you are, I'm afraid I'll have to slap you around again."

Leigh's mouth curved into a small, sad smile. "I was sorry Carmen got killed the first time—and I'm just as sorry the second. Even if she did kill Kristin and Stacey. But I'm trying not to feel guilty about it. I didn't even know she was going in the cage until it was too late. If I had known—"

"You couldn't have done anything then either," Maura said firmly. "She had a knife to your neck and Kristin's keys in her hand. She was going to do what she was going to do."

Leigh sighed. "I do wonder, though, if she would have actually hurt me. It sounded like she just wanted to make me look guilty to divert attention from Kristin—"

"Don't delude yourself, Koslow," Maura said sternly. "The woman killed one of her oldest friends in a fit of jealousy and didn't think twice about it. In fact, she used the situation to her advantage—to get out of debt and probably to get away from some pretty dangerous creditors."

Leigh sighed. Maura was probably right. "It's ironic that my getting arrested was her lucky break, don't you think? I mean, nobody would have ever suspected Kristin if it hadn't been for Stacey's murder and the tie-in with the tan Eldorado. But once the police started on Kristin's trail, Carmen's scheme was in trouble. And I made the perfect scapegoat."

"That's why you shouldn't delude yourself," Maura said heavily. "I think Carmen planned to make it look like you were guilty and had skipped bail. She would have taken you away somewhere, forced you to make a phone call or write a confession, and then you would have disappeared. If you get my drift."

Leigh got it. But the whole scenario was still hard to fathom. Carmen had switched her clothes and jewelry for Kristin's, leaving behind just enough of the body to prove someone was dead, yet nothing that would give away its identity. She had even thought to tear out some of her own hair at the scene. "Carmen was pretty clever, wasn't she?" Leigh thought out loud.

Maura scoffed. "She wasn't clever. She was damned lucky. The scheme would have blown up in a day if her blood type hadn't matched Kristin's."

"Then why didn't they do DNA tests or something?" Leigh asked critically.

Maura looked at her sternly. "DNA tests aren't free, Koslow. They cost money, and a detective has to have a darn good reason to request them. Carmen had no relatives crying foul, and there was a fair amount of evidence pointing to the body being Carmen's, and not a shred pointing against it."

Leigh didn't argue the point. She looked at her watch and threw a glance at the door.

"Who are you waiting on?" Maura asked suspiciously. "Don't tell me Warren invited Tanner over."

Leigh looked up in surprise. "No—I mean, I don't think so." Perhaps they should have invited Tanner—after all, the charges against him were going to be dropped too. The state police were now convinced that Carmen had killed Stacey after the two ran into each other at the cabin hideout. Stacey had probably threatened to blow the whistle, and that was that.

"So you're over the guy, eh?" Maura asked hopefully.

Leigh considered. She owed the man a nice dinner and a beating, but her desire to deliver either was gone. Perhaps she should do nothing and call it a wash. "Yeah," she answered. "I guess you could say that."

The buzzer buzzed, and the first guest headed up. It was Katharine Bower, looking especially attractive in a close-fitting turquoise suit. "It's official!" She smiled, looking at Leigh. "The charges against you have been dropped."

A cheer commenced, and Leigh promptly offered Katharine profuse thanks and a large Coke on the rocks. "Will anything happen to Dena Johnson?" Leigh asked, curious about the accuser she had never remembered meeting.

"Probably not," Katharine said, sipping thirstily. "She says now that she and Tonya met Kristin on their way out of the zoo that night. Apparently, Kristin had just found out she was pregnant and couldn't wait to tell Tanner—and rub Carmen's nose in it. She was heading for the tiger shed when they left. When they heard the next morning that Carmen was dead, they thought that the two had fought again, and that Kristin must have killed her. Since they were the only other people who knew Kristin had been at the zoo, they figured they'd do their pregnant friend a favor and not mention it. And when they found out the police suspected you, Dena foolishly decided to go a step further."

Leigh scowled. "I still think Dena was afraid of Kristin doing something to her if she didn't help."

"Maybe," Katharine answered, smiling slightly,

"but you're the only one I talked to who had anything really negative to say about Kristin Yates. Everyone else at the zoo seemed to like her."

Leigh sighed and shrugged. Her confidence in her character-judging abilities was flagging of late. The door buzzer rang again, and she headed toward it. "I hope that's the pizza," she announced.

A male voice came over the speaker. "Henderson Floral. Delivery for Leigh Koslow." Skeptical, Leigh walked over to the window, and was pleased to see a floral van parked below. She buzzed the young man up and accepted a beautiful fall bouquet with amazement.

Her cheeks red, she put the flowers on her coffee table and extracted the card. Mao Tse, who had been in hiding since Warren arrived, promptly popped up on the table to investigate. Leigh read the card and couldn't help grinning. *Sorry I misjudged you. Gerald Frank.*

She made a quick mental note to send a similar offering down to the bureau tomorrow. She knew just what it would say: *Ditto.*

"Now *that's* got to be the pizza," Warren announced when the buzzer rang again. "I'll get it. It's my treat."

"He's so generous, isn't he?" Katharine asked, standing at Leigh's side and watching Warren adoringly.

"Yes," Leigh answered a little tightly, "he is."

"You've got to respect a man who'd go to such lengths for a friend," Katharine continued. She started to say something else, but stopped herself.

Leigh followed Katharine's eyes to Mary Polanski, and wondered what Katharine knew that she didn't. Then a thought dawned. Warren had told her that the fund at Maplewood had been set up by a small group of wealthy benefactors. Could this have been a recent phenomenon, and could they have had a little urging, perhaps?

She looked at Maura, who was as happy as Leigh had seen her in months. Yes, that was what had happened. The Harmon magic. And probably a little chunk of the Harmon bank account as well. She smiled, but kept her thoughts to herself. Warren was right to keep it a secret. Maura could never know.

"Thanks for getting that package to him the other day, by the way," Katharine said cheerfully, trying to change the subject. "I don't think it worked, though."

Leigh looked up. "And what exactly was it?"

Katharine laughed. "What do you think? A beanie baby elephant with a 'Vote Republican' button on its tail, of course!"

Leigh laughed, but with a touch of chagrin. So, they shared the same sense of humor too.

Cara's family and the Koslows arrived en masse, and soon Leigh's small apartment was buzzing with activity—and pizza consumption. Even Mao Tse seemed to be in a festive mood as she risked the horrors of a crowd to get a closer look at the bizarre bundle in Cara's arms. Katharine announced to the newcomers that her client was now a free woman, and cheers went up from all except Frances, who was busy cornering Warren. Probably, Leigh thought, to ask about her legal bills.

Little Mathias took the whole affair in stride, alternately yawning and peering out at the big black furball that kept popping up into his field of vision. "She's always liked you," Leigh said to Cara, pulling Mao Tse away from the baby's head. "I guess it figures she'd like your son too."

Cara smiled, but her eyes were on Katharine, who had finally managed to wrest Warren away from Frances. "I'm glad I finally got a chance to meet your lawyer. She seems quite competent."

"Oh, she is," Leigh said anxiously, looking across

the room to where Katharine and Warren stood close together, laughing. Warren put an arm around her waist, and she leaned comfortably into his side.

Leigh felt her face get hot, and she looked away quickly. Unfortunately, Cara had been watching her, and was now wearing a humongous smirk.

"What's that for?" Leigh asked irritably.

The smirk increased. "Well, I'll be damned. You're jealous."

Leigh sniffed. "Me, jealous? Of what?"

Cara rolled her eyes. "You know exactly what I'm talking about. 'Just friends' indeed."

More annoyed than ever, Leigh left Cara's side and went to the counter for another slice of pepperoni. She was *not* jealous. She was merely concerned. Katharine was at least ten years older than Warren, even if she did look good in biking shorts.

Leigh watched as Katharine settled close to Warren on the couch, her hand resting just above his knee. The pizza Leigh had just eaten churned uncomfortably in her stomach, and her cheeks were practically on fire.

Well, damn.

She turned away again, nervously refilling her Diet Coke to the brim. There was no more point in denying it. She *was* jealous. She was jealous as hell. And she was going to have to do something about it.

She just hoped it wasn't too late.